THE Heart OF THE MATTER

REBEKAH ISERT

 Formatted with Vellum

*For all the girls
who found love
a little later
than expected.*

Content Awareness

I try very hard to make all of my books appropriate for all audiences.

However, there are some thematic elements that certain people might prefer to be aware of. Please refer to the guide at the back of the book, labeled "Content Guide" in the Table of Contents for further details.

For those of you reading this as a physical book, the content guide is found right before the "About the Author" page, immediately at the back of the book, on page 307 in the print edition.

Contents

1. The Problem Pt. 1 — 1
2. The Truth — 6
3. The Fallout — 12
4. The Solution Pt. 1 — 17
5. The Meeting — 29
6. The First Appointment — 42
7. The Second Appointment — 63
8. The Grill — 80
9. The Friend — 93
10. The Sister — 101
11. The Third Appointment — 113
12. The Mutual Friend — 126
13. The Fourth Appointment — 146
14. The Lesson — 162
15. The Dinner Pt. 1 — 188
16. The Dinner Pt. 2 — 197
17. The Talk — 208
18. The Fifth Appointment — 218
19. The Plan — 228
20. The Mountain — 237
21. The Coworker — 251
22. The Sixth Appointment — 260
23. The Problem Pt. 2 — 272
24. The Problem Pt. 3 — 286
25. The Solution Pt. 2 — 294
Epilogue — 299

Acknowledgments — 305
Content Guide — 307
About the Author — 309
Also by Rebekah Isert — 310

Chapter 1
The Problem Pt. 1

SUMMER

They say karma comes for us all. It's true. Doubly so for me. I'm not sure what my grandmother Claire was thinking when she named her daughter Karma, but ol' Claire's name must have been short for 'Clairvoyant' because that's what I'm experiencing right now.

The scene: My thirty-third birthday, December 21st. I'm sitting at the dining room table, over my favorite meal of Kalua pork and grilled pineapple. My dad sits next to me at the head of the table, with Mom across from me. Aunt Zen sits to her right, and my older sister Joanie is at the other end of the table. It's cozy. We're missing my brothers, who live in California, but I'm surprised that my brother-in-law and nieces and nephews aren't here.

That should be my first clue.

"How are you, Summer?" Mom's voice is pleasant. And yes, I was born literally on the winter solstice. Mom clearly doesn't have Grandma's affinity for names, though her wishful thinking is strong. "How's your boyfriend?"

"Okay," I say breezily. "We're both doing good. He told me

to say sorry for not coming." I don't intend to say anything more than that. I don't like talking about the guy. I nod toward my mom's right hand. "Could I have the pineapple?"

This is how I know Dad loves me—grilling on the back porch in sub-freezing weather is absolutely insane, but he does it every year.

"Sure, sweetie," Mom says, handing it over. She is studying me, gray-streaked brown bangs hanging over green-blue eyes the same color as mine. I can tell she's gauging something, and I don't like it. I turn my attention back to the fruit, and dish myself a small mountain. I eat a couple of slices. No one says anything.

The world screeches to a stop. Something has to be wrong. Not because of the pineapple—it's my birthday—but there's something about Mom's look that sends a small shiver up my spine.

"Is ... everything okay?" I frown as I glance around the table. Serious faces stare back at me. Even a glance at Dad isn't comforting. He isn't frowning, but he does look solemn.

"Sunshine," he says quietly. "We're a little concerned about you."

I run through the possibilities in my head: I haven't lost my job—actually, I got promoted last month to team lead. I have my own apartment. I'm not behind on bills. I'm not sick. I haven't done anything to embarrass the family name. So ...

"Why?"

"Honey," Mom says, her voice cloyingly sweet. "We're worried about your boyfriend."

The worry turns into a nauseating, nautical-strength knot in my chest and drops from my heart to my stomach with a horrible sploosh. "What about him?" I try to keep my voice as casual as possible. Unfortunately, acting is not my forte.

Mom flutters with her hands, her mouth opening and closing. Apparently, the discomfort she's also feeling is refusing to congeal in her brain enough to become words. Sensing her discomfort, Auntie Zen—Mom's sister—speaks.

"We're concerned that he's not right for you." Zen's blue eyes are serious behind her black rimmed glasses, corkscrewing their way into my soul.

"Why?" I asked, looking between my mother and my aunt. I shouldn't have had the pineapple. I can feel the acid making its way through my stomach floor. If one of my organs ruptures, would that get me out of this conversation?

Mom's words come out in a rush. "Oh, honey. It just doesn't seem healthy to us. He never comes with you to any events. I haven't seen a picture—sweetie, I don't even know his name. And with everything else ... I don't think I've heard a positive thing about him in all the time you've been dating him, and well ..." Her hands flutter around as she gestures helplessly, and then she turns to Aunt Zen.

I glance at Dad. He's quiet, but I can see silent agreement. His eyes are pleading under furrowed grey brows. As I glance around the table, everyone at that table has clearly come to the same conclusion.

Am I at an intervention?

On my *birthday*?

"But ..." I trail off, my mind trying to race faster than my heart and falling flat. "He's not that bad."

"He's missing your birthday," my sister says, her tone flat and unconvinced.

"He's got a project he's finishing." My voice is more defensive than I expect. "He couldn't put it off because of the holidays."

"He's worked every holiday since you started dating," Joanie shoots back, avoiding all pretense of tact. It's on brand for her.

"He's a leader at work. It's bound to happen." It's an excuse, one I've used before, and it doesn't work nearly as well this time.

"Name a time where he put you first over work." Joanie leans back in her chair, her arms crossed over her chest. "Go on. I'll wait."

I stare at her. My older sister, with her blue turtleneck and bleached blonde hair looks like she's the one who should be named Summer. She's also exactly right about my boyfriend. But what are they—

Realization smacks me in the forehead like the proverbial palm.

"Are you trying to get me to break up with him?" My head whips around to Mom and Zen. Surprising anger percolates in my chest. "Are you serious?"

"We're not trying to do that," Zen says quietly. "But ... we were going to ease you into this, but Summer, we really think something needs to change. So ..." she pulls out an envelope from under the table and slides it across the table to me. "This is a voucher to one of the couples therapists in my office."

Horror drops into the pit of my stomach like a bucket of angry eels. I can't look away. She keeps talking. "There's six appointments. If nothing else ... Summer, could you please take him?"

"To therapy?" I'm breathless. I don't even know what to think. Who buys someone therapy? Isn't there an ethical boundary in there somewhere?

If there is, Zen has done an absolute swan dive over it.

"But—" I look around the table. Everyone's expressions have changed from concern to a spectrum of pleading and hopefulness.

"Sunny," Dad's voice is quiet and piercing, my hand tight

in his like he's my landline, and he's trying to pull me in from the sea. I turn to him, my heart sinking. "We're a bit worried."

And that's the moment I lose.

The fight building in my chest dies a quick and merciless death. I can't refuse Dad. His quiet words are the proverbial knife in the gut. Twisting so slowly that I can't help but whisper. "I'll ... I'll think about it."

He gives me a gentle smile and nods. "Thank you."

I stare at the table and nod, unable to do anything else.

This is apparently what my family members are waiting for. With what sounds like a collective sigh, the mood shifts. Forks start scraping against plates and conversation—almost not awkward—strikes up and the party around me goes back to normal. Except for me. I take the cake Mom hands me as she wishes me a happy "big three-three" like she didn't just take a harpoon to my conscience.

And it *is* my conscience. Not my heart. Because the truth is, despite all of my protests, complaints, and general negativity, there is only one problem with my boyfriend.

He's not real.

Chapter 2
The Truth

SUMMER

The truth draggles after me like a miserable, soggy muppet as I crunch through the new snow on my parents' front walk, wondering how I got into this situation in the first place.

I'm not a liar by nature. I'm usually not even that great at it. I'm definitely not great at lying to Zen, who seems to have a nose for it—like the creepy Child Catcher from Chitty Chitty Bang Bang.

I unlock my car and slump into my seat, pinching my eyes closed against the deep ache in my chest. Guilt and a sharp sense of loneliness swirl through me as I try to center myself.

Freaking Karma.

Its her and Zen's fault that I have the fake boyfriend in the first place. Two years ago, my mother, in all her infinite sympathy and well-meaning, decided that at the ripe age of thirty-one, I was about to tumble off the Cliff of Spinsterdom.

In her desperate rush to Save My Soul, she drafted Zen. Zen has never married, and she was probably worried I would end up alone as well and didn't want me to be like her.

But that did not—and does not—excuse the twelve blind

dates over the course of one month. It was November, too. Did they consider how busy November is? No.

The dates were accompanied by reminders of all the single friends I had, and a subscription to a dating app. My mother, who can barely answer a video call without assistance, managed to buy me three months on LonelyHeartsofUtah.

My mother.

A dating app.

LonelyHeartsofUtah.

It was clear that I needed to do something unless I wanted to be chased by my mother through the online dating world until the end of time. She clearly wasn't going to stop on her own, or take no for an answer, no matter how many dates I managed to get out of.

So … I created a fake boyfriend.

I didn't think I used him that often. Or well, I hadn't until tonight. To be perfectly frank, he's been a convenient excuse. I've used him for everything from getting out of work events to contributing to the conversation when Joanie wants to complain about her husband and I didn't want to feel left out.

It's that last one that's probably gotten me in trouble. As much as my boss and friend, Ana, would worry about a bad boyfriend, Joanie's the one who would internalize things if I complained about a boyfriend occasionally.

Actually … have I ever *not* complained about him?

I drop my head onto the steering wheel with a thump, my gloved hands resting in my lap.

I am so, so dead.

I've got to get out of therapy somehow.

Maybe I should spill my guts to Mom and Zen. If I do, they'll know exactly how far they've pushed me, right? I mean, how insane do you have to be to make up a boyfriend?

Dad's face flashes in my mind, and guilt rolls over me like an enormous, unsympathetic rolling pin.

I wish he didn't know the fake boyfriend existed. Lying to Mom is bad enough, but Dad is so ... trusting. Not in a bad way. The man is savvy and totally not naive, but he trusts *me*. So, if I say that I have a boyfriend ... he thinks that I have one.

But I don't.

I want to date. I've gone on every date I've ever been asked on. All six of them. And the seven or so blind dates I couldn't avoid during that terrible November. It would be really nice to have someone to lean on. To enjoy life with. To start a family with. But relationships just ... haven't happened.

I raise my head and see the glow of the clock on the dashboard. Mom is going to come out and get me if I stay out here much longer. I plug the key into the ignition, and with a twist, my car chugs to life. Pushing the cassette into the tape deck, I plug my phone into the converter and slip it into the holder clipped into the air conditioning vent.

Then I call Lacy.

My roommate answers right away. "Hello?"

"Lacy, I'm in trouble."

"Has Jennie finally bit the dust?"

Way to manifest a catastrophe. Please, oh please, not today. "No, she's fine," I say, steeling myself for the next sentence. "My ... the boyfriend came back to bite me."

There's a long pause while Lacy undoubtedly tries to suppress the words, 'I told you so' from bubbling out of her throat.

She lasts about three seconds.

"I TOLD you," she says, her vindication filling my car to suffocating levels. "Didn't I tell you? This was a terrible idea."

"This was *your* terrible idea," I point out.

"Yeah, but I told you not to do it later, so I'm clearly absolved. How did your mom find out?"

"She hasn't yet."

"Huh?" Lacy sounds unbelievably confused, but I don't blame her. I still don't know how I got into this myself. "If she doesn't know, how can it have bit you?

"Because ..." How do I even explain this? "Zen ... bought ... therapy." The last word was so sigh-filled that Lacy makes another noise of confusion.

"Sorry? What did Zen get you?"

"Therapy."

"What?"

"Therapy, Lace. As in, with a therapist. In a counseling office. For me, and my very, very non-existent boyfriend."

There's a long pause. "Hmm. That's awkward."

"Lacy!"

"What am I supposed to say? Let's talk more when you get home." Lacy's tone doesn't indicate that she's taking this super seriously. It's annoying, but to be fair, she's right—this is all my fault.

I choose to move on. "You're already back from Renner's?"

"Yeah, he's got the early shift," she sighs. "But such is life."

"Fair enough."

"I told you to not complain about him so much." Lacy's voice is slightly tinny over the phone. The reception isn't great as I drive through the canyon, but it's more likely my slightly older car.

"You complain about yours all the time."

"Yeah, but you also hear about all the good stuff that he does for me. The flowers, the snuggles, the absolutely mind-blowing kisses--"

"Yeah, yeah, yeah," I say, hurrying her along. Lacy doesn't

deliberately rub her relationship status in my face, but she can make me feel single in other ways. "We've talked about this, Lace. If I brag about the boyfriend, at some point my mom is going to ask for evidence. 'Where are the flowers? Where's his picture?' At least she hasn't wanted to meet him up to this point."

"Yeah, but now she's sending you to a professional," Lacy points out. "Which is unarguably worse. What's the therapist going to think?"

"I'm going to have to get out of it somehow," I say, running a gloved hand over my hair. I'm almost always cold, even with the heater blasting in my car. "There's absolutely no way I am going to go to therapy with an imaginary boyfriend."

I pull up to my apartment building twenty minutes later. When I pick up my phone to text my dad that I've gotten home, there's a notification. I unlock my phone and click on the message.

It's from work. Or rather, from a coworker. Louis is another team lead. Why was he texting me after hours? I furrow my eyebrows as I turn off my car and walk up the salted sidewalk, my long black coat swishing around my legs. I'm also praying fervently that whatever it is, it is not an emergency. Not tonight.

> Louis Granger: Where did the Haggerty file go?

I stop at the base of the stairs, frowning. My team is in charge of the Haggerty file, why does he need it?

Then again, I had asked him to take a look at one of the

coding passages earlier. But why is he looking at it at—I check the clock—ten thirty at night? Four days before Christmas?

I shake my head. We're in IT. Sometimes we pull long hours. I should just be thankful it's not me.

And I am. I text him the answer and slowly start walking up the stairs to my apartment.

Chapter 3
The Fallout

CHASE

I think it's safe to say my life is falling apart.

It's not obvious yet. I haven't started to miss work, or even that much sleep. I'm eating well and still going to the gym. My dishes are in the dishwasher, not dirty in the sink. In fact, no one but the most discerning person, already very familiar with my life, would be able to tell. Avery, my sister, is one of those people.

She's currently sitting in my office chair, feet up on my desk, staring me down like I'm a particularly ugly piece of art: examining it for the sake of fairness, but overall, not even close to impressed.

While fair, it still stings.

"You're gonna have to tell me what you're thinking," I tell her, "because unless some sort of magic has started to exist in the last two minutes, I still can't read your mind."

"I don't think you'd want to even if you could."

Great. "I'm sure of that."

The office is silent for a long moment. I stand in front of the window, which shows almost the entirety of Utah Valley. It's an ugly, gray day. January has slumped in like a petulant child. It hasn't snowed since Christmas, leaving it dull, dirty, and dismal.

"I don't know, Morkie. You've got to let her go."

You've got to let her go.

She's talking about Amanda. And I did let her go, six months ago, when we broke up. It wasn't a hard separation either. The relationship had been slowly souring over the six months before that. She left me with a stiff speech about my general toxicity and "gym of red flags" and trotted off to her other boyfriend who was no doubt going to treat her better than I was ever capable of.

Yeah.

I have let her go. And it wasn't that hard.

"Do I look like I'm pining after Amanda?" It's a fair question, and she knows the answer is no. I'm pulling my weight at work, I'm taking care of myself, and everything is moving forward like it should.

Avery is sitting back in the chair, her dark hair the same color as mine spilling over her shoulders, spinning a pencil in her fingers. She's never completely still, but this amount of calm is a clear tell that she's mulling over her words.

I wish she'd just put me out of my misery.

"No, not really." Her bright blue eyes are piercing, and it makes the pencil she points at me feel like a gun. "But you're not happy."

We'd been having a perfectly normal lunch before this. Now the empty Chinese food cartons lining the edge of the desk seem to mock me. No hiding from it now.

I give it my best shot anyway. "Of course I am. Never better."

Avery scoffs. "That's a load of steaming horse manure and you know it."

"What makes you think I'm not happy?" I try to make the question patient, but even I can tell it's petulant.

"Oh, I don't know, the fact that you never smile anymore?"

"It's not like I'm constantly beaming at everyone regularly, Gills."

Avery squints at me, disgusted. "Chase."

"Avery." I glare back, but there's no real heat in it.

I drop the act. I can pretend I'm as tough as I want to be, but she knows me better than anyone else. We've been all the other has for years.

"It's not her that hurts," I admit. "It's what she said."

Avery frowns. "She was cheating on you. You can't take anything she says into account."

She's probably right, but that doesn't stop my ex's words ringing in my ears. *You're unreachable. Even if I wanted to have a deeper relationship with you, it would be impossible, because you don't want to be reached. You want to hold people at arm's distance, shoving gifts and things at them because you don't know how normal people connect emotionally. You're toxic, Chase. You're just toxic.*

"But what if she's right?" I ask. "You know better than anyone that it's hard for me to reach out. I'm not trying to shut people down or keep people out, but what if that's happening?"

Avery sighs. She's not typically the touchy-feeling kind of person, and would probably rather talk about almost anything else, but I'm kind of touched that she's doing it anyway. "Chase, Amanda was only herself when she was around ninety perfect strangers, and you have a hard time recharging around me. That doesn't make you toxic, that makes you an introvert."

"Yeah, but even introverts can have satisfying relationships," I point out. "And well ... that hasn't happened." Clearly. With my long-term girlfriends or otherwise. You'd think it would have happened with *one* of them by now. To increase the odds, lately I've been trying to go on at least two dates every week in an attempt to run into someone I'd click with.

Avery shrugs. "Then go to therapy."

"What?"

"Go to therapy," she repeats. "Stop this... whatever you're doing with women—which, by the way, makes you look like a straight-up player—and get some actual help."

I shake my head in disgust. "What, a therapist is going to wave his magic wand and tell me what's wrong?"

"Or they can give you a few more coping mechanisms than you have," Avery leans forward in my seat. "Considering that would give you at least *one*, it wouldn't hurt."

I sigh, and slump into the chair opposite Avery, frustrated. I don't want to go to therapy.

No, that's not quite accurate. I'm not sure how to get *into* therapy. I've done a bit of research, and aside from a couple of online platforms, I'm not quite sure how to ... start. Do I message someone? How do I check their credentials properly? What if I don't get along with them? There are certainly hundreds, if not thousands of horror stories of when a therapist and client don't match. What happens then? There are a finite number of therapists in the state of Utah. If I got through them all, what then?

Or, on the flip side, what if I start meeting with one and they confirm that I am as toxic as Amanda claims?

"Chase?" Avery's serious voice permeates my thoughts, and I look up at my sister. "Will you at least think about it? Nothing's going to change if you keep on doing everything the same."

I rub my forehead. "Are you talking as a friend or a sister?"

"I can be your friend and your sister," Avery says quietly. "I know it's not affecting your work right now. But how long will it be before it does? Your company is super well established now, and your staff is experienced and good at their jobs. You can afford to slow down a little bit. Take care of yourself."

I nod absently, not entirely sure what to say. She has a point, but the idea of picking over my emotions with a stranger doesn't feel that inviting. And yet, on the other hand, it has felt like the thing I need to do for a while.

"I'll think about it," I finally say.

"You promise?" Avery points the pencil at me.

"I promise."

"Good." She leans back in my office chair. After a moment of silence, she tilts her head to the side, like we didn't just have a heart-to-heart. "Did you hear about the new Indian restaurant they've opened in Orem?"

I roll my shoulders, trying to shake off the conversation, and settle into the chair on the visitor-side of my desk. "As a matter of fact, I have. I booked us a table for Friday."

"Sweet!" Avery says. "Am I a third wheel, or is it just us?"

I think about it. As uncomfortable as it is to admit, Avery has a point. Nothing will change if I keep on doing the same thing. And if that means going on less dates ... well, it's a start. It'll help my social battery in the long run, anyway.

"Just us," I said. "And I'm buying."

"Double sweet."

We lapse into quiet, but it's not uncomfortable. For being all up in my business all the time, she really is looking out for me. I'm lucky she's my sister.

"Well, I should probably be headed out soon," Avery says, looking at her watch. "Your lunch break is almost over, and I've got to get back to work."

"What are you doing for the rest of the day?" I ask.

Avery brightens, and I can't help the smile as I listen to her plans, a brief, soothing interlude to the churning inside my brain.

Chapter 4
The Solution Pt. 1

SUMMER

I slam the door, and stalk inside. I kick my boots off in the entryway and stomp through the kitchen, dispassionately dropping my purse on the counter. As I pass, I wave half-heartedly at Lacy and stump into my room.

I need to change. This is not an evening for anything with buttons or zippers, or anything even remotely fitted. Gathering my hair on top of my head, I scrunch my curls into the messiest top knot to ever mess, and swaddle myself in my softest sweatpants, oversized hoodie, and cabin socks.

Much better.

When I walk out, Lacy's still at the counter, her phone propped up against the paper towel holder, eating something that looks good and smells better.

She looks up from her phone, and nods toward the crockpot, and a pan on the stove. "Chili and cornbread. Ready, set, go."

I don't wait. In two seconds, I'm seated beside her on one of the barstools. After saying grace for my food, I start to inhale.

Lacy waits until I'm on my second bowl before she tries to talk to me.

"You okay?"

I look up at her with a frown. "I guess."

Lacy raised an eyebrow. "Convincing."

I add some more cheese to my chili and stir vigorously. "I aim to please."

"Work?"

"Yeah."

"Wanna talk about it?"

I groan but shake my head. "No, it's just Louis."

Lacy pulls a sympathetic face. "Forgetting he's not your manager anymore?"

"Weird, it's like you know him," I grumble.

Lacy nods sympathetically, then puts her phone down on the counter.

I look over, expecting to see a reel, and pull in my chin when a man's face stares back at me. It's some sort of social media profile. I register dark hair and hazel eyes and look up at her. "Lace?"

She looks down, and instead of correcting herself, she nudges the phone toward me a little more. "I think I found a solution to your problem."

My problem.

To be fair, I have more than one, but Lacy is only helping me with one that would involve social media.

Long story short, I haven't found a way to get out of therapy. No matter what I try to use as an excuse—money, time, whatever—every time I bring it up, Zen reassures me with excruciating kindness that she can definitely afford it, or the therapist is very flexible, or my boyfriend and I absolutely won't be wasting the therapist's time. She'll then flip it around and ask what I've done.

And oh man. I've done. To my horror—not only did I reassure Zen that I was working on it, I have actually talked to the therapist—mostly to see if I could back out on grounds of incompatibility—and instead committed to schedule an appointment by Friday.

I'm down to two choices now: break up with my fake boyfriend, or go to therapy.

The third option is praying for the apocalypse, but that would affect Lacy, and this situation is my very real consequence of my own terrible choices. She doesn't need to be involved.

The temptation to break up with my fake boyfriend is real, but LonelyHeartsofUtah keeps on floating through my head like a malignant blimp. I can't imagine how Mom might react to the truth if—heaven forbid—she found out the truth. Forget LonelyHeartsofUtah—she'd arrange my marriage before the beginning of March.

I was briefly tempted to play hooky, but if I do, Zen will hear about it. Probably from the therapist.

Because they work in the same office.

Ethical behavior clearly runs in my family.

So, my real choices are either admitting to my dad that I've been lying to him for the last six months or finding someone to go to therapy with that isn't weird, dangerous, or going to accidentally tell my family the truth at the first possibility.

Apparently, Lacy has a candidate.

"'Chase Merrill?'" I read the name, scrolling down his profile. There's not much there. His profile picture is nice. He's got a strong nose, a bit of scruff, and broad shoulders, creating a very pleasant effect overall. Not that appearance is what I'm strictly going for. I mean, it would be a plus to have a good-looking man to pretend to be my boyfriend, but I am fast approaching willingly taking anyone with a body to come with me. I don't have to look at him, I just need him to come sit with me while I lie to a professional.

Great googly moogly. There is definitely something ethically wrong with this.

"Who is he?" I ask, yanking my attention back to the present.

"He's an old college buddy of mine," Lacy says, spooning another huge scoop of chili into her mouth. "We still keep in touch. He lives here in the valley."

"Well, that helps," I say absently, scrolling through his profile. There's next to nothing except for people wishing him a happy birthday last September. "But why him?" I scroll back up to the top and tap on the 'about' section. I frown. "It says he's in a relationship."

"It's old," Lacy says around another mouthful. "He hardly ever goes on social media."

I frown. "So ..."

"I want you to see his face."

"I see it. He has one."

Lacy rolls her eyes. "I think he's a good candidate. Chase goes on a lot of dates—he's even raffled them off for charity before. He even took me out a couple times in college before I met Renner."

"Really?"

"Really. And right now, he's one of my clients. I'm on his support team. He's a really good guy. If nothing else, he can come sit in and look manly while you work things out with the therapist."

"But—"

Lacy scoffs and turns back to her chili. "C'mon Summer, it's not like you have to actually be on good terms with him after all of this. You could probably even go to half the therapy sessions and break up if you wanted. You'll have to do that anyway at the end of this, unless you want to actually date whoever you find."

I push my chili around in my bowl, frowning. She has a point, but there is a big difference between having a real, corporeal man to break up with and just being able to say, 'Oops, he's *gone.*' A sudden breakup would make my family ask questions, and it was only a matter of time before the truth caught up with me.

And then Dad would find out. And Mom would arrange my marriage.

Great googly moogly.

"I know," I mumble, a little too late.

"Unless you're *doing* this to find a man," Lacy says, a comically concerned look on her face. "In which case, we need to talk, because there are better ways."

"You know I'm not, Lace."

"Then choose a guy and go for it!"

I drop my head in my hands, and stare down at the chili. It smells delicious, but this whole business is well on its way to giving me an ulcer.

The last thing I want to do is rope another person into the absolute dumpster fire that is my life right now. Aside from the whole therapy fiasco, at work today a team member made a fairly minor mistake that took less than an hour to fix and didn't affect any of our clients. However, Louis spent the majority of the day following me around, helpfully reminding me that I needed to talk to the team member in question about it. He'd continued to do so until I'd told him quite curtly that I'd talk to him and he didn't need to remind me anymore.

He'd ignored me the rest of the day. I *probably* should be put out about it, but frankly it was a relief. I'm not afraid of conflict, but he's been kind of overbearing the last few weeks. I am praying that this is not a trend. Louis knows his stuff, and I want to learn, but I don't need him to micromanage me the whole time.

I sigh again.

"... Aaaand I think I've lost you."

I look up at Lacy guiltily, who's holding her phone out. It's open to the phone function, with Chase Merrill's name staring back at me.

Is Chase a micromanager? I hope not, because me and the deep seated exhaustion settling into my bones has just about had it for today, and I cannot see another way forward.

"Do you want me to call him?" Lacy asks.

"Yes," I say, and turn back to my chili.

I don't expect her to call him right then. On speaker.

"Lacy, right now?" I whisper desperately.

"Yes, now," Lacy whispers back unsympathetically.

Cold explodes over my head like I've been dropped into the deep end of the pool without knowing how to swim. I shouldn't be shocked. Lacy's not one to beat around the bush. My plan, my terrible, terrible, plan, has truly come back around to bite me.

Would Chase be implicated as an accessory if I'm found guilty for unethical therapy sessions?

What if he's the one to turn me in?

... Would the cops be called for a breach in ethics?

I hold my breath as it buzzes and then picks up on the third ring. The third ring.

Who even answers their phone anymore?

"Hello?" I can hear Chase's voice clearly. It's deep and pleasant, even after being electronically transmitted, which is either a credit to his voice or the phone maker.

I don't think Samsung can take that much credit.

"Hey, Chase, it's Lacy!" Lacy's voice takes on that tone that is more cheerleader than IT. It has confused many a person unacquainted with the wide variety of people in Information Technologies. It usually lasts until she fixes the issue, optimizes the hard drive, and completes all available updates within thirty minutes, all the while chatting about you and your dog.

Yeah, she's that good.

"Hey, Lacy, how's it going?" His tone has changed. It's definitely not dislike, but maybe ... caution?

... Fair, I guess, but I can't help the judgement that swelled instinctively in my chest in defense of my friend.

Lacy is unbothered. "Always a party! Hey, I have two questions. Renner wanted to get in touch with you about a possible project?"

"Oh, yeah. Does he still have my work email?"

"If he doesn't, then I do. Can he drop you a line?"

"For sure. I'll have Ed look at it when it comes in. He's in charge of acquisitions this month." His voice has shifted from cautious to conversational. "You said you had two questions? Is the other business related?"

Lacy casts a look at me. "Mmm, not really. Hey, do you remember me talking about Summer?" My stomach drops. Has she been talking about this with him already? The nervousness surges.

"Was she that redhead you were trying to set me up with in college?"

"Huh?" Lacy looks confused for a moment and then shakes her head. "No, that was Gina. A bullet dodged, looking at it now. No, Summer's one of my coworkers. And my roommate, coincidentally."

"Okay?" The word comes out a little harsher. "I'm going to tell you right now, Lace, I'm on a hiatus from dating for the time being."

"Oh, good, that will make this less complicated. I'm not asking you to date her."

"You're not?"

She's not?

Actually, again, fair. It's not like I'd actually have to be his girlfriend for this to work. We'd only have to meet up at therapy six times. We could realistically be strangers at the end of this.

"No. You wound me, Chase," Lacy's voice is heavily ironic. "It's not like I've pushed you into a relationship before."

"No, but you've certainly given me more opportunities than I have ties."

"So, like... two?"

"I have a lot of ties, Lacy." His voice is tired, and I hear a sigh. "So, what about Summer? What do you need?"

What about Summer? This suddenly feels like being set up on a blind date. While I'm in the room. Something approaching a medical emergency twists in my stomach, and I push my chair back to leave. Lacy can take care of this on her own. I might be attaching myself to this poor hapless man, but at least I can have the decency to let Lacy lead him to his doom in private.

Lacy grabs me by the back of my hoodie. It's not hard, but I have to stop to keep from wrenching her arm. I scowl at her. She sticks her tongue out at me.

"So, we have a sticky situation."

"Lacy—"

"I promise you, I have nothing romantic in mind. Her family is under the impression that she's dating someone toxic, and so they've paid for her to go to therapy, and we're trying to find someone who will stand in as her boyfriend."

"And you immediately thought of me?" Chase sounds faintly insulted. I bury my head in my hands.

"Only because of your singleness," Lacy says, completely unconcerned. "I won't trust my roommate to just anyone and not only do I know you're not weird, you're also trustworthy and a gentleman. There aren't a lot of people that I'd set her up with for something like this."

"And I lucked out?"

"Sure did, pal." Lacy's voice has lost none of its enthusiasm.

There's a long pause. He obviously has questions. He's smart, then. It'd be weird if he didn't. I'm glad he has questions.

"Why is she pretending she has a boyfriend?"

Except for that one.

"Family stuff. You should ask her yourself when you meet with her."

"Wait. Why isn't she making the call?"

"You'd take this kind of request from a stranger?"

Another pause. "Good point."

"She's home right now, if you want to talk to her," Lacy says. I stare at her in horror and shake my head violently.

"I have one question first," he says. I stare down at the phone, dreading the question. He's going to ask if I'm insane. I'm about eighty ... seven percent sure.

"Go for it."

"It's got two parts."

Lacy doesn't sound bothered. "Technically that's two questions, but I'll allow it."

"Is it real therapy?" he asks. "Like with a real therapist?"

Lacy looks at me. I nod. Zen gave me the packet. It's very, very real therapy, with a licensed therapist.

"Sure is. Was that both of your questions?"

"No, my second question is ... Lace, you sure you're not trying to set me up?"

"I promise," Lacy says solemnly. "Cross my heart. In fact, I'll bump up the stakes. If you manage to woo Summer Weathers, I will personally pay for a date to the most expensive restaurant in the valley."

There's a long pause, and I bury my head in my hands.

Chase's voice is hesitant. "Summer ... Weathers? Lacy ... is this a prank?"

I've had enough of this. "Give me that." I swipe the phone from Lacy. "Hi, Chase, this is Summer."

"Oh. Hi, Summer." He doesn't sound like he's on the verge of laughter. He actually sounds a little embarrassed, which is vaguely mollifying.

"Sorry for not saying something earlier," I say, brushing over the fact that I wasn't supposed to be in the room yet. "Look, I know it's weird, and I'm not proud of being in this situation, but if ..." I steel myself. "If you're willing to help, I'd really appreciate it."

"What would it involve?" His voice is serious. It's vaguely similar to the businesslike tone he had earlier, and it's weirdly comforting. I can handle business. I'm good at business.

I take a deep breath. "Well, not a real relationship for starters. I'm mostly looking for someone to go to therapy with. I'm..." I'm decided is what I am, "I'm not going to carry this ... thing—" lie, the word is lie "—past the visits. I more or less need a real person to break up with. So, essentially, it'll be therapy, and then a breakup."

There's another long pause, though this one sounds more contemplative than ominous. "How many sessions?"

"Six."

"How often?" His voice is definitely contemplative. I'm not sure if I feel better or worse about this.

"Probably once a week, or once every two weeks. The therapist is flexible."

"Do you think anything else might come up?"

"Such as?"

"Family visits, business visits, parading me in front of real exes?"

Like I had any of those. "No to all, as far as I know. My

parents plan everything out two or three weeks in advance, so even if that changes, you'll have plenty of time to make other plans to get out of it."

He sounds confused. "... why?"

Lacy jumps in, her voice matter-of-fact. "Because that's what her 'boyfriend' always does, Chase. That's why they need therapy."

"Ah."

It's not exactly judgment that I hear in his voice, but it's not that far off. I don't know whether it's for me, or the fake boyfriend.

Am I technically both? I feel like I'm technically both.

I'm jolted back to reality at the sound of his voice. "Do you know when the first appointment is?"

"I still need to schedule it," I admit, "but I've committed to get back to them by the end of the week. I can't put my aunt off any longer than that."

"Make it Thursdays at lunch, if possible," he says. "I take a long lunch those days and can slip away from work. But I would like to meet you in person before that to nail down a couple of details, and to see your face at least once before we go do fake therapy."

My conscience gives me a plaintive whine as it withers, and I wince. "Well, it is real therapy."

"Right, sorry."

The conversation lapses for a moment. I scramble for something to say. "What about this Thursday? I work in the north part of the valley, but I can take a couple of extra minutes at lunch that day."

Chase sounds a little impressed, though I'm not sure why. "Sounds good. Here, take down my number."

I punch it into my phone and send him a text.

Me: This is Summer Weathers.

A text comes back immediately.

Unknown: Chase Merrill. At your service.

"Got it," I say, saving his name into the contacts. There's another moment of silence. It's probably for my soul.

"Well, then," Chase says. "I'll see you on Thursday."

Chapter 5
The Meeting

SUMMER

WE DECIDE TO MEET AT A COFFEE SHOP IN LEHI. IT'S innocuous enough—other than the fact I'm not drinking coffee—and it's a shockingly normal place to meet. I don't know why I've gotten it into my head that we would meet somewhere more cinematic, like a pier or some gardens. But my wallet and Jennie, who is running on over four hundred thousand miles, say a hearty prayer of thanks for the little shop instead. My nose does as well—the closest pier is in Utah Lake, and ... no thank you.

The quaint little shop is relatively empty at this time of day, with only a business meeting or two happening along the walls. I suppose I'm there for one as well, but this feels different from a normal stocks-and-contracts visit. I'm there early, and the hot chocolate in my hand is warming me up when the door jingles. I look up.

It's Chase.

He's taller than I expected, easily topping six feet, his dark scruff accentuating his jawline as he looks around, his eyes still mirrored by sunglasses. My stomach twists, halfway between mildly infuriated and amazed. He looks better than his profile photo, and he didn't look shabby in his picture.

I am suddenly concerned.

While I did send him a picture last night, it was the photo from my last visa application when I went to India. On the plus side, I also look better than in my photo today. On the other hand, I'm not sure what I was thinking. It's not like it's the last photo I took. But, well ...

I can't send a picture of me in a hippo onesie and a top knot to a man that I've never met. It is a privilege for close friends only, and the only way I even know Chase exists is because of Lacy.

Speaking of Chase, he's still looking around for me.

If I'm this unrecognizable from my photograph, I fear greatly for national security.

"Um, Chase?" My voice is quiet in volume but seems to ricochet around the shop. It's probably my imagination, but it feels like every eye turns on me, like they know I have bad judgment in picking positively-identifying photographs.

Thankfully, with the rest of the hopefully-imagined stares, Chase also looks in my direction. Nothing on his face betrays what he's thinking as he stills, taking me in. It's possible he's thinking that I—hopefully—don't look like a crazy person. Or he could be wondering which exit is the closest, and if he could make it out before I caught up to him.

I think he could. His legs look long, and I'm sitting down.

"Summer?"

With everything going on in my head, I'm almost surprised when he takes a step toward me, holding out his hand for a handshake.

Relief floods through me, and not only from the fact that he's not bolting for the door. He's acting businesslike. I can do this.

His eyes follow me as I stand. This, at least, I'm used to. At five foot ten, I'm not the tallest girl out there, but I'm well-proportioned, so from a distance or sitting, I don't look as tall as I am. The good news is, given the look on his face, my height doesn't seem like a dealbreaker for him.

I take his hand. He's got a comfortable grip and matches the strength I put into it. An experienced businessman, then, and good at reading the room.

I can do this.

"Have you ordered?" Chase asks, nodding toward my drink. "Something to eat, I mean?"

"Um, no, not yet." I am way too nervous to be hungry. Plus, isn't it good manners to wait? Wait, is there coffee shop etiquette? There must be. They've been in existence since the 1500s. Anything that passed through the Regency period had to have etiquette attached.

Have I been rabbit hole-ing through Wikipedia to keep my mind off things lately?

Maybe.

Chase, unaware of the downright intrusive commentary going through my head, smiles at me and gestures for me to go ahead of him in line. "Well, then. If you're okay with it, my treat."

"Oh, you don't have to."

Chase's eyebrows raise, but he doesn't look offended. "I'd like to. I'm under strict instructions from Lacy to not be weird or creepy while we're working together." He thinks for a moment. "Think of it as a business lunch?"

"Aren't I the one employing you?"

Chase smiles. Oh dear. It looks good.

"I think it could be classified as a joint venture. Even if you are my employer, could I not give you a thank you?"

To help me lie to someone?

He sees the flicker in my expression. It doesn't seem to bother him much. "Maybe a better way of putting it is a gesture of good faith," he amends.

That makes more sense. If he's lingered on it for this long, it's probably important to him. I shrug. "If you'd like, but you're not obligated. I hope you know that. I know I'm kind of dragging you into my ... situation. Making you pay for everything from this point wouldn't make sense."

He shrugs. "If we were in a real relationship I would be anyway."

"Not for everything," I protest. It's a little too loud, and I look around sheepishly.

"Oh? Are you a fifty-fifty person?" He doesn't seem to be implying that I'm a raging feminist, but there's a concerning flickering behind his eyes.

"Not necessarily," I say truthfully. "But I don't like the assumption. It's not fair to you."

We're almost to the head of the line now. Chase's expression smooths, and for a moment, I see the ghost of a smile playing around his lips.

It's our turn to order, and I choose a sandwich. He also gets one, plus a brownie, and water. He looks at me. "Do you need anything else? Refill on that hot chocolate?"

My eyes go down to the cup in my hands, with its large 'HC' on the side. The casual offer is just that, but a confirmation that he's not saying it to be polite or guilt me into doing it. "No," I say, a small smile creeping up my cheeks. "But thank you."

Chase returns my smile and pays, and we head back to the table with the remote buzzer.

"I don't think I've been to this shop yet," Chase looks around.

I mirror the action, taking in the little shop. "It's pretty new, but I like their lunches. They don't do bad on their desserts, either. Most of my team usually orders from here at least once a week."

"You work nearby?"

"Yeah. I work for Banff Technology Services, like Lacy. She's on one of the other teams now, so we don't work on the same projects anymore, but she and I go way back."

"College?"

I smile. That would have been a riot. Probably literally. "No, she went to university here, but I was over on the other side of the country. We met in high school."

"Where did you go to college?"

"Georgia Tech."

"Wow." His expression is sincere, and I can't help the pleased curl of warmth in my chest. Some men get a haunted look in their eyes when I tell them, but there's nothing like that on Chase's face. "Why did you choose to go into IT, versus programming or something?"

"I had a hard time choosing between programming and something more people interfaced," I say. "I enjoy working with people, I just also like to work with computers. Considering what Banff does, helping companies keep everything online, creating back-end programming for specialty programs, it's kind of perfect."

Chase's smile grows, and he settles back in his chair. "Well, I'm going to pass on asking you what's your favorite programming language in the hopes of avoiding any sort of debate," I smile at the joke, "but I'm glad it's working out for you. I know that it doesn't always work that way."

"I feel like a bit of it was a fair amount of luck, but I agree. I feel really grateful to be where I'm at right now."

The buzzer starts going off, and I stand up to get our food. Two minutes later, I'm taking a bite of my sandwich. It's just as good as I remember, and I can't help but relax a little. Even if it all goes downhill from here, nothing can ruin the taste of my sandwich.

We take a moment to eat, and then it's down to business.

"So, I thought I'd give you this," I say, handing him a plastic folder that I pull out of my purse. "It's probably overkill, but it's a short profile of me, stuff that you would know if we were dating."

He takes the folder and takes the papers out. "Summer Sunshine Weathers," he reads. He has a smile on his face, but it's not mocking or anything.

I'm still a little defensive. "My mother had a little bit of seasonal depression going on when I was born."

He looks confused, until he notices my birthday. "First day of winter?"

"During a snowstorm," I say. "Shortest day of the year. It was kind of a bunch of little contributing factors."

He shakes his head. "No, no. I like it. It fits you."

I don't know how he could possibly tell, but he hasn't cracked any summer jokes yet, so I'll take what I can get.

"Thanks."

Chase reads through it aloud. "Thirty-three, born here in the valley, favorite color is yellow, favorite food is Hawaiian—good choice."

Chase gives me a smile and lowers the portfolio. "Well, I'm sure you know, I'm Chase Merrill. I don't know how much Lacy told you, but I'm thirty-five, born in California—don't hold that against me, I was raised here—my favorite color is blue, and my favorite food is probably Chinese—not ethnic. The plain, boring American kind."

"Pretty sure most Chinese food is good."

"It takes a lot to ruin it, for sure. I also like to travel, but with my start-up, I haven't had the chance to do it much. Do you like to travel?"

My shoulders relax just a bit more. "Yes, actually. I go on a big trip almost every year to visit a different country."

"Really? Do you have this year planned?"

"Not specifically yet, but it's a toss-up between Italy and Peru."

"Pompeii or Machu Picchu?"

"Machu Picchu or the Villa d'Este."

"Where's that?"

"Near Rome. I've seen pictures, and it looks really cool."

He smiles and looks down at the papers again.

"And what is this?" he says, flipping over to the next page. And the page after that. And after that.

My stomach drops. And this is where I might lose him. "Well," I say. "That's ... I should probably explain how we got here in the first place."

He frowns. "Didn't Lacy say that you faked having a boyfriend, and that he's toxic?"

"Yeah, pretty much," I'm undoubtedly flushing red right now. Maybe by refusing to acknowledge it, I can negate the consequences? "But ... this has been going on for like ... half a year."

His eyebrows raise. "That long?"

"Yeah." I put out a hand. "I promise I had a good reason. I'm not a liar by nature. It just kind of ... happened."

He looks down at the list. "So, what's this?"

"A list of the stuff that I've ... complained about."

A line appears in between his eyebrows as he keeps reading.

I can't stop myself from talking. "I'm—this isn't because I'm neurotic or anything. This is more so I can keep track. I only see Mom and Auntie Zen every month or so, but ..."

He keeps reading. He must have a million questions.

I have a million regrets. Why didn't I just come clean to Mom and Zen when they came up with therapy as an option? Why is it so important to have a boyfriend? He probably can tell *why* I don't have a real boyfriend.

"Does this boyfriend have a name?" Chase asks, flipping back a couple of pages. "I'm not seeing any identifiers in here."

"No," I say. "I tried to keep it as ambiguous as possible. I didn't want my mom googling him or anything."

"That's fair. Well, it does make things simpler, although I'm not sure I want to be the person that's forgotten your birthday *and* Christmas."

"It's not that he forgot, he had wo—" I cut myself off as I feel myself swinging into Deal-With-Mom mode. "Sorry."

"You're okay," he waves the paper at me. "At least I know why we're going into therapy. Mostly because of me, looks like."

I shake my head. "I'm sure I have stuff I need to work on. If I attract a guy like that, doesn't that mean I've got issues?"

Chase's expression changes. I can't tell exactly what he's thinking. Possibly that he knows *exactly* what kind of issues I have. Thankfully, though, Lacy is right, and he is too much of a gentleman to actually say anything.

"We should talk about our game plan," he finally says, putting the papers down on the table. "Have you set up the appointment?"

"Yeah. Next week with a Dr. Jacobson for Thursday at lunch, like you requested. They told me up front that Dr. Jacobson already has a couple of appointments on Thursdays at or around lunch time, so it might be every two weeks."

"That's okay," he confirms. "As long as I know the dates in advance, it shouldn't be any problem. I'll let you know as early as I can if that changes."

I nod and he turns to the last page of the document.

"Ah, I see this is the contract part," Chase says.

"I didn't want there to be any misunderstandings," I explain. "It's less of a contract, and more like guidelines."

"'No need to meet outside of sessions, all monetary expenses to be paid by Summer, minimal physical touching necessary.'" Chase looks up at me seriously. "Please don't take this wrong—I know you're not looking for an actual relationship any more than I am—but that last one might not work in actual practice."

"The touching?"

A dimple pinches in his cheek as he frowns. "We're supposed to be in a relationship. You probably know from your previous boyfriends that couples tend to touch quite a bit."

Did I? Then again, looking at Lacy and Renner, that was something I hadn't considered.

"I didn't want you to feel obligated," I say, trying to cover my tracks a little bit. "We aren't actually in a relationship, and even our pretend relationship is on the rocks."

"I understand that, but if necessary, we might need to freestyle a bit." At my faint look of alarm, he shakes his head. "I'm not talking making out or anything, but being physically closer. Knee touches, arm around the shoulder, stuff like that. Absolutely nothing inappropriate. If I cross a line, tell me immediately."

It doesn't shut down the tiniest bit of anxiety that has built in my chest, but it keeps it from growing. I'm a grown up. I can handle that. "It makes sense. For therapy."

The corner of his mouth curls up. "For therapy," he agrees. "Which brings me to another question. What is the point of us going to therapy? I mean, you need to have an actual face to break up with, and to deal with your family stuff, but what does Summer-with-a-boyfriend need the outcome to be? Are we going to make up and you suddenly have a good relationship with a fictional boyfriend who has my name and face, or is it going to be messy and fail? What am I looking at here?"

It's a good question, and thankfully I know the answer. "We're going to complete the therapy," I say. "It's weird, but I kind of feel like I owe it to Aunt Zen. She's paid in advance, and ..." I shrugged. How did I explain to a stranger that going to the appointments for my aunt felt like it made up for lying to my dad?

He blinks at Zen's name but doesn't comment on it. I continue. "So, let's have the therapy, and then breakup amicably. I don't need it to be messy or anything, but let's go, and then realize we're not good for each other anymore."

It's not ideal for me—nothing about this is ideal for me—but maybe going through a breakup will help give me enough wiggle room to figure out how to keep Mom and Zen off my back for the foreseeable future. I will never use a fake boyfriend again—the thought of getting into this situation *again* makes me feel like throwing up—but it'll hopefully give me a couple of months to figure out what to do while I 'mourn'.

Do they still do arranged marriages? Or maybe arranged boyfriends? A boyfriend for hire. No, that was exploitation.

Pull it together, Summer.

"Got it," Chase says. The frown is back, but this time it's concentration as he writes something down on the paperwork and underlines it. "Therapy, then break up. If it's six appointments over every one to two weeks, that would put us at the middle-end of March or so when we finish this, does that sound right?"

"Give or take a couple of weeks, yeah."

"Sounds good." He makes another note on the paper. "Do you have any questions for me?"

"Well, I would like to repay you for your time—"

Chase puts up a hand. "Don't worry about it. With you covering your own costs, I get free therapy, and who couldn't do with a bit of that?" His smile is genuine, but it seems a little too big for his face. I don't know what to do with it.

"If you're sure," I press.

"I'm sure."

"You can change your mind at any time."

His smile softens. "Summer, I'm sure."

"Just let me know."

He leans back, and smiles. "I'll let you know."

CHASE

Summer finishes her food and leaves the restaurant so fast it's like she's qualifying for the Olympics. I try not to notice, but it's difficult not to notice Summer. She's very pretty, from her reddish-brown hair, to the bright sparkle in her green eyes as her pink lips curl up into a smile.

She's so genuine as well. I'm used to people trying to leverage me, but that's not the vibe I get from her at all. She's simply a woman with a problem, trying to figure out how to fix it without diving into further trouble.

What I can't figure out is why she's in this amount of trouble in the first place.

It's clearly not her lack of organization—she's given me a written profile.

I can't help but smile as I read it. The photo is clearly a government photo—and not entirely flattering to her—making her face seem wider than it actually is and dulling the color of her hair to a flat brown. I almost hadn't recognized her sitting at the table, until she'd raised one hand. Even then, it was a little hard to believe the woman in the photo was the same as the one sitting in front of me.

Then again, if it is actually a government photo, the fact that it looks anything like her at all is borderline miraculous.

I only hope she can't tell how excited I am about this. It's not because of her. As out of touch as I apparently am, even I know that would be creepy. But free therapy? Free *relationship* therapy? Is there a downside to this? The boyfriend that I am supposed to be portraying seems to be just as out of touch as I am. I look down at the list again.

- Worked through Christmas and my birthday (for obvious reasons)
- We haven't gone on any super fancy dates (I'm not going alone on my own dime.)
- Wouldn't let me get a puppy. (Common Sense. I also don't really want one. Do not gift pets. <u>Ever.</u>)

Summer's annotations in blue ballpoint pen make me smile, and I skim through the other complaints. They all boil down to not being present and controlling of Summer's time and choices.

I frown. It's not quite the same verbiage that Amanda used, but it's not far off. Amanda never accused me of not providing for her—that I am confident I know how to do—but I was emotionally distant. I frown and try to focus back on the paper.

- Wanted me home by nine on a Friday during volleyball season. (I really wanted to get out of watching volleyball with my mom. She's ... it's not fun.)

- Wouldn't buy me a stereo system that my MLM friend totally recommended.

I smile as I realize she's used this boyfriend to get out of every single thing she didn't want to do for the past six months.

Maybe I need a fake girlfriend. Clearly there are some perks.

However, I know even as I read this list that there is one thing that Summer doesn't have that a fake boyfriend can't provide. An actual, living, breathing, human man that can go to therapy.

Thankfully, I can help with that.

Chapter 6
The First Appointment

SUMMER

I'm not usually a nervous person. Really, I'm not. This whole business has been an anomaly, stretching my nervous system like a mischievous pre-teen with a rubber band. If things keep going this way, I'm probably going to end up in therapy for anxiety.

Except it's therapy that's triggering my anxiety in the first place.

For crying out loud. You'd think they'd have an intro-to-therapy course somewhere.

There isn't. I've checked.

More than once.

Google has failed me.

I run my hand over my clothes as I sit in my car, making sure everything's in place. I'm never careless in how I dress and today is no exception. I had wrestled my curls into waves, used lipstick a shade darker than I normally wear, and pulled out my camel wool coat in preparation for the day. I'm glad I did—it feels like I'm wearing armor.

It's already been put to good use. Before I left my house this morning, I'd received a text from Joanie telling me good luck. When I arrived at work, Louis was waiting for me by my cubicle to 'touch base with my progress on one of my projects,' only leaving when I gently reminded him that he has his own projects. Gratefully, since then it's been a quiet Thursday.

Aside from the carousel of monkeys continuously screaming in the back of my mind.

It's so ridiculous. This appointment is simply talking to a professional about a boyfriend I've had problems with. The fact that he's not real doesn't mean I haven't had problems with him. Ergo, this appointment should be a cinch. It doesn't matter that I'll have Chase there. Although, he's the one who will probably bear the brunt of everything.

Poor guy.

What did he do to deserve this?

This is all my fault. Despite what I said to Lacy, there were ways I could have prevented the need for therapy. Spending a random holiday at home or having The Boyfriend go on business trips.

But ... I didn't want to stay home on holidays. Intervention notwithstanding, I did actually love my family.

But if I was on good terms with The Boyfriend, where were the gifts? Where were the pictures? Honestly, I'm surprised the picture thing hasn't come up yet. Or the fact that he doesn't have a name. Dad hasn't even asked, which means he's probably been waiting for me to tell him. I *have* actively avoided the conversation, but unlike my mother, he hasn't tried to corner me about it. He's kind like that.

It also makes me feel like more of a slug than I already do.

And I do. Today, for the first time in my life, I found myself hoping that Jennie wouldn't start. If I couldn't drive to therapy, it wouldn't be my fault that I'd missed it, right?

But Jennie works perfectly all day, with nary a clank, whistle, or thwack all the way to therapy. In fact, I would venture to claim that she has never worked better since I bought her as a sixteen-year-old. And so, here I sit in the parking lot of the office, a whole five minutes early.

It's not what I envisioned a therapy place to be. My regular primary care doctor works in a big red brick building with a huge glass entrance and the name over the door. I more or less expected the same to be true here. There's no name over the door, though; in fact, I have to go searching through my phone for the suite number so I can make sure to enter the right building.

I'm so engrossed in my phone that I don't see Chase approaching my car, and when he raps gently on the window, I jump, scream, and am halfway across the bench seat before either of us can register what's going on.

"Sorry!" I hear his muffled voice say as I recognize his concerned hazel eyes as he leans down. I reach over, cranking the window down.

"Oh, hi, Chase," I say, desperately trying to pretend that I'm not out of breath or that I may or may not be fighting tears.

I scare easily.

"You okay there?" he asks.

I nod, taking a deep breath and clearing my throat. "Yeah, you, um, surprised me."

He's too much of a gentleman to say that everyone within a five-mile radius is now aware of that. He's also fortunate that I'm a flight-over-fight sort of person. Instead, he shrugs a little self-consciously. "Sorry about that."

"Not to worry," I say, my heart rate finally dropping below 120 beats per minute. "What time are we looking at?"

"We're on time. We probably shouldn't wait out here much longer."

It's not exactly a hint, but it's close enough for me. I nod and roll up the window. Once the glass fits into the frame, Chase opens the door for me, which gives me an unobstructed view of him. It's a clear day for once, and the blue sky frames him as I look out of the car.

He extends his hand out to me.

I stare at it.

It's ... it's not what I expect.

I mean, it's not what my boyfriend would do. The fake one. The one Chase is supposed to be. He's supposed to be neglectful, right? Or at least self-possessed?

Maybe he's trying to turn over a new leaf? A hopeful little voice speaks up from the back of my mind. *He did agree to come to therapy with you.*

That could be true, except for the fact that this boyfriend didn't exist until he inhabited Chase's body. But where did that leave me? I couldn't exactly refuse it, but was this how Chase treated all of his girlfriends?

This man was hopelessly miscast as my boyfriend.

Move, Summer. The part of my brain in charge of rational thought speaks up. *He's still waiting on you.*

So, after a brief turn back to grab my purse, I reach out and take his hand.

His hand is gentle but strong, like his handshake last week, and he has no trouble pulling me to my feet. Once I'm on my feet, only a foot or so away because, y'know, physics, I raise my eyebrows in a half-questioning look.

He subtly nods to one of the buildings.

Our therapy facility is in Suite 302, in Building Four. The walls are almost entirely windows. Chase leans in a little, and I can smell his aftershave. It's subtly familiar, like I've smelled it before, but I can't place it before I'm distracted by his voice in my ear.

"The therapy offices are on the first floor. We'll need to be sure we keep up whatever we have in there out here as well."

Somewhere in the middle of the second sentence, I realize that he hasn't let go of my hand yet. His hands are warm. It's delicious in the freezing January air, but it's also incredibly distracting. He probably hasn't realized that he's held on, so I drop my hand.

He lets it go.

"Makes sense," I say, giving him a gentle smile to let him know that I understood it was an accident. "Well, in that case we should probably get going, huh?"

He smiles in return. "Let's do this."

CHASE

Maybe handing her out of the car was a mistake. In my defense, it's an old, old habit. Despite having spent my childhood in a lower-middle-class neighborhood, Mother and Father had insisted chivalry would not die with me. From the moment I turned twelve years old, I had been responsible for handing out any female within a one-mile radius should she try to leave her vehicle, be she toddler, college student, or grandmother. My sister was not exempt, her friends were not exempt, Mrs. Steinway across the street was not exempt. The only one who was exempt was my mother, and that was because it was Father's job.

What was a definite mistake, though, and definitely could not be attributed to any kind of habit, was holding Summer's hand afterwards. We did agree some touching would be necessary, but maybe I should have given my explanation for holding onto her ice-cold fingers first, instead of waiting until she started to pull away.

I don't blame her hesitance. At the very least, I've unnerved her. I've probably accidentally internalized our couple-ship too much. She doesn't actually know me apart from a lunch date last week, which means I should keep my hands to myself for now. Anything else would just be weird and uncomfortably predatory.

Still, the moment has passed, and we're heading across the parking lot side by side. Even since last week, I forgot how tall Summer is. She's not quite my height, but she's at least six feet tall in her heels, and dressed to kill in a camel wool coat, green turtleneck and black slacks. The turtleneck sets off her clear, pale complexion, and in the fifteen seconds that I was close enough to see, her eyes match the deep green almost exactly. She moves comfortably, her posture upright and confident, and at such a speed that she's either nervous, or trying to outpace me in a vain attempt to get away.

She does slow down as we get to the door, giving me enough time to pull ahead and open the door, gesturing for her to go through.

"Thank you," she says, giving me another tentative smile. It's the same one she gave me as she pulled her hand from mine. There's something about her smile that makes me nervous, like something's wrong and she doesn't want to tell me about it.

Well, it's her right. We're not actually dating. She doesn't need to confide in me, and I don't really have a right to ask. But there's something about the set of her shoulders, and the straightness of her back that tells me that she's deeply uncomfortable. It's probably something I've done, because it seems to cross her face in stages, but I'm not sure what 'it' is.

You're not a mindreader, Chase, I remind myself. *Just because you can tell she's uncomfortable, doesn't mean it has anything to do with you. It simply means that she's uncomfortable.*

It would be a lot easier to believe if I didn't have Amanda's voice screaming counterpoints in my head.

Maybe it would also be easier if I knew what Summer actually thought about this imaginary boyfriend, but her complaints don't really speak much to how she feels about this person. Or if she even feels anything for him at all. I wanted to pump her for information, sit her down and pick her brain about this, but if she wanted to give me a character sketch, wouldn't she have included it in the portfolio?

I'm going to have to freestyle it, which makes me feel even less confident.

The foyer of the building is blessedly warm, and to our left, I can see the sign for Valley Family Therapy. We turn as one, and she lets me grab the door as we enter. I bring up my hand to her back, intending to guide her through the door, but I remember myself at the last minute and let the limb drop to my side without touching her.

Summer makes a beeline for the check-in desk, and I follow at a slower pace, drawing even with her as she gathers the paperwork from the receptionist.

"You're Chase Merrill?" the receptionist asks, a bright look on her face.

"Yes, that's me."

The receptionist tips her head toward Summer, who holds two clipboards. "I need you to each fill out an intake form. Please be as honest with your answers as possible and give them to me when you're done. They are meant to be completely confidential. Dr. Jacobsen will be able to see you as soon as you're finished."

An intake form? Summer is looking at the clipboard with a furrowed brow and pushes one of the clipboards into my hands before wandering to a seat by the corner of the room. I copy her but sit a few spaces away to give her privacy.

Silence reigns in the waiting room as we fill out the questionnaires. It's fairly simple, but not what I was expecting from a relationship therapy appointment. It's all, well, kind of generic—mostly mental health history.

- During the past four weeks, have you had any problems with your work or life due to any emotional problems, such as feeling sad, depressed, or anxious?
- Have you felt particularly low or down for more than two weeks in a row?
- When was the last time you were really happy?
- Do you feel content with your relationship and family?

In other words, exactly the questions I'm not really comfortable answering.

Still, if I don't answer, how will they know how to help me? If they're going to be confidential, they probably won't be sharing these answers with Summer. She still doesn't know how much I need this appointment, and I'm not going to be the one to tell her. She's already nervous enough about coming with a near stranger. Knowing me and my history would make it ten times worse.

I answer as truthfully as I can and take the clipboard back to the check-in desk. Summer follows suit a couple minutes later. The receptionist takes our surveys into the back almost immediately, and Summer and I are left waiting in the foyer.

It's quiet and awkward. Summer chooses to sit beside me, but she's sitting on the edge of her seat like it's made entirely of nails, her hands clasped firmly together on her knee, biting her bottom lip absently.

I'm feeling nervous now, too, and I'm glad that Summer is here. Stranger or not, it's reassuring to have someone with me. Besides, she's not a *total* stranger. I know a few things about her.

Her favorite color is yellow.

I wonder what she likes to do for fun. Interestingly, that wasn't on the list. I open my mouth to ask and catch myself in time as the receptionist makes her way back into the foyer.

Summer notices my mouth opening, and raises her eyebrows, as if to urge me to go on. I shake my head with an uneasy smile, not having the brainpower to think of something else on the fly.

How in the world is this so intimidating?

Also, why is there no one else here? Summer made it sound like they took lunch appointments all the time, but this waiting room is more abandoned than a post-apocalyptic grocery store. Maybe they're making an exception for Summer since her aunt works here?

I don't know how I feel about that. We aren't cutting into someone's lunch hour, were we?

No. No, we aren't. Summer said something about there being another client that took our Thursday spot sometimes, right? Besides, no matter what time we're being seen, it doesn't change the quality of the therapy, right?

Again, why is this so intimidating?

"Summer and Chase?" We both straighten and turn toward the voice. Summer looks faintly relieved, but I feel like I am being stabbed with something hot and uncomfortable. Is it too late to back out?

So, so, so too late, Chase.

I push away the thought and focus on the speaker. It is an older woman—at least, older than us—probably in her mid-fifties, and her light brown hair is swept with gray. She's standing in the hallway entrance.

I was expecting her to wear a white coat, or something to denote her doctor-hood, but instead she's wearing slacks and a cozy looking sweater with some sort of low-res animal woven into the wool. It kind of looks like hedgehogs, but I wouldn't have bet my life on it.

Her smile is genuine, and something in my chest loosens. It's a little easier to stand up.

"That's us," Summer says, a smile mirrored on her face. "Dr. Jacobsen?"

"Yes, that's me. You can call me Andie, though. No need to stand on ceremony. Will you join me?" Dr. Jacobsen walks forward with a hand outstretched, and she shakes both of our hands.

Summer and I exchange glances, and follow Andie back to the offices.

Andie's office is as cozy as her sweater, ten feet by ten feet, with a desk, an armchair, and a loveseat, with shelves across the back wall.

I angle myself toward the armchair, but Dr. Jacobsen gestures toward the loveseat. "Please, take a seat."

Summer eyes dart between me and the couch before choosing a spot. I follow her lead, stepping up to the sofa and lowering myself onto the seat as Andie closes the door behind us.

To the doctor's credit, it is an extremely comfortable loveseat, soft as down, and completely sucking me in.

The problem? I am probably *actually* stuck. Seriously. I have little to no confidence I'm going to be able to extricate myself at the end of this appointment. One glance at Summer shows that she realized the hazard before she sat down. She's perched on the edge of the cushion, her legs tucked neatly in a way that keeps her center of gravity forward. Maybe if this goes well, she can help me up when it's time to go home.

If not, I'm going to be asking the therapist for more than mental help.

"So, I took a moment to read your evaluations," Andie says brightly after we've gone through the formalities of legal disclaimers and making sure Summer's insurance information is correct. "If you don't mind, though, I'd like to get to know the two of you a little bit better."

"Of course," Summer says, "What would you like to know?"

Andie gives us a big smile. "Well, how about we start with a little bit about you both, kind of like a short sketch of each of your lives, a brief history of your relationship?"

Right to it, then. Summer looks at me. "Would you like to go first?"

Not really, but I'd have to share eventually. No time like the present. "Uh, sure," I say, my throat drier than Utah winters usually make it. "I'm, uh, Chase Merrill. I'm one of the CEOs of Merrill and Victor, and ..." I glance at Summer. "I'll let Summer handle the history of our relationship."

Andie's smile doesn't diminish. "Being a CEO is a big responsibility, Chase. I'm glad you could make time for this. Where did you grow up?"

"I was born in California, but I grew up here in Utah," I say. "Murray."

"Pretty close, then." Andie's expression is pleasant. "Did you go to college?"

"Yes," I say with a short nod. "BYU. Got my MBA. Graduated a while ago."

Andie glances to my right. "When did you meet Summer?"

Oh no. I didn't know this. I knew we started dating six or seven months ago, but when did we meet?

Freestyle.

"Um ... summertime," I say, nearly choking. "At a ..." Think, think, think, Chase. Where's an appropriate, not creepy place where I could have met Summer and she would have given me the time of day?

Why would she? The snide voice is not helpful. *There's a reason you can't get in a permanent relationship.*

Be quiet, I command my thoughts.

"We met at a barbecue a year before last," Summer says quietly, looking over at me with what looks like concern. Can she tell how much I'm struggling? Can I get fired from our agreement? I sincerely hope not.

"That's a lot of fun. You've known each other about a year and a half, then?" Andie sums up.

"Yes." I don't know if I'm relieved or if my heart has given up. "Sounds about right."

Andie reaches for her phone and pauses. "Sorry, from time to time, I'll make notations for myself. They're just questions I want to ask the two of you in the future. Please continue." The therapist makes her note, but I can't think of anything else to say. We should have talked about this at our meeting last week, or even over text at *some* point since then.

Hindsight was truly 20/20.

I'm not blaming Summer—I have her phone number as well. I'm not afraid of asking questions. Normally, I wouldn't even be afraid of making something up on the fly, but there's something about Andie that inspires complete and utter honesty from me, which is something Summer doesn't need right now.

I open my mouth, and force something out, hoping that it's good. "It was a barbecue. In August. Sorry, Summer, I can't think of the day right now. I was dating someone else at the time, so nothing happened, but after that ended ... a mutual friend told me she was interested. I reached out and asked her out. We had lunch the week after at a ... coffee shop, I think."

Andie looks at me with a thoughtful expression and nods. "Thank you, Chase. Now, I'll ask you both these questions, but if you need a moment to think about it, let me know, and we can catch up with Summer."

I gesture for her to continue. I'm happy to let her take over.

I regret it almost immediately.

"My questions are," Andie says, "what was the moment you decided to come to therapy? What was the incident that—even though you knew someone else was paying for it—really made it worth it to come? The other question I have is what do you hope to achieve by being here?"

Man. How honest can I be? How can I say that the real motivation is a relationship that only ended six months ago? Summer and I have only supposedly been dating for about that long, but how can I keep cheating off my rap sheet? Inattentive and domineering is one thing. Infidelity is something completely different. The one thing I have going for me is that Amanda broke up with *me*.

"Can I answer after Summer?" I ask. Maybe her answer will give me some inspiration.

"Sure." It doesn't seem to bother Andie at all. She turns to Summer. "Summer, how about you?"

Summer shifts. "Well, I was born in Utah as well, down in Provo, but I graduated from Georgia Tech. I've been working in Information Technologies ever since. Like Chase said, we met in August two years ago. I think it was some sort of end-of-summer bash." She sneaks a look over at me. "We were only friends for a long time. Then after about a year ... well, he asked me out." There's a small smile on her lips. "He was cute. I said yes. We officially started dating in July."

I almost don't register the compliment. When I do, it's a little too late, and she's not looking at me anymore.

"Have you had therapy before?" Andie asks.

Summer shakes her head. "No, but my older sister has. It's definitely a new experience."

"It can be intimidating," Andie agrees. "I remember my first appointment with my husband was a bit of a circus."

"You had couple's therapy?" Summer asks.

Andie's grin isn't self-conscious. "I was even a therapist at the time. Sometimes we need a hand up, no matter our background. So, Summer, I'll extend the same question to you: what convinced you to come to therapy? And what do you want to get out of it?"

Summer shifts in her chair, her hands still clasped together. She glances over at me, then straightens her back. "Well ... things haven't been great recently. I've been feeling like ... like Chase might be prioritizing things over our relationship." She starts to speak faster, like she's trying to get it out as quickly as possible. "I know he's got to make a living and stuff, and I'm fine with that being a priority for him, but I kind of ... I don't know." She doesn't look at me now.

It hurts. I know it's not about me—couldn't possibly be about me—but it's a glancing shot to an already tender place, and I can't look at her anymore.

"Summer, what are you hoping to get out of therapy?"

"I don't know," she says, and I look up when I hear the vulnerability there. "I guess part of me wants to see if we can still make it work. We're both busy. We've both got separate lives, but ... can't we mesh them?"

She does look over at me then.

And then I take a deep breath. There's no way I can follow up sincerely after that. I've forgotten—I'm the negligent type in this scenario, right? I'm not the type of person who would really want therapy, right? "It ... yeah. We've kind of grown apart. She pointed it out to me, and I agreed. I want to try to make it better."

It's lame. It's SO lame, but I want to keep coming and undermining her won't help either of us.

Andie's smile lessens for the first time, and she nods carefully.

The rest of the time blurs together. She mostly wants to know more information about each of us individually. I don't know how much to share, not wanting to work against whatever narrative Summer has going on, but still giving as much accurate information as possible. The balance is hard, and it ends up sending me into an insecure silence. It's not me, and I hate it. I'm usually a confident speaker, adaptable and even a little glib, but the uncertainty of the situation has undercut me entirely, leaving me floating adrift in the conversation.

It's bad and uncomfortable, and it shows.

By the time we're done with our introductory visit, I'm down to single-word answers, and Summer is shifting in discomfort at least once a minute now. Andie gives us a professional smile, and we stand to go.

After I struggle out of the quicksand couch, I'm first out the door, and once I'm over the threshold, Andie looks at me with a calm expression. "Chase, would you mind if I talked to Summer privately?"

My heart sinks. Andie knows. She knows we're faking it.

Can we be sued for fraud over this? My brain says no, but

my already-frayed lizard brain says, *Yes, absolutely. Wait for the papers at your office.*

"Sure." I clear my dry throat. "I'll wait in the lobby."

Andie's expression softens a little, and she nods. "Thanks, Chase."

She reaches for the door, and I turn tail, trying not to feel too relieved to get out from under the therapist's assessing gaze. I am never going to lie again. Ever. It is not worth it. I'm starting to reconsider whether therapy is, either.

It's only a moment before Summer comes out, her cheeks a little more rosy than before. She glances at me nervously, before striding quickly toward the door. She's moving fast, and I barely make it in time to grab the door for her as she practically runs out of the building.

By the time I catch up with her, it's by her car, and her arms are crossed tightly across her chest. She's not looking at me, and her back is to the building.

"Summer? What happened?" I ask, stepping quickly to her side. My hand moves to her elbow, and I barely catch myself before dropping it back to my side. She's already uncomfortable, no need to make it worse.

Summer pinches her forehead, and it's clear she's either frustrated or embarrassed. I'm not sure if I can help, but I need to ask, because whoever I was in the office, I am Chase out here.

"Summer?"

"Andie ..." she trails off, her cheeks pinking up. "Well, she thinks we should break up."

"What?" It's almost a gasp. "What did she say?" Could a therapist do that?

Summer can't look at me, and squints against the cold wind that's pulling the clouds over the sun. "Not in so many words, but when she pulled me aside, she told me in a Very Gentle

Tone, that I could remember I didn't have to be in a relationship, and she and I could meet privately if that's what I wanted."

For crying out loud, Andie had been in my presence for an hour, and she agreed with Amanda.

Summer exhales hard, her cheeks puffing out. "She said it wasn't an actual recommendation, just an option." She doesn't look over. "But she also said was for me to take the next week until our next appointment and really think about whether or not I even want to be in a relationship."

Silence reigns heavily between us. Summer pinches her lips together and shakes her head. "I felt so bad lying to her. I know that I don't know her, and it shouldn't matter to her, but even only telling her I'd think about it, instead of confessing upfront ... She just wants to help, and—ugh." She shakes her head and finally looks at me.

"I could tell you were uncomfortable in there, Chase. I'm sorry. This is way harder than I expected it to be. If you want out, we can break up and be done with it. I ... I thought this would be the better option, rather than dealing with Mom and Zen's pitying stares and sighs for the rest of my life, but watching you in the appointment, and knowing we're lying to Andie ... I don't know if it's worth it. I'm sorry for putting you through that."

For essentially having just admitted to having a fake boyfriend to keep her family off of her back, it's oddly not self-pitying at all. It's almost like she's weighed the options, done the experiment, and it had failed. Time for the next option.

I believe that until I look into her eyes. There's defeat there, like she had really hoped this would work, and it's terrifying that it didn't.

"Why me?" I ask.

It's quiet. The wind almost drowns my voice out entirely,

but Summer definitely hears. Her chin lifts, and there's confusion in those deep green eyes as they meet mine.

"What?"

"Why does that boyfriend have to be me?" I ask. "Summer, you're very pretty. If you want a boyfriend, you could probably go out and get a good one and avoid therapy altogether. Why does it have to be me?"

I almost expect her to get defensive. It's not really very sensitive to ask a girl why she's single. But under the circumstances, it feels important.

She doesn't get defensive, though. She seems to weigh the question, and answers carefully. "It's not that I don't want a relationship. Really," she finally says, her lips pressing together. She looks around the parking lot, before centering her eyes back on me. "But there's a very big difference between theoretically being able to get a man and actually catching one."

It still doesn't really answer my question, and part of me wonders what the issue is. Confidence? Effort? Priorities? But really, it's none of my business, and whatever the case may be, Summer does have a point. Real relationships take two people. That's what my problem is, too, apparently.

It's also why, no matter how awkward today was, I really still need to go to therapy, and I don't want to give up this chance. And if what Summer says about her family looking down on her for being single—or whatever is going on—is true, then I don't want to leave Summer at their mercy. She chose to come today, as an honest, forthright person, rather than to come clean with her family, and that's starting to carry a lot of weight with me.

We have to at least try. Even if we're going to just break up at the end.

But I can't do what we did today again, and I don't think Summer wants to, either. Something needs to give.

I check my watch. "How long do you have until you have to get back to work?"

Summer checks her phone. "About twenty minutes. I asked for an extended lunch."

I nod. "How far?"

"About fifteen minutes away."

I nod again. Here goes nothing. *Treat this like a follow-up meeting. We've tried something, it didn't work. What now?* "Okay. This probably sounds crazy, but ... I don't think we should give up just yet."

Summer looks up, her eyebrows drawn together in confusion. "What?"

"This—today—was awkward," I admit. "Very, very awkward."

Summer's shoulders slump, but a look of relief—mixed with a decent amount of chagrin—crosses her face. "Yeah." It's almost more sigh than voice, but it's clear enough.

"I think we can do better," I say. At her look of confusion, I explain. "If this were a trial product at work, where we're invested in how it ends, we'd take a look at the situation, see what worked and what didn't, and then adjust right?"

"Yeah, we would."

"So, we do the same here. You don't want to deal with your family, and I've committed to helping you. What could we do better?"

"Communication," Summer says immediately. "We fell apart when she started asking about our relationship. We're going to have to tighten down the details—thank you, by the way, for not making us start dating immediately after we met each other."

"You don't like love at first sight?" I ask lightly.

"I don't believe in it," she admits. "I've definitely had

crushes at first sight, but you can see by my singleness how well that's worked out."

"I imagine it takes a certain type of person," I say, nodding. "I am not one of them."

She huffs a laugh.

"Okay, then," I say, "Communication. I think we should also sink as much of ourselves into our ... well, roles, I guess. I know you're probably already doing that, but I didn't quite know what to do in there."

"Really?" Summer says, sounding quite surprised. "I thought you were just going for 'sullen boyfriend.' You were doing so well it was throwing me off."

It's my turn to laugh now. "I don't think I've ever been so uncomfortable. I was so worried about messing up whatever narrative you'd set up beforehand that I didn't know what to say."

Summer bites her lip and pats me on the arm. "Sorry about that."

We're silent for a moment longer, and then she shakes her head. "So how do we do this? I mean, nailing down dates and stuff is one thing, but ... how do we ...?" She trails off, but I know what she means.

"Honestly," I look over my shoulder at the office, and then down at my watch. A minute more until Summer has to go back to work. "I think if we get to know each other a bit better it might work out better. Knowing how each other works, and even general facts might help." I check my watch again. Time's up. "Look, I don't want you to be late for work. I'll pull up some internet questionnaires tonight and text them to you. Fill them out and we'll do a video chat or something."

I reach toward her car to open the door, before I realize Summer's car is the oldest Crown Victoria I've ever seen, and requires a key to enter.

I look up at Summer, and she's biting back a smile.

"Sorry," she says, fighting a smile. "Let me introduce you: this is Jennie. We go way back. I've thought about getting a new car, but it always feels like a betrayal. Hold on." She pulls the single key out of her pocket and sticks it in the door. It clicks open. She reaches for the door handle, but I'm already there to pull the door open.

She looks at me a little questioningly, and I smile, nodding toward the therapy building, with all of its windows facing right at us. "For therapy?"

She returns my smile.

"For therapy."

Chapter 7
The Second Appointment

CHASE

I'M FEELING MORE PREPARED THIS TIME AROUND. SUMMER and I met over video chat Tuesday night, and I feel like we've gone over and decided at least the most important things. Officially, we met on August fifteenth and started dating eleven months later—almost seven months ago, a few weeks after my breakup from Amanda. No one knew we were dating until a few weeks later—coincidentally when Summer first announced it to her family—and things started going sour around Labor Day, when I chose to work over the holiday weekend rather than go to the lake with her family for a last summer hoorah.

Thanks to the questionnaires, I know that she loves all food except for eggs and Turkish delight—whatever that was—and enjoys Korean dramas. I know she's a night owl—same as me—and loves the fall the best—same as me.

In short, I am feeling much more prepared.

I'm sitting in my car, reviewing her answers when my phone rings. I glance at it, fully intending to ignore it if it's anyone except for Ed, Summer, or—

"Hey, Gills," I say into my phone.

"Hey, Morkie," Avery says, yawning a little.

"You just getting up?" I glance out the window to see if Summer's pulled in yet. I've gotten here early on purpose, but that'll be for nothing if I miss her.

"No, got the lunchtime sags," Avery's voice isn't super convincing. I might be a night owl, but if it weren't for the regular work schedule, Avery wouldn't exist before noon most days.

"I thought you had a day off today?" I say, checking my watch.

"I do," Avery says, "but I had to squander it to get on the road."

"Road?"

"I went up to Salt Lake for a history tour. I told you about it at dinner last week, but only in passing." Avery's voice squeaks like she's stretching. "Unfortunately, my friends don't seem to realize that a.m. stands for 'absolutely miserable.'"

I snort and pat the steering wheel. "The monsters."

"You're telling me. I'll have to complain one of these days," she says with a sigh.

I frown a little in concern. Avery is not the sighing type. "All good, Gills?"

"I heard from Mother this morning."

I pause. "You okay?"

"Of course." Her voice isn't untruthful but still seems a little more subdued than normal.

"Are they?"

"Both of them are fine. I dunno. You'd think I'd get used to five-minute calls with my mom every few months."

"Maybe if it weren't our quarterly call, it would be different," I say, trying to keep the bitterness out of my voice, and failing miserably. "Still, it's good to hear from them outside of social media." It's the only reason I have it anymore. Our calls are basically proof-of-life. Any real life updates come from outside sources.

I can almost hear Avery's frown. "Yeah, I guess. Well, enough with feeling sorry for myself. What are you up to?"

I freeze and look up guiltily. Despite getting wrapped up in all of this, I haven't told Avery about Summer, or the rather confusing situation I've found myself in. It's not that I want to hide what I'm doing—at least, not from Avery of all people—but I'm not quite sure how to explain it to my sister.

But I can't lie to her.

"I'm at a meeting," I say, looking toward the almost empty parking lot. It's less than five minutes to, and Summer still hasn't shown up. I'm a little concerned. She was over fifteen minutes early last time. I know because I was twenty.

"What? Right now? I'm so sorry. I thought you were taking your long lunch—"

"No, no, I am," I say, reassuring her quickly. "I'm going to help a friend."

"... with a meeting?" Avery asks dubiously. "That doesn't sound like a long lunch. Well, actually it does, but not in the way long lunches are supposed to be long."

I laugh and look toward the road just in time to see Summer's Crown Victoria round the corner.

"Nah, it's cool. They actually just pulled up, so I'm going to have to go."

"No worries. Love you, Morkie."

"Love you, Gills. Hang in there."

"I will."

I step out of the car as I hang up, heading toward where Summer is easing into her parking spot. She looks up guiltily as she turns the car off and then gathers her purse as I open the door.

"I'm sorry I'm late." Her pale cheeks flush as she reaches

back for her wallet, which has slipped out of her purse and is stuck at the far side of the bench seat. "I got held up by a coworker on my way out. I ... may have used you as an excuse to get out of there on time."

"Me?" I ask, before I realize what she means. "Isn't that my purpose here?"

"Well, I will admit, it felt different before I put a face to the name," Summer says, sitting up straight. I offer my hand, and she takes it, standing with a smile. She lets go almost immediately, but her left hand comes up, patting the back of my arm, apparently in thanks.

"I thought he didn't have a name. Or face," I say musingly, popping the push lock closed and shutting the car door.

"Like I said," Summer says, putting her keys into her purse. "It feels different now."

"Well, since the whole point of this exercise is for you to have a real—meaning corporeal—boyfriend for the duration of this, don't stop now."

Summer huffs a laugh and looks at me. She's not wearing high heels today. I peg her at about five foot ten or so, but her posture is upright, her expression confident. The powder-blue turtleneck she's wearing brings out the red in her hair, and the black coat accentuates her natural height well.

I'd tried to ask Lacy about her over the last couple of days. Nothing weird or overly personal, but ... background information. Given that they've known each other for upward of fifteen years, Lacy would know better than anyone what makes Summer tick.

Because that's the thing, even after having Summer take two questionnaires and talking with her—in therapy and out—I'm still not sure what drives this woman. Not that I'd have expected to know everything about her right away, but usually I can read people better than this. She's a businesswoman, and most businesspeople are after one of three things: glory, money, or a relationship.

But I don't get the feeling that any of those things are accurate for her. She's success-driven, but not obsessive. Well-to-do, but not greedy or excessive. Personable, but not ... personal.

And that's why I outsourced.

Or I would have, if Lacy had been cooperative at all. Every time I asked—and for my pride, I stopped at three times—she referred me back to Summer. "You want the skinny, Chase? Ask her yourself."

I can't imagine that going particularly well, especially given our current closeness and strange relationship, but maybe I'm wrong.

We walk toward Suite 302 and Summer slows to let me get the door for her—I explained the door rule during our video chat earlier in the week.

She steps in and I follow, both of us walking over to the receptionist. She checks us in, and we barely have time to sit down before Andie comes through the door.

"Chase, Summer! Welcome!" Andie smiles genuinely as we walk toward her.

Summer checks her phone. "Sorry we're almost late. I got caught up at work."

Andie waves it off. "If you're not late, there's no need to apologize." She motions to the couch as we pass her into the room. "Please have a seat."

We do, and the couch sucks me in just like last week. I feel like it's strategic at this point.

"I'm happy that you're back," Andie says.

Summer nods and looks at me. "Thank you for letting us come back. Last time ... well, I think we might have not been at our best."

"Therapy can be stressful," Andie says kindly.

It's a very generous statement.

Andie looks carefully between the two of us. "How's it going now?"

"It's better," Summer says, her voice a little quieter. "We've talked about what you suggested last time. It's been a little tough lately between us, but we've both decided that, no matter what the outcome is in the end, we want to try and make this relationship work. We're willing to put the effort in to see if we can make it."

Andie looks pleased. "I'm very happy to hear that. Hopefully the discussions we'll have and the exercises I have for you two will help. The fact that you're even here today is a really positive sign." She assesses the two of us. I smile at Andie, trying to come off as confidently as I can. I think it works.

Andie waits for a moment and the silence sinks into my skin, tempting me to fidget. Before I do, she continues. "I think the best way to start all of this is to start with communication patterns. Now, I hope you realize this is only what I've picked up from our session last time and your surveys, but I believe it will help."

She crosses her legs and picks up a clipboard that's sitting on the shelf beside her. "Now, communication and all the different types of it is something that's constantly being worked over and discussed in the field of psychology. For the most part we've narrowed down communication into four different types —passive, aggressive, passive-aggressive, and assertive. Are you familiar with these?"

I am. As a member of my company's management, I've tried to go to as many seminars as I can to help communicate with my team in the best way possible.

Summer nods as well.

"Good," Andie says. "The good news is that you're both assertive communicators. It would be a lot more difficult if one of you were passive and didn't stick up for yourself, or if one of you were aggressive and attacking the other all the time. I'm not saying that that can't happen, but even when you were both uncomfortable last time, you treated each other respectfully, even if it seemed like there was friction there. This is good. I also think we have room to grow."

That's putting it *mildly*.

But this is what I'm here for. I try not to let the trickle of excitement show on my face. If Amanda was right and I have difficulty connecting with people, this is a massive step forward. What if this unlocks everything?

Andie continues. "Now, you two have a couple of differences in how you communicate. Chase, you're probably more assertive than Summer, but you're more emotionally detached."

The excitement that was building is squashed flat, dying with an undignified screech like it was hit by a falling piano.

Amanda was right.

I try to keep the stricken silence in my chest off my face, but Andie isn't done. I hope it's over soon. It feels like I'm being dissected. But I'm here to learn and to grow, so I inhale and try to take it on the chin.

"It's because you're a strong communicator." Andie's tone is probably supposed to be comforting, but I'm feeling the sting. "You keep your emotions out of a conversation, so you can communicate more clearly and effectively, but it can come off that you don't care, particularly when you do start to care, and start withdrawing to keep your emotions level."

She'd picked that up from one conversation? I'd been talking for the last thirty-four years—give or take a couple of months—and hadn't realized anything of the kind. Was this something inborn, or—

"Summer," Andie turns and gives the woman beside me a kind smile. It kind of feels like a trap at this point, and I can feel

Summer shift beside me, her shoulders tensing. "You are very kind."

The shoulders release, and Andie continues. "You are very able to express what you want and need, and given what we've already talked about, I think you think very deeply about what you're going to say and how it's going to affect people. It naturally makes you more reserved, and less likely to say much about how you're feeling emotionally. You try to get a feeling for a situation before you engage with it in any way."

I steal a glance at Summer. There's now a slight pinch between her eyebrows. Now that Andie's said something, it kind of fits. Have I ever heard her actual opinion of things? Not just facts about her. I guess if we're being didactic about things, she's given me her preferences about the seasons or foods, but it's not exactly personal.

"Now, we're not going to change everything about how you communicate, nor do we want to," Andie says with a smile. "You both are good at being yourselves, and that's something to respect and cherish. However, your relationship consists of two people. Sometimes adjustments are necessary to create the greatest outcome."

It makes sense, and I watch Summer. Her chin bobs, the small line in between her eyebrows pinching as she frowns.

"What are your recommendations?" Summer asks.

Andie studies Summer. After a moment, so do I. Summer's frown has turned into a focused stare. It's the look of someone who's about to take on a challenge. Then Andie turns her eyes on me.

I'm sure I don't look as hungry for information as Summer, but I definitely want to know.

Scratch that, I *need* to know.

Andie is teaching us how to communicate, right? Even if

my real relationship isn't going to be with Summer, I can always use this, right?

"Well," Andie says, her eyes back on Summer. "My first challenge is this: Give each other a little more to work with. Summer, you feel deeply. I can tell when I talk to you. But you don't necessarily show a lot on your face. Now, I'm not going to tell you to start making more expressions but do give Chase something to work with. If you don't like something, speak up and let him know. He can handle it, I promise."

Summer glances at me, and back at Andie and nods. "I will."

"Chase?" Andie says, and I look up at her. "I need you to *listen* to Summer."

I should have seen that one coming.

She's not done, of course.

"For what it's worth, I think you've been trying, but especially since Summer is going to be trying to open up more, I want you to respond in kind. Don't let it be a mystery what you're thinking and feeling, but keep in mind the tone of your voice and how your words could be perceived. Summer is not your business partner, and your relationship is not a corporation. Your words can directly affect how she feels, and you should carry that responsibility wisely."

Summer shifts, her lips parted. Andie speaks first. "This includes how you speak about each other while you're apart. How we talk about things, especially to ourselves, colors everything else. If you want to make this work, you're going to need to invest in each other to make it really worth it."

I stare at Andie, floored. I hadn't expected her advice to be so specific. I hadn't particularly thought I'd been so businesslike, but as I look back over the last few months—especially with Amanda—I see the proverbial light. Amanda had gotten distant, and instead of being curious, I'd gotten polite.

I swallow, and turn to Summer, whose expression has gone completely blank.

"Where do we begin?" She clasps her hands on her knee.

Andie smiles. "Well, if you're up to it, we can start with a couple of practice sessions."

"Practice sessions?"

"Yeah, kind of like a role-playing session. Troubleshooting, if you will, to make sure you know what kind of communication you're looking for in certain scenarios," Andie says.

Summer hands clasp a little tighter and bites her lip for a millisecond. "What ... kind of scenarios?"

Andie waves her hand reassuringly. "Normal situations. We can even pretend you're meeting for the first time today if you want. Just to get the hang of things."

Summer considers this. "What do you think, Chase?"

"Me?" I ask. It's not that I'm surprised that she asked me, but I ... okay, yes, I was a little. She was the leader here in therapy. Was my opinion really that important?

Summer presses her lips together. "You're half of this relationship," she says softly. "If you're not up for it, then we don't have to do it."

"Do you want to?" I ask, digging for more time. I have no idea if I'm up for it. I'm still not sure what this will entail.

Her hands relax a fraction as she mulls it over. "I think I do. We want things to get ... better," a deeper smile surfaces, and I realize it for what it is—a reference to our charade. Summer squares her shoulders. "It'll be good practice."

I'd decided before we'd ever began therapy to follow Summer's lead in these sessions. It was a given that if she wanted to do this, I would follow. But the intensity of her gaze, how she's leaning toward me slightly, focused on my answer, all confirm she's actually concerned whether I really want to do this.

I don't know if I should be, but I'm touched.

"If you want to," my voice is quieter than I intend it to be, "then we'll do it."

Summer sits back, her eyebrows furrowing into an expression of quiet determination, and she presses her lips together.

"Thank you." She shifts, as if a new thought comes to her mind. "If you're uncomfortable with this at any point, let me know and we'll stop."

I settle back into the couch. It's probably a mistake—it sucks me in like it's entirely made of octopi—but it's a statement. I'm not going anywhere.

"Only if you do the same," I say gently. "If it doesn't work for us, then we'll stop."

Summer nods. "Agreed."

Andie's looking between us with a smile that may or may not be slightly teary. "For the record, that's exactly what I'm talking about. But let's run through a few scenarios. The first one, Summer, you meet Chase for lunch. You've had a hard day at work. How would you begin?"

I only see the flash of mischief on Summer's face, when she holds out her hand. To shake. She then continues in her pleasant but neutral voice. "Hi, Chase. I'm Summer. I've had a bad day, and I would like to have lunch with you."

I can't help it, I snort. I reach out and take her hand. Pumping it up and down once, I don't let it go, holding onto her fingers. They're cold, and I adjust her fingers in my palm to warm them up. I expect her to pull them away, but her thumb curls around my hand. I meet her eyes. She's not looking at our hands, she's looking me in the eyes, gauging my reaction.

"Hi, Summer. I'd love to have lunch with you. What made it a bad day?"

I get a real smile for that. "Oh, you know. Annoying coworkers."

"Sounds miserable," I say, making sure to soften my tone so she knows I don't mean it as too much of a joke. "Anything I can know about?"

Summer's eyebrows lift microscopically, but then she smiles. "My work isn't top secret. Or all that important. He's just annoying." Her expression flickers a little bit. "Don't feel like you have to do anything about it."

I squeeze her hand, and she looks down at our hands for the first time. Her fingers aren't quite warm yet, but I drop them. I'm about to spew some kind of bravado about beating him up— I would have, a couple of months ago. But then I think of her words from a moment ago. "Would you let me know if you want me to do anything about it?"

"I will," she says quietly. There's something different about her posture now, and for the life of me I can't pinpoint what it is.

"Well done!" Andie says. "Summer, great job at expressing something to Chase, and Chase great job at showing care without being overbearing. Let's try another scenario ..."

By the time we're done with three more scenarios, our hour is almost up. We're wrapping up when Andie hands Summer a journal.

Summer frowns. "What's this?"

"This is a couple's journal," Andie said. "Over the next few weeks, I'm going to be giving you some homework assignments, especially for the times where we have a couple of weeks between appointments. Once you're done with each assignment, I want you to each write your impressions of how it went. After you're done writing, read the other's entry. When you come in next, we can go over it together, and if there are sticking points, or situations where maybe things didn't go as well as you wanted, we can talk through those.

"I also want to encourage both of you to keep your own

personal journals. In my experience as a therapist, journaling can really help you process whatever you might be feeling about any one given situation—negative, neutral, positive, or what you don't understand.

"Of course, with anything like this, it will be on the honor system. I can't follow you everywhere—and I think probably everyone here is glad that I won't. It only works if the two of you are completely honest with each other."

I meet Summer's eyes. She nods, and I turn back to Andie. "We'll do it."

"Awesome," Andie says. "Now, your homework assignment is to have two face-to-face conversations before your next appointment, where you practice your communications skills. This probably won't be hard, since you probably see each other more than that, but dedicate two meetings for this specifically, and journal about it."

Summer nods. "Okay."

Andie's smile is huge as we all stand up. We start heading toward the door. This time, Andie touches my arm and says to Summer, "Do you mind if I have a word with Chase for a moment?"

Summer looks at me in alarm, and then back at Andie. "Is everything okay?" she asks.

Her concern is obvious, and I don't really blame her, considering the last time this woman spoke to one of us privately, the therapist told her to break up with me. Still, Summer and I are in this together. I can plead my case with the best of them if that's what I need to do.

"I'll be fine, Summer. Would you wait for me in the lobby so I can walk you to your car? We've got enough time, right?"

Summer checks her phone, and then nods, looking up at me.

Andie smiles, and pats Summer's arm. "I promise to bring him back in one piece. We'll just be a moment."

Summer nods again, then turns and walks down the hall, her black coat swinging. Andie waits until Summer makes it to the lobby and then closes the door. She then looks up at me.

I give her a winning smile. "How can I help you, Andie?"

Her expression sobers a bit, and I felt my expression dim of its own accord.

"What's wrong? Is everything okay with Summer?"

"Everything is fine with Summer," she says gently. "But I was hoping you'd answer a couple of questions."

"Of course," I fight the urge to clear my throat. I'm not a person who runs from their problems, but I can feel the urge to bolt building. Is Andie suspicious? Can she tell that we're faking things?

Is she going to tell me to break up with Summer?

Andie is still weighing her words, which makes me feel even worse, if possible. She stands barely taller than my shoulder, and yet I can feel her presence looming over me. "I was just wondering what your priorities are."

The feeling of doom lifts slightly, and I shift. "My priorities?"

"Yes."

My mind races. "With my relationship with Summer?"

"In general, actually."

I exhale hard and study the room as I think. "I have goals," I say, as though I'm admitting a fault. "I want my work to be successful, and I want to help my company grow. But I ..." *Want to keep coming to therapy?* "I want to do right by Summer. I don't know if what's already happened between us will keep us from having a long-term relationship, but I want to make sure that we've tried everything."

Andie's face softens. "Do you not want to stay in a relationship with Summer?"

"That's not it," I assure her as sincerely I can. "There's just ... history. With me. With an ex."

She thinks about this. "I understand what you're saying. Relationships can be a really difficult business. Sometimes, even after trying everything, they don't always work out. Would you care for a little advice?"

"That's why I'm here," I say honestly.

"Know what you want out of *this* relationship, and what you need from Summer. It's going to take work, compromise, and sacrifice from both of you. Things won't always go your way, and you'll need to decide what you actually want your future to be like. But you *can* decide."

I shuffle my feet a little. "Easy to say."

"Sure," she says kindly. "But if it helps, if you didn't care, you wouldn't be here."

My shoulders drop. "I am trying to be better."

She pats my elbow in a motherly way. "And that's why I think you two will make it work. You're a determined guy, Chase. I have a feeling that whatever goal you set for yourself, you'll eventually get."

I felt the corner of my mouth curl in a self-deprecating smile. "Thanks, Andie."

"You've got this, Chase."

Somehow, I feel a little better.

The air seems heavier as I leave the building, enough that it's actually a relief to step out into the late January air. We make it to Summer's car, and she unlocks it before turning around to talk.

"I know that Andie's asked us to meet outside of therapy, but we didn't agree to that originally," she says in a rush. "I'm not going to hold you to it."

I consider this, folding my arms. She has a point, of course, but we've also both agreed that we're going to put in the work for this. I, especially, need the help.

"Do you not want to?" I tilt my head to the side. Summer's leaning back against her car, her arms folded across her chest, staring into the middle distance.

"Huh?" She straightens, "No, I mean that in the deal that we had, you only agreed to do the therapy sessions. I'm sure that I could fake the journal entries or something."

I think about this. "I'm not sure whether I should be impressed with your lying skills or concerned about your offer of forgery. But no, I think we should do the assignment."

"Why?"

I smile ruefully and nod back to the office. "Because I just got a very kind talk about needing to make sure my priorities were in line with my goals, and I think it would help establish our actual couplehood." When Summer's mouth drops open in horror, I shake my head. "Don't worry about it."

"But what did she say?" Summer whispers.

"She told me to work for our relationship, and that if I didn't work at it, it wouldn't happen at all."

Summer grimaces. "This is such a nightmare."

"Summer, I'm not taking it personally. In fact, it was kind of helpful."

"Yeah, but ... to actually say that ..." She trails off, pressing a hand to her head. "Who does that?"

"A doctor," I say evenly. "Who's looking out for your mental health and mine. It makes sense, Summer. From what she knows, I'm the one that wasn't pulling my weight in this relationship. That was our story. I'm not taking it personally." At least not where it pertains to Summer. Where I'm concerned ... well, it's not comfortable, but it is intriguing. *Have my priorities been skewed all this time?*

Summer sighs and folds her arms again. "I still don't like it."

I turn and lean against the car beside her. She glances at me but doesn't move away. "Well, as far as I can see, we both don't like lying very much. It seems like the best way to keep being convincing is to keep meeting up."

She nods. "I think you're right." She looks up at me with a squint. "Sorry for being a dealbreaker."

"Sorry for making you keep the deal," I joke. "As for actual meet-ups, there's a new restaurant I want to try. They're open at lunchtime. Do you want to meet up next week?"

"What kind of food?" she asks.

"Chinese."

She bites her lip.

I hold out my hand. "For therapy?"

She sighs, but there's a bit of a laugh behind it. She reaches out and her fingers close around mine, a smile growing on her cheeks. We shake. "For therapy."

Chapter 8
The Grill

SUMMER

Thursday sneaks up on me like a big cat on a gazelle in the Serengeti. One minute, I'm climbing into bed Thursday night, and the next it's a week later, and I'm about to leave work for lunch, wondering how late I can get away with being.

And then I laugh and scold myself. It's not like Chase is an unknown entity anymore. Actually, I'm starting to feel more comfortable around him. Weirdly, the roleplaying conversations actually helped. Because we agreed to keep our therapy-selves as close to our real selves as possible, I felt like I was able to talk to him like I would anyone else, namely, without feeling like I was at a job interview.

It was ... fun. Actual fun.

Fun enough that I scold myself again about feeling nervous. Chase is a good guy, and he knows just as well as I do what this is all about. This is doing our homework, and he knows that.

I make it to the restaurant on time. Chase is waiting out front, and when he sees Jennie entering the parking lot, he steps into the snow strewn street lot to meet me.

I grab my purse and stuff my phone inside before lifting my

eyes to see out the windshield. Chase hasn't made it to the car yet, so I sit on the bench seat for a moment, watching him approach. He grins as he jogs the last couple of steps and opens the door for me. Extending his hand, I let him pull me up.

"Thank you for waiting," he says, his white smile broad across his face.

I can't help but return it, shrugging. "It's not hard when you're so prompt." I nudge his shoulder with mine. "You'd better be careful. One day, when all of this is over, I'm going to have forgotten how to open doors, and then where will I be?"

Chase's smile doesn't fade, and he shakes his head ruefully as he leads me across the parking lot. "I highly doubt your ability to forget anything, but if you do, keep my number on hand. I'll come open your door anytime."

I can't quite help the smile, and I duck my head to keep him from seeing.

"You were waiting for me," I say as we stomp the snow off our shoes outside the door. "I hope it wasn't for long. It's pretty cold."

"It's fine," he assures me, "but I was only just coming inside when I saw you. Thankfully Jennie's distinctive. If you were in a random sedan, it would be much harder."

The blessed warmth washes over us as we walk in. Although, my right hand didn't take being outside too harshly. It—

I look down.

Great googly moogly.

I'm still holding his hand.

I let go, gently trying to ease my fingers from his. Chase notices, and with a slight lift of his eyebrows, releases my hand without comment, not even pausing as he talks to the restaurant host. Once the host walks away to check our table, he looks back at me a little chagrined.

"Sorry. This is going to sound like a terrible excuse, but I kind of forgot I was holding your hand. I'm ... well, the not creepy way of saying it is I am a hugger."

I bite my lip to try and kill the grin that's building on my face. My efforts fail. "Touchy-feely?"

"In the least creepy way possible, yeah." He shifts his weight like he's self-conscious.

Interesting. "That makes sense."

His eyebrows raise. "Does it?"

"Yeah," I say. "Not in a creepy way, don't worry. I was thinking about all the doors you've opened, and how you nearly held my hand going into therapy the first time as well."

His shoulders lose some of their tension. "Well, the doors are more of a family thing than a touchy-feely thing, but please let me know if it gets to be too much."

I shake my head, remembering at the last minute what the therapist said about letting him know what I'm thinking. "It's not too much. Please don't be worried about it."

Chase's expression relaxes. "Let me know if it changes."

"I will," I say sincerely, reaching out and patting his arm.

Once we're seated, the conversation turns to our jobs. He's got the advantage on me since he uses our company for IT support. Lacy and I have never been on the same team at work, which in some ways has been nice, because even when we have to work late, it's almost never on the same night. It's how we came up with our dinner schedule.

On the negative side, as I am currently discovering, I know almost nothing about her clients or what she's working on, including anything to do with the man in front of me. Sharing isn't forbidden, but usually at the end of the day, apart from generalized complaints, the last thing we want to do is talk about work.

Then again, it certainly gives me an opening to ask him all the questions my little heart desires.

Which is surprisingly a lot. Enough that it takes four consecutive buzzes from my phone for me to even hear it, and even then it's with sincere regret that I excuse myself and reach down into my bag. Chase doesn't seem to mind. His plate of food is almost untouched. I wince inwardly. He probably felt like he was in an interview today.

It's embarrassing, but his work is interesting. Building software in any capacity has always been fascinating to me, but the way he's integrated it into filing and organizational tools that already exist is incredible, and worth all the questions.

Not that our conversation has all been business. He's mentioned—briefly—that he has a younger sister.

I look at my phone. There are four texts, all from the same person.

I make a face and turn the phone face down on the table.

"Wow, I don't think I've seen you make that expression before," Chase says, sipping his soft drink from a straw. "Which is interesting, considering I've been talking non-stop for the last forty-five minutes.

"You talking about programming is one thing," I say. "Four texts from my mother asking how therapy went in varying degrees of boldness is quite another."

"Four?"

"In about two minutes, looks like."

"Are you going to answer her?" Chase's voice is soft, and his head is tilted to one side, like he's studying to me.

"I try not to text at the table." My voice is even. I'm proud of myself "Besides, I don't think I want to involve her any more than she already is."

His eyebrows draw together. "I'm sure she's just worried

about you. You're trying to figure out a relationship with someone that she doesn't particularly like."

"Yeah, well, I don't want my mom's worry," I snap. "I'm an adult and am more than capable of doing things on my own. It's Mom's fault I'm here in the first place." I take the phone and stuff it into my purse. "It doesn't matter that I have three university degrees under my belt. It doesn't matter I'm a Team Lead, or that I've lived on my own for fifteen years without a single handout or have almost zero debt. According to Karma, I am absolutely missing out on *everything* important because I Don't Have a Man."

It's bitter.

Really bitter.

My heart freezes in my chest, and Chase stares at me, eyebrows pulled together and shoulders uncomfortably hunched. I flush to the roots of my hair.

"I-I'm so sorry," I stammer. "I didn't—" I take a deep breath. "I'm sorry. That has nothing to do with you. I didn't mean to take it out on you. I'm sorry."

Chase's expression softens, and he reaches across the table, stopping just short of my fingers. He's about to say something, but I'm finding I don't really want to hear it. I inhale and start talking right before he opens his mouth. "I, uh, thought we could try another restaurant for our other conversation. For our therapy assignment, I mean."

Chase's hand stops, and he sits back in his chair, his eyes tightening around the edges. For a terrible minute, I think he's going to ask about me and my mom and everything else that has happened, but then he nods. "Sounds great. Got anywhere in mind?"

I release the breath that's being held hostage in my chest. "There's a good Indian place down the road. Interested?"

"I love Indian. Good tikka masala?" He raises his eyebrows.

"To die for." I speak softly, not meeting his eyes, trying to make up for my outburst. "Their naan is great as well."

"Fantastic. Well, we don't have to wait until next Thursday. Got another hour where you can do lunch?"

"Tuesday work?" I offer, still shaken. "If not, I can look into the evenings, but we're finishing up a couple of projects, so I'm not sure when I get off."

Chase nods, the corners of his mouth curling upwards. "Tuesday works great. Text me the address?"

"Sure." I start to reach for my phone, only to retract my hand from my purse as the device buzzes again. I'm not going to look at my phone until I can read my mother's texts in private. "Remind me if I don't send it by seven or so. I should be home by then."

"Sounds good."

The rest of the meal passes in peace. He tells me about the little Chinese place down the highway, and I tell him about my favorite Hawaiian restaurant. When we get up and pay, the cashier is surprised we split the check, but I'm more than a little relieved that Chase respects my decision on that.

Alongside my relief is a hefty bit of regret. Chase is already here because of my mom. It is absolutely unacceptable to make him have to deal with any of the rest of the situation. That's why, as we walk out of the restaurant, I put my hand on his arm.

"Chase?"

He stops and looks back at me. I pause as I tilt my chin up to look him in the face. It's more than I'm used to; I keep on forgetting how tall he actually is. He's not exactly unassuming, but while I think he could totally command a physical presence if he wanted, he's unobtrusive. He's not trying to stick out or make himself the center of attention, he just is.

It's kind of nice.

"Summer?"

And I have gotten lost in my thoughts.

"Thank you for today." I can feel the curve of my lips, but it diminishes as I speak. "I'm so sorry for snapping at you. Like I said, it has nothing to do with you, and it wasn't appropriate. I won't do it again."

Chase's hand covers mine where it's still holding onto his arm, keeping it in place. It's warm in the cold air.

"Thanks for apologizing, Summer," he says with a sincere smile. "For the record, I'm not offended, and I know it wasn't directed at me, but I appreciate you looking out for me. I'm sorry you've had difficulties with your parents."

My stomach twists, a knot building in my throat. I turn my head to survey the parking lot, but I don't move my hand. He doesn't know the half of it, but I can't help but feel like he's saying it from a place of experience. "Thanks, Chase."

When I get back to work, I head to my cubicle. I'm only about fifteen minutes late from my normal start time—well within the half-hour Ana, the assistant manager, gave me to do my therapy appointments. There's a sticky note on my computer that wasn't there when I left.

It's probably from one of my team members, asking me to look at one of their completed sections of work when I got back. When I look a little closer, though, It's not from Jason, Jack, or Dave. Or even Marvin, even though the world would probably have to end before he used a physical note instead of the online work chat.

It's from Louis.

I sigh. Louis was my team lead before I was promoted.

When that happened, the teams were reorganized, and I'd taken two of his more experienced programmers with me, Dave and Marvin.

I don't think he's actually upset over that, but it is becoming very apparent that he doesn't trust me as a team lead. Whether it's my newness or what, I don't know. I don't think it's because I'm a girl—he doesn't give Lacy the same treatment, though I'm pretty sure the entire male population of Banff Technology Services, and possibly Utah County, is simply terrified of her—but he knows as well as the rest of management that I've never been in an official leadership position before.

I kind of get it, but I wish he didn't make it so obvious.

I read the note.

> Summer, I need to talk to you about Jack. Please let me know when you're back from lunch. - Louis.

I frown at the little sticky note, and go in search of my fellow team lead.

He's at his desk.

Louis, so he has informed me, was named after Louis Jourdan, a famous French actor. I looked him up once—the actor, not my coworker—and they look nothing alike. It makes sense, no one names a baby after who they resemble, but I don't think Louis has realized this. While Louis Jourdan is tall, dark and handsome, Louis the Coworker is sort of blond, exactly one and a half inches taller than me, and is ... almost handsome.

I know, I know, don't come after me. It's very possible that someone else finds him absolutely devastating, but for the life of me, his nose is ever so slightly too large, as is his propensity to micromanage. I think even if I had found him attractive in the beginning, I was cured shortly thereafter.

I don't think Louis has noticed. Up until a month or two ago, when I was promoted, he tried to act very suave and gentlemanly. Since then, by all appearances, he's tried to keep putting on all the affectations and gestures, but his words have been sharper, and his critiques are a little less carefully worded.

I'm not sure he's noticed that either.

I don't take it personally. I've had way too many "math is for boys" professors over the years, and frankly speaking, I've been waiting for it to crop up in my professional life, but it is a little disappointing, especially after Louis's treatment while I was on his team.

I watch from around the corner. Do I really want to engage with him? I can always claim that his knock-off sticky notes didn't stay stuck to my screen, and I didn't see it until—oh, I don't know—fifteen minutes before closing.

But I've already yelled at Chase today, and as much as I don't want to deal with Louis, I would feel guilty for ignoring the note, and I would have the meeting hanging over my head for the rest of the day.

Pass.

This way I can at least have the meeting at his cubicle so I can actually leave when I'm done.

I approach. "Hey, Louis." He looks back, and I hold up the note. "You wanted to talk?"

"Hey, Summer. Yeah." He looks around. Jack is seated across the room on my team's half of the space. He's focused on the computer, and has his earbuds in, but if we talk in here, we'll be heard. "Let's grab a meeting room."

"Sure," I say.

He picks up his laptop and walks into the room. I close the door, and slide into the chair nearest to it. "What's up?"

He has started to lower himself into a chair about four seats away, but stops and moves back toward me when he sees I have no intention of going further than I am.

"I wanted to talk to you about some of Jack's work," he says, pulling his laptop open. "I was going through the YellowPlay project, and I noticed a problem in the code."

He turns the computer toward me, but I don't look down at it. I'm staring at him.

"Why were you in the YellowPlay project?" I ask. "The file came with me when the teams got divided."

He rolls his eyes a little. "Touchy much? I was double-checking some of my code. I want to use it on one of my team's products, and I knew it was in here. But I found this."

I have a hard time looking away from him to the computer screen, but I see the problem immediately. "This code isn't going to work."

"There are whole passages like this. Wasn't Jack in charge of this part?"

"He is," I say, scrolling down the screen a little more. "This isn't like him."

Louis leans back in the chair, the springs of the chair creaking loudly as he does. He folds his arms across his chest. "He has been going through a lot of girl trouble lately. I wouldn't blame him if it's affected his work."

I'm still reading. "Well, be that as it may, thank you for bringing it to my attention. I'll discuss it with him."

"The YellowPlay project is due by the weekend, Summer," he says, his blondish eyebrows lifting. "There's a lot of work to do."

I furrow my eyebrows. "And I said I'll discuss it with him."

"It might be a team job," he says, with an apologetic smile on his face. It doesn't look, or feel, sincere.

"Well, then," I say to him lightly, "I'll have my team look at it. Thank you for bringing it to my attention."

"You'll have to go over all the code yourself. Your week-nights are pretty much shot—"

I stand slowly. Louis stops talking, but doesn't move, looking up at me expectantly.

"Thank you, Louis." I don't break eye contact. "Is there anything else?"

He doesn't say anything.

"Then I'll head back." I say, and head out of the room.

It is a very great pity, but Louis is exactly right. I'm not sure what happened to Jack—I'm not sure Jack knows what happened to Jack, because he looks just as mystified as I do when he looks through it—but a good twenty-five percent of the code we've been working on for the last three months is corrupted, rendering a patch that we've been making for YellowPlay completely inert. It's fixable, but after broad corrections, it is now clear that we're going to have to go through the whole program line by line.

And then, as team lead, I'll have to go through the whole thing myself again. My team's fixes can happen during the regular eight a.m. to five p.m. workday. Mine ...

Well, so much for any free time this weekend. Good thing I have a lunch date—or rather, therapy session—with Chase during the day. Next week. After the project is due.

I check with Ana, the assistant manager, to get approval for overtime and to work from home for the evening.

Ana forehead crinkles. "I thought you'd mostly completed that project."

I shrug as I head toward the door. "Someone must have bumped something. It happens."

"Doesn't mean it's not the worst," Ana says, sliding her own laptop into her bag. "Everything else going okay? With therapy?"

I think about my possible responses. It's not necessarily better than I expected, but it's also not bad. "I think so."

"The boyfriend at least treating you better?" Ana says, standing and coming around the desk to stand by me.

Chase's face flashes across my mind, and for a moment I'm confused why he wouldn't be, until I come to myself. "It's getting better," I say. "Little bit by little bit." We start walking out of the office together. "I'm not going to lie, it's a little weird going to a therapist. I'm sitting there telling all my secrets to someone that I don't even know."

"Yeah, but isn't that the beauty of therapy?" Ana says. "They don't have any stake in the game. It's basically troubleshooting for your brain."

"I suppose." I hike my purse a little higher on my shoulder. "I guess it's a little interesting when I'm going with ..." Was I actually about to say 'someone I don't know?' Was I actually insane? I pause and then fumble out. "Chase."

Ana's eyebrows lift.

I frown. "What?"

"I didn't know your boyfriend's name is Chase."

"You didn't?" Of course, she didn't. I hadn't told her.

"Nope. First I'm hearing of it. Does that mean you don't mind me asking about him now?"

"I don't think you couldn't before."

"Oh, please, Summer. Anyone could tell you weren't comfortable talking about him. Frankly, it's a relief. Therapy must be working."

My frown doesn't shift. Was it really that obvious? Didn't the therapist just say I was hard to read?

Then again, Andie's only known me for about two hours. Ana's been watching me for close to three years, and she's been pretty intuitive from the beginning. It's undoubtedly why she's one of the assistant managers.

"So ..." Ana draws the word out. "Chase. We'll start with the basics. What does he look like?"

"He's, um, tall."

"Like ... taller than me? Or you?"

She looks up at me. She's wearing four-inch heels and is still about four inches shorter than I am.

"Taller than me," I say quietly, unable to keep the smile from crawling up my cheeks.

"Hair color?"

"Brown."

"Eyes?"

"Hazel."

"Hot?"

"Ana."

"Do you have a picture?"

"Ana!" I exclaim, a laugh escaping my lips as I turn toward her. "Really?"

"Summer, I'm curious!" Ana laughs in return, dropping the subject. "You've never talked about him before, and I am dying to know what type of man turned your head, especially after keeping him private for *forever*."

I shake my head, the smile still on my face. We're at the door of the building now, and I hold my laptop case. "Okay, ma'am, it has only been six months. Now, I'm going home," I say with another laugh. "You have a good evening."

"Bring pictures!" she calls after me, and I shake my head as I walk away.

Chapter 9
The Friend

SUMMER

I have completely forgotten absolutely everything except for this project by the time my phone buzzes a little after at seven. I look away from my computer screen, pretending I'm not going a little cross-eyed, and check my phone. I expect it to be Lacy, asking what's for dinner—a question I absolutely do not want to address right now—but it's not Lacy.

It's Chase.

"The address." I smack myself in the forehead, wincing. I open up the text, and sure enough:

> Chase Merrill: Hey! Just bumping you for the address.

I can barely remember that it was an Indian restaurant that we talked about, let alone the name. I sigh, and text.

> Me: Can I push it off for another couple of minutes? I'm sorry. Work has swallowed me whole.

I put my phone down on the desk, and turn back to the

computer, covering the screen of my phone with my arm. I'm going to have to figure out what to do for dinner tonight. Neither Lacy nor I have had the chance to go grocery shopping, and I have no idea whether I'm hungry or not, let alone what I want to eat.

My phone buzzes under my arm, but I don't check it. It's probably Chase saying it's fine.

I'm wrong, but I don't know it until five minutes later, when my phone starts ringing. Not buzzing with a text message, but actually rings.

I nearly fall out of my chair, while scrambling for my phone, which has suddenly adopted the physical characteristics of a greased pig, and falls off the table. When I pick it up, I am not expecting the 'CM' in the little circle.

Chase is calling me?

What?

I stare at it for a moment, and then—more out of curiosity than anything else—answer the phone, holding it up to my ear. "Hello?"

"Summer, this is a video chat."

"Oh!" I yank the phone away from my face, and look around, making sure that my surroundings are Chase-appropriate. I've never appreciated the fact that I'm almost neurotically organized until now. "Sorry about that. I forgot to check."

Almost as an afterthought, I run my hand over my head, and realize—to my horror—my hair is in a top knot. Some girls can really carry them off.

Not me.

It's only a matter of time before I make a baby cry or something.

"Oh, sorry," I say, and pull the elastic out of my hair, sending my waves of hair around my shoulders.

"Don't worry about it," Chase says, looking slightly

concerned. "Don't feel like you have to ..." he trails off and clears his throat. "Never mind. You called?"

"Huh? No, I didn't."

"Uh, my phone has been resting on the counter for the last five minutes since I texted you, so it's either you or the little FBI dude monitoring your phone."

"Nah, I doubt it was him." I run a hand over my hair again, willing it to behave. "He of all people should know we're fake dating."

Chase snorts and shakes his head.

I look at the phone. Sure enough, I started the call. "Looks like I arm-dialed you." I look at my loose sweater. "Through my sleeves, even. Which probably means it's providence." I prop my phone up against the computer screen and rub my forehead. "It's probably time for a break anyway."

"A break? I thought you finished work before seven?" Chase says. The room he's in—maybe a kitchen?—is bright. He's rested the phone somewhere where I can see him from the chest up, but not much else. I rest my chin on my hands, watching him as he looks down. His shoulders are broad, filling out the grey t-shirt he has on nicely. He's probably cooking his own dinner.

Ugh. Dinner.

"Most days," I say quietly. "Not today."

Chase looks up at the phone and raises his eyebrows. "Not today? What's going on?"

I sigh, and shake my head, feeling the corners of my mouth turn down. "One of my team members messed up somewhere on the code of a project that's due Saturday night. My 'favorite' fellow team lead was the one who found it, and so I get to spend the next three days checking code. Which includes overtime."

"Are you salaried, or do you get actual overtime?"

"Thankfully, actual overtime," I say, glancing up at the computer screen, and then pinching my eyes closed. "But I'm getting my money's worth out of these blue filter glasses."

He glances up and smiles. "Yes, I like the circle rims."

"Normally, I'd take them off for a call," I rest my chin in my hand, "But you're on a screen."

"I'm not complaining." His voice is gentle, and I smile in return. "Do you think you're going to be able to get done with the project on time?"

I take a deep breath and shrug. "I hope so. As long as I lose the need to eat or sleep or shower."

Chase frowns a little. "Oh? All of those sound like they're going to help you code better."

"Yeah, but they all take time," I say, running a hand over my face. "Ah, well. It'll work out. At least I know when it has to end."

"Anything I can do to help?" Chase asks, tilting his head to the side.

I lean back in my chair and sigh. "Nah, not unless you want to send dinner to me and Lacy. It's my turn to make it and I have no energy, desire, or ideas. If it were Monday my dad would probably ask if he could send something, but ..." I trail off with a shrug. "It'll end up being takeout anyway."

Chase gives me a half smile. He puts whatever he's doing down and leans against the counter. It makes his arms look nice. I look at him for a long moment, appreciating the view.

"Say no more. Any preferences, or should I surprise you?"

I bolt upright, realizing what I said and what I was doing in the same instance. "What? Oh! Chase, no, that's not what I meant!"

"Really?" he says with a smile. "Because it kind of sounded like a plea for help."

"No—well, not a serious one."

"Sure," he says, apparently unconvinced but equally unconcerned, picking up his knife again. He looks up at me with a far-too-innocent smile.

"Chase, don't you dare get me anything," I say emphatically. "I'd have to explain to Lacy where I got it."

"Lacy knows what's going on, Summer," Chase says lightly, "It's not like she'd get the wrong idea."

"I know, but you don't have to."

"I know," Chase says soothingly. I don't trust this man as far as I can throw him. Except with, y'know, the majority of my secrets.

"You really don't have to," I repeat.

He's looking straight at the phone, and there's something soft in his gaze. His expression turns a little more serious. "I know, Summer," he repeats, the soft tone of his voice soothing me without permission. Then he nods at me. "Well, I'm about to the point where I need to start cooking, so I have to go now, but you work hard. And get something to eat, okay? And get to bed at a sort-of reasonable time tonight. I've been there, and it really is worth it."

I chuckle ruefully, but dip my head in agreement, conceding the point. "Okay."

He leans in toward the camera, his eyes twinkling. "Have a good night, Summer."

I return his smile. "Good night, Chase."

And then he hangs up.

Half an hour later, the doorbell rings. When I open it, there are two grocery bags full of food from my favorite Hawaiian restaurant. The receipt is stapled to the outside, and at the bottom of the receipt is a note from the sender.

Summer,

> Take care of yourself.
> For therapy.
> Chase
> P.S. Some of this is for Lacy. Or maybe not. I won't judge.

I can't help the smile that spreads across my face. Shouting my thanks to the delivery driver, I walk inside and start unloading the food. I'm not sure how much Chase thinks Lacy and I eat, but with every single side dish I open, my heart grows a little warmer.

I load up a plate, piled high with pork and chicken goodness, and then pull out my phone. I hold up the plate, take a selfie with it, and send it to Chase.

Me: Thank you.

Chase Merrill: Of course. I've been where you are, and friends have helped me out. I'm glad I can be that friend.

Friends? Are we friends?

I guess we are. If nothing else, we're in cahoots, and that's about as good as friends.

Lacy gets home fifteen minutes later. She looks over the huge spread on the counter, and then up at me.

"I thought you said you weren't going to order from them more than once a month."

"It wasn't me," I say, snatching a piece of pineapple from

Lacy's portion. She doesn't know how much there was originally, so she can't complain.

"Summer, your budget!"

"Lacy, honestly, it wasn't me!" It comes out as a laugh, and I'm not entirely sure why. "Chase sent it."

Lacy looks utterly confused. "Chase?"

"Yeah, you know, the fake boyfriend? Chase."

Lacy looks down at the food with a curious expression, and then back at me. She's going to start teasing me at any moment now. Part of me would rather die, but there's a part that knows I'd joke right along with her. I'm feeling oddly happy for a woman who has at least three more hours of programming checks to do.

"How do you feel about this?"

It's not the question I'm expecting, and I look up from where I'm about to take another slice of fruit.

"Me?"

"Is there someone else in this room I don't know about?" Lacy challenges. Then she looks a little unsure. "There, um, isn't, is there?"

"No, there's not," I reassure her. "I ... I guess I'm happy. I accidentally called him earlier, and I told him not to, but he still sent me dinner when I told him about Jack and having to program this weekend. It was ... It's my favorite food. And it's a ... really nice thing to do."

"It *is* a really nice thing to do." She looks up at me with a mischievous smile. "And he's kind of hot, isn't he?"

I roll my eyes and turn away. "You're already in a committed relationship."

"I'm stating this as a perfectly objective opinion."

Despite my best efforts, my cheeks are flushing. "Chase being hot doesn't have anything to do with his ability to send food."

"So, you do think he's hot."

Yes, but there's no way she's getting it out of me now.

"I plead the fifth," I say, grabbing my plate to carry it back to my room.

"You know, technically, he is still single! You could take your lease and make it a rent-to-own!" Lacy shouts down the hallway as I turn into my bedroom.

I pop my head out the door, frowning. "First of all, who are you, Shania Twain? No more dating/real estate metaphors, please. Second of all, Chase couldn't possibly be my real boyfriend. His follow-through is too good. This was literally just a nice thing he did for a person in need."

"Yeah, but that person is you," Lacy reminds me.

"And we're friends," I remind her right back. "You can be nice to your friends."

"Uh-huh," Lacy says, shoveling Kalua pork into her mouth.

"Have a good evening, Lace."

I retreat into my bedroom.

Chapter 10
The Sister

CHASE

"Sorry again about all of this," Summer says, grasping my hand and standing up out of the car. It's icy, and I hold onto her hand tighter as she steps away from the car.

"No problem. Thanks for letting my sister come. Careful, it's super slick. I don't think they salted the parking lot."

"I—oop!" Summer slides and grabs for my free arm. I reach forward, gripping her as she slips even more. She catches her balance and looks at me with a suddenly breathless, unsure smile. "Nearly got me."

"You okay?" The parking lot is a little darker than what is probably allowed by Utah law, now that the sun has long since disappeared, but the one streetlamp a couple of cars down gives me good enough light to see her face.

She dips her head in agreement but still looks worried. "It really is slick. I don't know if I'm wearing the right shoes for this."

I look at her footwear. They don't look too bad with the low heel, and I say so.

Summer shakes her head, her expression a little guilty. "There's no tread. These are super old."

"Well, then," I say, offering my elbow. "Lock up Jennie, and we'll see if I can get you to the restaurant in one piece."

She hesitates for only a moment, and then does exactly as I've said, locking the ancient Crown Victoria, and then grabbing onto my elbow with a grip a tourniquet would be proud of. As one, we turn toward our destination—the Indian restaurant Summer recommended last Tuesday. She'd gotten the address to me late Thursday night as proof that she was going to bed on time. We'd originally been aiming to go as our regular lunch date, but I'd had a meeting crop up last minute, and so we'd pushed it to this evening.

And why was Avery coming?

Well ...

"What did you tell your sister?" Summer asks, her gaze trained firmly on the ground. "About me?"

She doesn't say it out loud, but I know what she means. Did I tell her that we were faking it? The answer is no. I know, I know. It feels all sorts of weird and wrong, especially considering how close Avery and I are.

In my defense, I had no intention of inviting her. I had called Avery to cancel our regular Tuesday dinner date, or at least move it to a different day of the week, and somehow, I had ended up including her on my date.

Therapy date.

Therapy assignment.

Thank goodness I'm not a spy. I am really terrible at this.

"Chase?"

"Sorry, she's under the impression that we're dating. I wasn't—I didn't know ..."

"How to explain?" Summer asks, looking up at me.

"Yeah," I admit with a sigh, and she nods.

"Don't worry. Of all the people in the world, I understand more than most. Sorry to put you in this position."

"I think I did the work all on my own, but thank you," I say, grimacing.

We shuffle closer to the building and pause on the meticulously-scraped sidewalk to catch our breath.

"So, she thinks we're dating," Summer says, not letting go of my arm. "What else does she know?"

"Well, she knows it's new. I had to put it that way—she knows I haven't dated anyone since Am—" I break off, suddenly realizing Summer knows almost nothing about my past. "My last girlfriend," I amend. "We broke up last summer."

"I'm sorry," Summer says, the line between her eyebrows appearing as she studies my face. "What you've told Avery is just fine. It's closer to the truth, anyway, and that'll make it easier to keep track of. I'll make a note in my file."

I pause. "You have a file for what people know?"

She shrugs, guilt coloring the smile on her face. "Do you know the little poem 'Oh, what tangled webs we weave/when we practice to deceive?'"

"I've heard of it."

"I've been doing a lot of practicing." She grimaces at the confession. "But considering what I've been doing has been for a good cause—at least for me—I figured I'd at least be organized about it."

"Is it a good idea to write down your crimes?"

"It's only a crime if money is involved. I'm not scamming anyone, laundering money, or defrauding anything. Anything else is only a breach of ethics." Summer stares off across the parking lot, biting her lip. "I checked."

I grin. "I'll let you keep track, then. But back to your question, Avery knows it's pretty new, but she doesn't know about the therapy. I wasn't planning on telling her that part yet."

Summer doesn't seem overly troubled. "That's fair. If we're asked, we can just say we met in the sandwich cafe, through a mutual friend. That's more or less what happened."

I blink. She notices, pulling herself up a little taller. "What? The best lies are the complete truth, but only the most useless parts." Summer winces. "And with that, I would like to reiterate that I really don't like to lie."

"I know." I squeeze her arm, still hooked in mine. And I do. Aside from going to therapy itself, nothing that she's done has been close to dishonest. She never tried to pass the therapy off as something that it wasn't. She hadn't told me exactly why she was doing it, but at this point, did that really matter?

I'm about to say more when I see a mint green Miata driving into the parking lot. There are a lot of cars in Utah Valley, but I haven't seen anything resembling my sister's car yet. I nod toward the car and look down at Summer. "Here comes Avery."

"She's on time," Summer notes, pulling her phone out of her coat pocket. Today's coat is dark green wool, setting off her eyes as she looks up at me under the pot lights that illuminate the sidewalk.

"An enforced habit in our family," I say, smiling. I look down at Summer. "Would you mind if I leave you here for a moment?"

Summer shakes her head and drops her hands from my arm. "No problem."

I start my way carefully back across the parking lot where my sister has already popped her door open and is laughing uproariously. "I beat you, Morkie! First time this year!"

"It's barely February, Gills," I protest, picking my way across the Northern Utah/Antarctic Ice Field over to my sister's car. "Don't get out yet, it's slick."

"And dark," Avery says, looking around. "Hey, is that

Summer? Hi, Summer!" Avery's half out of her car before I can make it over to her and waving at the woman on the sidewalk.

Summer smiles and waves back. "Hi, Avery!"

Avery smiles and waits for me as I round her door and hold out my hands. She grabs them and levers herself up. She's wearing high heels like normal, and they act like little ice picks. She told me once she picked it up while she was an exchange student in Russia before the sanctions took place, but I'm still not sure whether or not it's as good as she says.

It probably is, though, because she only keeps one hand on my arm as we make our way across the parking lot. Avery looks between me and Summer, and grins.

"So, *you're* the meeting that Chase keeps going to on his lunch breaks."

Summer glances toward me, her eyebrows lifting. "I ... yes?"

Avery laughs and throws her arms around me. "I've been trying to get an appointment with this guy for weeks. It's a pity that I know it's not even a competition."

Summer laughs, her eyes flicking up to mine. "Well, I have been hanging out with your brother on Thursdays. I'd apologize, but I'm having a little too much fun."

Avery's grin only widens, and she opens her arms for a hug.

I look between them, a little curious. Summer doesn't strike me as a super touchy-feely person, at least not with people she first meets, but her expression doesn't change at all as she reaches out in return for Avery.

"Hi, Summer," Avery says. "It's so good to meet you! I have heard absolutely nothing about you."

Summer laughs. "At the risk of getting Chase in trouble, same. But I'm glad I get to make my own opinion of you first."

Avery's blue eyes crinkle at the edges as she smiles a deep, genuine grin as she backs away. "Oh, I think I'm going to like you, Summer." She holds out a hand. "Avery Merrill."

Summer sticks out her hand. "Summer Weathers."

Avery doesn't bat an eye, and gestures toward the restaurant. "Shall we eat?"

The smell that rolls out the door as I pull it open is divine. Since the meeting went long, I've been running on one of my emergency granola bars since breakfast this morning, and I'm about two feet too tall, a hundred pounds too heavy, and in possession of one too many stomachs for that to be sufficient.

Avery sits across the table from Summer and me. She and Summer pick over the menu. They've both been here before and share recommendations back and forth before making their choices. I stick to my tikka masala, but Avery gets aloo gobi and Summer gets chicken vindaloo and some naan for all of us to share.

Considering how hesitant Summer was when we first met, I'm a little worried how Avery and Summer will get on, but it's less alley cat and more like a house on fire. Avery peppers Summer with questions—how did we meet, where did we meet, how did Summer convince me to come on a second date, etc.—and Summer completely sticks to the truth. We did meet through Lacy on a blind date to a sandwich shop. She convinced me because I wanted to meet her again.

"What have you guys done on dates?" Avery asks, sipping on her strawberry lassi.

I frown. "Gills, bug out."

"It's okay," Summer says, lifting her eyebrows at Avery's nickname. "It's not like we've done anything except talk. But that's what we both want to do."

"Really? Because Chase usually tries hiking or something on the second date." When I make a noise of protest, Avery looks over me with an unimpressed look. "Only, like, one in five women would go hiking on a second date, and those are the ones who have never in their lives consumed true crime."

I make a face back at my sister. Summer looks contemplative as she glances between us, clearly amused. I pose the question to her. "Would you have?"

Summer thinks about it, and flushes a little bit, though to be fair, that might be her vindaloo. "Maybe not the second date. But knowing you now, I would."

That raises my eyebrows. From where I'm sitting, Summer looks pretty sincere, and I'm not entirely sure what to do with that. I shake myself internally. *Summer is very good at pretending,* I remind myself. *Besides, you're not actually looking for a girlfriend. You're learning how to be a better boyfriend.*

"How many dates have you been on?" Avery asks.

Summer thinks about it and looks over at me. "Four?"

"Five, if you count dinner on Thursday," I point out.

"Um, can you count it if you weren't there?" Summer's question is innocent on the surface, but I can hear the playful challenge.

"Um, I'm providing dinner for my girlfriend, and we video chatted. Shouldn't that count?"

Summer squints good-naturedly at me, and I pull a face at her. She laughs and bumps me with her shoulder.

And then she doesn't move away. I bump her back, half returning the gesture, and half seeing if she'll move away, but she doesn't, settling in a little more. My heart stutters.

I don't want to move.

I'm a touchy-feely guy. I know this. Enough that I got slapped a couple times in my teens without really realizing what I was doing wrong. I'm not entirely sure where I get it from either, considering I can't ever remember my parents doing so much as touching hands, apart from when Father was helping Mother out of the car. I'm happy if Summer is giving contact willingly, but it's not like I'm going to take it from her if she doesn't realize that she's doing it.

But if she's not going to move away, that means it's okay, right?

You're overthinking this, I scold myself. Summer is an adult. Normal adults don't just lean on each other—something that I am very, very aware of. I am able to follow normal body language cues, and Summer isn't telling me to back off. She is leaning into me.

"I guess when it's time, love can move along quickly, can't it?" Avery is saying, resting her chin on her hand.

"I guess so." I shift a little, putting my arm around the back of Summer's chair. She still doesn't move away.

Instead, she smiles up at me. "Yeah."

SUMMER

Chase helps Avery back to her car, the two of them slipping and sliding all over the place. At least, Chase is. Avery, all five foot six inches of her, looks like she's walking on normal tarmac, her stiletto heels not hindering her in the least. When they get to the green car, Chase says something that has Avery shoving at him. He tweaks her nose, and then she laughs and shoves him harder.

It's nice watching them. It's not that I don't have a relatively good relationship with my siblings, but I don't think we've ever been like this. Laughing, joking, pushing. Mom wouldn't have allowed the pushing, but Chase and Avery look like they're well aware of just how far they can push each other before they lose their balance.

I haven't seen Chase around someone else before—aside from waitstaff and Andie—and it's nice to know he's as good to his sister as he is to random people. It makes it a little easier to trust him.

Chase makes his way back to me, only slipping once, the laughter bright and shining in his eyes and apparent on his rosy cheeks. I can't help the grin on my face as he steps back up on the sidewalk and comes to stand in front of me.

How do I keep forgetting how tall this man is? The first time it was a little bit intimidating, and I was glad I was wearing taller shoes. But now, in sort-of sensible—if a little old—boots, it's kind of fun to tip my head back to look up at him.

"You made it back alive," I say, twisting side to side, my hands deep in my pockets to keep them warm.

His grin only intensifies. "Were you worried?"

"More about you than I was about Avery," I admit with a sheepish smile. "Then again, if you'd fallen, you'd probably would have grabbed onto her and taken you both out."

"Avery played rugby in college," Chase says with a smirk. "If she wanted to stay upright, she would have dumped me off in a heartbeat."

I can't help the laugh, and Chase's smile deepens. "That tracks," I say, with a mock contemplative face. Then it turns real. "I do have to ask, though ... Morkie?"

Chase throws back his head and laughs. "I was an exchange student in Norway for a year in high school. The word for 'dark' is mørk. I have dark-ish hair, and so one of my friends nicknamed me Mørk, and Avery caught on. Clearly, it's never left."

I grin in response. "And Gills?"

"Before rugby, Avery was a swimmer. She was in the water

so much, our mother told her once she wouldn't be surprised if Avery grew gills, and that stuck."

"That's awesome." I mean it, too. Only Dad had ever called me anything other than 'Summer.' Actually, among all of us, only Joanie broke free of her given name. Sort of.

Chase hums in response, and it goes quiet between us. For the first time, it's not an awkward quiet, but a natural lull in the conversation. I don't feel like I have to talk, but it's not weird when I speak up.

"Did you play sports?"

"In high school." Fondness fills Chase's voice. "I was the quintessential football kid. The basketball coach tried to get me as well, but I was never quite as good."

"College?"

"Just intramural stuff." He surveys the parking lot and exhales with a laugh, his breath billowing out in a big white cloud. "I was busy prepping for my MBA, but I couldn't give it up altogether."

He looks so happy as he speaks, and I can't help feeling the joy filling me up by proxy.

"How about you?" Chase turns to me.

"I was mostly in STEM classes," I admit, shrugging. "Most of those had after school programs, and there wasn't much else I wanted to do. I took weightlifting and track for PE, but I wasn't super competitive. It was just to keep in shape."

For a second, I was worried he was going to roll his eyes or something. I was definitely a stereotypical geek in high school—including braces, glasses, and an unfortunate stint with a bowl cut. Those pictures would never ever see the light of day again. They'd spent enough time on Mom's 'history wall' to last me a lifetime.

But Chase didn't roll his eyes. He actually seemed somewhat intrigued. "Have you always wanted to work with computers?"

I nod, twisting from side to side a little more. "My dad's always liked having them. He wasn't into programming, but he just liked the technology to see what it could do. I loved playing on them, and seeing how they worked when they broke. I usually learned it quicker than Dad did, and so I've been his IT service since I was about ten."

Chase grins and stamps his feet. "I have about ten more questions to ask, but I'm getting cold. Would you mind risking our lives and taking a walk?" He nods toward a sidewalk wrapping around the building that looks relatively snow-free. "We can start there and then make our way back."

I nod and turn with him. Our shoulders bump, and we smile at each other, but we keep walking slowly down the sidewalk.

Chase continues. "Were you a math kid, then?"

I snort. "As much as I resent the implication, yes. I think I'd rather eat nails than do another English class."

"What, you didn't like Romeo and Juliet?"

"And have like a million people die because two people couldn't have a conversation? The only book I hate more is Wuthering Heights—they didn't want to talk, and they still just tried to make each other's lives worse."

Chase snorts. "Not a reader, then?"

"Oh, I'm a reader," I counter. "I love to read. My e-reader is sitting on my nightstand at home, full of books, but just because I like to read doesn't mean I have to get all didactic about it. Save your reports and analysis. Just let the books be fun."

Chase smiles and nudges me in the shoulder. "Ms. Weathers, I think this is the start of a beautiful friendship."

I raise my eyebrows, tilting my chin up to see his face. "You think so?"

"Oh, I know so," he says, and he leans down to whisper in my ear. "You practically quoted the last paper I ever wrote for English. Also, incidentally, on Wuthering Heights."

My mouth drops open, and I turn toward him. "The fact that you remember the book and the paper does you credit, sir."

Chase does a mock bow, and I grin. Silence rolls over us, and we stroll along the sidewalk, the quiet street settling down for the evening as the odd car rolls by. The dim light is nice. As we walk, I tilt my head back and I can see the twinkling of dim stars above us. Reaching out, I loop my hand through Chase's arm, letting him be my guide as we walk.

"Anything good up there?" he asks.

I smile and turn my focus to him. "Not much that I can see. It's the price we pay for living in civilization. You're never going to have a great view, because of the light pollution."

"You studied that, too?" Chase asks.

"I had to decide—astronaut or IT support," I tease back, and then look forward again. "In all honesty, as much as I like the exploration aspect, the actual programming appealed to me more. That, and people, surprisingly enough."

"Surprisingly enough?"

I point at myself. "Introvert. I do not recharge much around other people. Usually, it takes a book or a movie and an evening alone. But it's really satisfying being able to help people at work."

Chase smiles and keeps walking forward. "I agree."

We're both completely frozen by the time we make it back to my car. It's been so long that the ice has frozen hard in the parking lot and is easier to walk on. He opens my car and hands me inside and then waits and watches until I drive away.

I know because I check.

Chapter 11
The Third Appointment

SUMMER

IF THERE WAS ONE THING THAT I DIDN'T ANTICIPATE going into therapy with a fake boyfriend, it was for the therapy to actually work. Somehow, between the Indian restaurant and the time we meet up for our Thursday appointment, Chase and I have texted more than I have ever texted anyone else, with the sole exception of Lacy.

It goes something like this: I text him that I got home safe on Tuesday night—which is a courtesy thing, and he had asked me to. He says he's glad and sends a gif along with his message. I send a gif in return. We both laugh about said gif, he sends another one, I send one back, and now we are having a conversation that is approximately sixty-two percent pictures.

And it's awesome.

And also—apparently—suspicious?

At least, that's what it seems like as I catch Ana sneaking smiles at me at work when she sees me reaching for my phone, and Lacy's eyebrows disappear into her bangs at dinner when I laugh at one of Chase's texts. I try to ignore them. I'm never texting when I shouldn't be, and it is completely appropriate to become friends with Chase. He's pretty much my partner in crime—or at least ethical ambiguity. The fact we get along so well is a blessing, and nothing less.

And it's because we're friends that I'm smiling as I pull into the therapy parking lot. Chase is already waiting for me, leaning against his black sedan with aviators on. Good grief, it's a good thing that we are permanently friend-zoned, because it is a very good look on him.

A smile crosses his face when he sees my car and starts to walk up as I pull into the parking place two spots over. The smile on his face doesn't dim as he opens my door, locks up Jennie for me, and then lets his shoulder brush mine as we walk toward the building

Andie is just as happy to see us, and the atmosphere seems to relax as the appointment begins. We share the journal entries, and talk about our dates, and Andie sits back in her chair, smiling at the two of us.

"I'm so glad that you two had a positive experience with this. I'm going to give you the same assignment for our appointment next week as well. Sound good?"

I look over at Chase, and he dips his chin. I turn to Andie. "Sounds good to me."

"Awesome," she says. "So, I do have a couple questions for the two of you today. I've already asked some iterations of these questions to let you think about them, but I would like to hear your thoughts today."

Chase is the one to answer this time. "Happy to. What's up?"

"Part of how I help therapy be the most effective for the both of you is figuring out what the two of you are looking for in a relationship," Andie explains. "Now, your answers don't have to be the same—you're both individuals trying to see if a life together will work. But even if what you individually need is different, your goals and how you support each other can help you grow together. Does that make sense?"

"Yes," I say, looking over at Chase. His lips are slightly pursed and he doesn't answer for a long time. I reach out and touch his knee. "Chase?"

"Hmm? Oh. Yeah, it does make sense. I guess I haven't thought about it that way before."

"A lot of people talk about relationships being two people becoming one," Andie agrees. "And that's true, but you're still talking about two different people with two different backgrounds trying to merge their lives. Without knowing what the other needs and being willing to help support them is ripe ground for misunderstandings to arise."

Chase nods, the edges of a frown tugging at his lips. It's not like him, and I turn toward him in concern. He notices, but when he meets my eyes, he smiles reassuringly and shakes his head just enough to let me know that he's okay.

"So," Andie says, looking at each of us, "I know that you two want to be in a relationship, but ... why?"

It is a very good thing that she did not ask me this question three weeks ago. If she had, I would have spilled my guts about fake dating then and there. Even now, my shoulder angel is metaphorically yelling into a bullhorn in my ear. If it's not the truth—or at least the realest truth—I'm not entirely sure what to tell her.

Was there a right answer to this? Surely at least some of this had to fall face-first into philosophy, and neither Chase nor I had specialized in that. Why did I need to be in a relationship?

At least I knew the answer to that question. "Well," I say, my voice more shaky than I anticipated it being. "This probably sounds kind of lame, but it was at least partially because of my mom."

Andie tilts her head to the side. Chase looks over at me but also doesn't seem surprised. He shouldn't be, I've more or less told him as much. This is solely for Andie.

"She got really persistent," I say quietly. "One day I'm twenty-nine and life is dandy and I'm getting started in life. And then I turned thirty. The first year wasn't bad. Then she bought me a dating app subscription for my thirty-first birthday. It's why ..." I shut my mouth and try to keep the truth from tumbling out. I'm stumbling for words. "I guess I don't really know what I want out of a relationship. Is it too little just to want someone to be happy to see me in the evenings? Someone who's kind and who loves me. Who wants the best for me. Someone who makes me feel ... cherished."

I press my lips together, feeling like I've said too much. I glance over at Chase. His eyes are soft, and he reaches out, and his hand squeezes my knee briefly before he leans forward a bit.

His expression is contemplative, as though he knows his answer but is trying to find the right words. We wait in silence for him. I don't know how he's feeling, but it's not awkward for me. I hope it's not awkward for him, either.

"It's never been hard for me to start relationships," Chase says quietly. "Meeting new people and going on dates has always been something that I can do and have fun doing. But ... I don't feel like I emotionally connect. Maybe that's what's happened here, that made everything go bad," his voice trails off a bit, and he clears his throat. He looks up at Andie, forehead creased, and deep sincerity in his eyes.

"I know I'm not perfect. I'm here because I want to get better, to help shave off some of my hard edges—or at least point out where the edges are, so I can work on them myself. But what I want ... I want someone I can share everyday life with. Not just the highlights. Not just to show off or be shown off. To experience the good and the bad, to be able to share it all, and come off the better for it."

Finally, Chase looks at me, his hazel eyes boring into mine. His expression is completely unguarded, and somehow, I know that every single word that he's spoken is the absolute truth. Warmth prickles in my chest. It's like I've never seen him before, and what I'm seeing now ... it's amazing.

I manage to focus during the rest of the appointment, but the look Chase gave me never quite leaves my mind. There was a question there, but I'm not sure if it was for me, or if I was simply the person there to see it. I don't know if I can even put the question into words.

There is one thing that is bothering me that I can put into words, but I'm not sure how to express it without falling more on the 'girlfriend' side of 'fake girlfriend.' But ... well, it was fair that we both knew what we were getting into, right? And just because it was fake didn't mean that I didn't care about Chase at all.

Besides, it wasn't the therapy part of this that was fake.

We make it to the cars before I have the guts to ask.

"Hey, Chase?"

Chase is walking slightly ahead of me but turns back at the sound of my voice. "Yeah?"

"Back in there ..." I motion over my shoulder. Then I pause. He should know I'm not demanding this information. It was a personal question. Really personal. "You don't have to tell me this if you don't want to, but you've told me before that you broke up with your last girlfriend last summer, and, well, with what you said in there earlier, it ..." *Spit it out, Summer.* "It sounded like it didn't go well. That it made an impression."

Communicate, girl. Ask your question. Give him something to work with.

"I just," I stumble. "It made me worry. And I wanted to know what happened. If you want to tell me. But only if you want to tell me."

Chase's expression is difficult to read. He's not smiling, but he isn't angry—which is what I'm the most worried about. I take in his pinched eyebrows and his relaxed shoulders. It also isn't quite relief or resignation. Maybe a combination of the two?

Who am I kidding? I'm not great at this—this is exactly the reason I am more than happy to do most of my client interactions over the phone or email.

Chase studies every inch of my face, and then his face relaxes. "I want to tell you, Summer. But if it's alright with you, could we maybe sit in my car? Or yours, if you want. It's cold out here."

I nod. "Yours is fine. Jennie sometimes forgets she has a heater when she's idling."

Chase's eyebrows pinch together in sudden concern. "What?"

Backpedal.

I wave him off. "Only when she's idling, Chase. Come on."

He thankfully allows me to herd him toward his vehicle. Once I'm inside, I realize it's far nicer than what I anticipated. It smells new, and it either is, or he is the most responsible driver known to mankind. It's also possible he gets it cleaned regularly, and I don't know which is most likely. I feel a little self-conscious putting my slushy outside feet on the clean mat, but Chase doesn't seem to mind. He presses a couple of buttons, turning on the seat warmer and the heater.

I don't say anything. I don't think I'm supposed to. I definitely don't want to, in case he decides to change his mind. I don't know why it's so important to me to know what happened. It's not my job to fix him—I know from my friends' experiences that that isn't my job even if I were his girlfriend—but maybe, if I know the pain, then I can at least be a part of alleviating it?

That was something that friends did.

Chase rests his head against the headrest. "I guess the first thing that I need to explain is that Amanda is almost ten years younger than me. We met through friends and hit it off. I don't know whether it was because I liked having someone to protect, or she liked having someone older and more mature taking care of her, but ... we made it work for about two years. Or at least I thought we were making it work.

"About a year ago, things started to get rough, but I figured I just wasn't paying her enough attention. I tried to take her out more—she never really liked nights in—and send her surprise flowers, but it always seemed like she was looking for something else."

Chase is drumming his fingers on the steering wheel. It's nervous energy. I haven't seen him do that before. He's being really vulnerable right now, and I feel the sudden desperate need to honor that. I feel like the best way is to let him finish.

"Well, it lasted until about June. I can't remember which day, believe it or not. Sometime in the last week of June. We were at dinner at an Italian place, and she sat me down and ... let me have it."

"What did she say?" My voice is small, and I don't intend to say it. The atmosphere is delicate, like it'll shatter if I make sudden moves or talk too loud.

His expression sobers, and he looks down at his hands. "That I couldn't connect with people, even if I wanted to. That she could do so much better than me. That I was ... toxic."

He starts to turn his head over to look at me, and then stops, as if he can't quite bring himself to look me in the eye. "That's why I said yes to coming with you, Summer. Because for the life of me I can't make Amanda's words go away, and the more I think about them, the more I think they're the truth. I don't want to go through my life unable to connect with people. I want to have good relationships—with a good woman, but also with my friends. I don't want to have to feel like I'm friends with people because I'm buying them, but whenever I look at myself, all I can see is the walking red flag that she was talking about."

I'm silent. I'm silent for a good long while. But not because I agree, or because I think he has a point. I am silent because I'm angry. Very angry. It's hot, sweet, and flashes through me like a match hitting a gasoline can.

"Are you kidding me?" I demand.

Chase almost jumps and finally turns to me. "What?"

"Are you kidding me?" I repeat myself, partially because I'm not sure if he was listening, and also because I'm not sure I can say much more without screeching like a tone-deaf barn owl.

"Summer?"

"You know she's full of it, right?" I say, my tone much harsher than what's probably needed for the situation. Well, right now if he needs kindness, he can go talk to Andie. He's in this fake relationship with me, so he gets what he gets.

"Who? Amanda?"

"Yeah!" I exclaim, somehow managing not to throw my hands up in the air. I'm going to need to calm down. The last time I got this animated I ended up breaking one of my fingers, and considering the projects I have in the near future, that is not going to do me any favors.

I take a deep breath and force my hands into my lap for my own protection. "I mean, don't get me wrong, Chase. I know you're not perfect. You're at least a little crazy, or you'd never have gotten into this situation with me in the first place. But ... you? Toxic?"

Chase closes his mouth and turns back to his steering wheel, the beginnings of a smile on his face. It's more of a self-effacing one, though, like he's humoring me, and I don't like it.

"Summer, I'm not perfect."

"I literally just said that, but let me tell you something, Chase Merrill, you are a fantastic person. And I'm not going to change that opinion even if we decide to ditch therapy and never see each other for the rest of our natural lives."

"You hardly know me, Summer."

"I know enough that you'd rescue a girl from her own ridiculous mess for no reason. I know you enough that instead of writing Amanda off as some crazy chick—which she clearly is—you're humble enough to weigh your own behavior and see if there's anything you need to change. I know that you have a sister that adores you and lets you call her Gills and basically worships the ground you walk on."

"Summer—"

"I know that you order dinner for random women when they're in over their heads at work and need a little help. I know that you respected my wishes for paying for myself most of the time, even though you could probably be sneaky and force the issue. I know you have," I get a little breathless at this point, and find myself getting oddly emotional. I clear my throat and start again. "I know you have a million things to do other than be here with me, but you're still here. And you have kept on going above and beyond over and over again.

"Chase, you might have rough edges—somewhere, because frankly they're pretty well hidden to me—but at least you *know*. At least you're trying to be better. That's not toxic, that's human. I've never been bored listening to you, in fact, I keep on thinking of new questions that I want to ask you because I want to get to know you better. You're—objectively speaking of course—incredibly good looking, and you care about and for the people in your circle. Chase ... Has it occurred to you that maybe she's the toxic one?"

Chase stares at me, his eyes far too wide. I said it as hyperbole, but it occurs to me that my note about parting ways and never seeing each other again might actually happen. At least for now I'm in his car. Maybe if I buckle my seatbelt, he can't kick me out so fast.

I'm not embarrassed about what I said, though. Not even close. Everything I said was one hundred percent true, and I will stand by that until the stars fall from the sky.

Great googly moogly. I need to lay off the drama for a minute. I sigh. "Sorry, that's probably really strong from someone who didn't know you at all three weeks ago," I say. It's not a sincere apology, per se, but if I, of all people, can pick up on that after so short a time, what other explanation is there?

"Summer?" Chase's voice is a little quieter than normal.

"What?" I can't stop my voice dropping low in dread.

"Thanks," he says quietly, and a genuine, if a little subdued, smile grows on his face.

"Do you believe it?"

He looks away. "Right now? I'm not sure." Then he turns back to me, the smile still present. "But I want to. And the fact that you believe it ... it means a lot."

I sigh and sit back in my seat. "I told you, I don't lie."

Chase's eyebrows lift and I frown at him. I point at the building. "You don't see me getting this emphatic in there, do you?"

He laughs, and the tension dissipates. "No, I guess you're right. So basically, check to see if your intensity is up to ten? Is that how I can tell you're telling the truth?"

"I—um," I stammer. "Sort of. Within reason. I am actually usually able to function in society on a normal basis. Usually."

He laughs again. "Summer ..."

"What?" I cringe as the embarrassment starts to sink in.

He puts his hand on my shoulder, squeezing it. I look up at him. His smile is broad and genuine. "Thank you. I mean it."

I mirror his expression, though a little more chagrined. "Anytime you need a reality check I guess." I laugh nervously.

His head dips down to make eye contact with me. "I'll come to you, every time." We sit there, taking each other in for a handful of heartbeats. Then he straightens. "Hey, we should talk about homework. Andie wanted us to find some goals, right?"

I take a deep breath and, grateful for the change in conversation. "Yep, think on our own what we'd like our relationship to be, and then meet together and discuss."

"Do you want to meet somewhere? Like the sandwich shop on Saturday?"

I think about it. "Actually, we could meet at my house, if you'd like. It's not too far from where you work, or so Lacy tells me. Lacy is supposed to be out with Renner for most of the weekend, so we could use the front room."

Chase raises his eyebrows. "You'd let me into your house?"

I copy him, challenging him. "Did you not listen to the embarrassingly emphatic diatribe earlier? I trust you."

He grins, and suddenly I realize that he's teasing me. The gears in my brain grind as I try to make sense of this, and I ultimately shake my head, laughing lightly as I purposefully fix my eyes on the purse in my lap. "Sorry about that."

Chase shakes his head. "Don't be. Really. I appreciate it." Then he squeezes my shoulder. "But, along with my extant faults, I have now made you late. You'd better hop back to work."

"Jennie only drives," I say drily. Then I sober, reaching up and covering his hand with mine. "Chase ... thanks for telling me. I'm sorry that she made you feel so ... that."

Chase smiles at me with quiet intensity. "Thanks, Summer."

I can't help the curve of my own lips. "Anytime."

Time. Work. I glance back at the door. "So, I don't know in-the-car etiquette. Do I open the door myself, or ...?"

He snorts, squeezes my shoulder one more time, and is already getting out of the car by the time I look back at him.

"Stay where you are," he orders with mock fierceness, and circles the vehicle to hand me out.

Turns out 'a little bit late' is more to the tune of twenty minutes than the five I reassure Chase about. I'm hoping I can slip in without too much notice, but Louis, like the bloodhound that he is, sniffs me out before I make it past the front door.

"You're late," he says, looking down his slightly oversized nose at me.

I look down at my watch and continue walking down the hallway. "Yes, I am. Which is why I'm hurrying back to work."

"You didn't look like you were hurrying in the parking lot," he says, still waiting at the door with his arms crossed. I turn back to him.

Mostly, I'm wondering why I'm having this conversation. Secondarily, I'm wondering what business of his it is, and thirdly— "The parking lot has ice patches, and I am wearing heels," I say. "I would be later if I broke a limb."

He frowns. "I don't think you need to be wearing heels in the first place."

"Well," I say, stuffing down all the many, far too delicious answers I could give to put him in his place. The interaction with Chase has left me a bit fired up, but I know better than to aim it at Louis. "That is my decision."

"You're way too tall to need them."

This is crossing over into territory I don't want to be in with this man, and I cross my arms. It's true that in certain heels I am over six foot, including the ones that I'm wearing right now. It's also true that it is none of his business.

"My boyfriend doesn't seem to mind." It slips out. Cool and collected, like a liquid nitrogen reality bomb going off in Louis's face.

It doesn't work the way I intend. "Boyfriend? You?"

My frown deepens. "Is it so hard to believe? I seem to remember that I've had a boyfriend for over six months now."

Louis snorts. "Yeah, right. A boyfriend with no name or pictures? Come to think of it, I don't think I've even seen you get a text from him."

I'm caught, smack dab in the middle of my own lie. When Ana asked me before, I shrugged her off, because I knew she wouldn't press the issue. Not everyone here shared details of their personal life. But Louis ... He really *wouldn't* believe me unless he saw a picture.

He might not even believe me if I did show him a picture, but at least I would have had proof to wave in his face.

But right now, I'm standing in the hallway, lost for words. He smirks. "I'll let Ana know that you're back," he says, and leaves me there.

Chapter 12
The Mutual Friend

CHASE

"So where are you off to today?" Avery's voice comes over the speaker in my car as I carefully drive through the winter wonderland of Utah Valley.

"Summer's." I'm sure I sound slightly preoccupied—I am. The roads aren't bad, but as is customary during a snowstorm, people have forgotten how to stay in their own lanes. I'm not an angry driver, but I am intimately familiar with defensive driving.

"Oooooo," Avery's voice is far too thrilled. "Meeting with your girlfriend during a veritable snowstorm?"

"This isn't unprecedented territory, Gills," I point out.

"It is for six dates into a relationship, sir." Her voice is altogether too delighted. I must have caught her in an especially good mood. "You must liiiiiiike her."

I roll my eyes. "Gills."

"Deny it."

I don't respond. I can't exactly explain to her that I'm going over to Summer's to make up relationship content for our therapist, can I?

126

I really need to tell her about therapy.

"That's what I thought." Avery's voice is smug now. "Well, I won't keep you from your true love much longer. I just wanted to let you know I'm off on a business trip for the next week or so."

I frown, and not just because of the Mini Cooper going at a snail's pace in front of me. "Have I heard about this before?"

"Yes, but you've got a girlfriend now. I don't expect you to remember everything." Her voice is light, but I know better. She's a little hurt. Avery is single, and with our parents physically and emotionally absent, she needs someone to look out for her, too. I want to be that person, but she's not completely wrong—with everything that's been happening with Summer, my focus has been elsewhere. But it doesn't feel right forgetting my real sister while I work out my fake relationship.

"I'm not going to forget about you just because I'm dating Summer," I say. "Would you send me the exact dates? I want to make sure I know when to report you missing."

Even over the phone, I can feel the pressure lift. Avery snorts. "Will do. Now, go have fun with your girlfriend. Don't kiss her too much."

"Gills—"

"Chase and Summer, sitting in a tree, K-I-S-S—"

"Bye, Gills." I roll my eyes, but the smile on my face is as real as it is involuntary.

"—I-N-G! Bye, Morkie. Love you!"

"Love you," I respond, and end the call as I turn into Summer's apartment complex.

It was easy enough to find—only about fifteen minutes away from my house by car, it's in one of the nicer apartment buildings looking over the valley. A valley that I can't actually see right now, considering the snow is falling in huge fluffy flakes as February throws her yearly temper tantrum. Finding a parking spot isn't hard, and after I shut off the engine, I look up at the building.

It's oddly intimidating. It looks normal—grey brick and siding, with lots of windows—but it feels a little like it's staring me down.

Avery is not wrong. It was a full three months after Amanda and I had started dating before I'd stepped foot in her house, and it's only been about three weeks.

Except this is a fake relationship, I remind myself as I leave my car, heading toward the entrance. Summer's apartment is on the third floor, and although there is a service elevator in an indoor lobby, I need to burn off some of the anticipation that's building in my chest.

My heart's beating like I've already run up one of the flights of stairs, my stomach is squelching uncomfortably, and I'm definitely warmer than I should be in the middle of a snowstorm. I honestly don't know why I'm nervous. It's been almost twenty years since I've felt this way about walking up to a girl's door. Isabel Porter had been sixteen, a brunette, and we had gone on exactly one date. In Isabel's defense, there was a rather unfortunate misunderstanding with a toad. It was Avery's fault.

At least I have a better track record with Summer. We're already in a relationship for one, albeit fake, and as of yet she has not run away screaming.

So, what's the big deal?

I make it to her front door without finding an answer, and even though my heart is beating twice as fast as is healthy to do so, I ring the doorbell.

There's a muffled voice from within, and a shuffle behind the door. A softer voice speaks, just distorted enough I can't make out what it says, and then the door opens to reveal Summer in a zipper hoodie, sweats, and cabin socks. She's looking to her left, looking a bit concerned.

Her teeth flash white in a grin as she catches sight of me. "Chase! You made it!" She glances over my shoulder, and her eyes widen. "Oh wow, I didn't realize it was snowing so much."

I shrug. "It's not that bad."

"You can't see the freeway," she points out. Then she pauses, as though reminding herself of something. "I'm a little worried the weather could cause you problems later."

I reach out, gently touching her arm. "I'm not worried about it, Summer. I've got winter tires, and I'm not afraid of driving in snow."

Summer looks relieved, and then her mouth drops open. "Oh! Come in. Look at me, worrying about the snow while keeping you out in it."

"All good," I say, stepping past her into the warm living room. Her house is cozy, with the light coming in from the front window, bathing the couch in the white, natural light. The couch and ...

"Lacy?" I ask the bundle of blankets. There's no reply.

"Shh," Summer says softly, beckoning me further into the house. I kick my shoes off in the entryway before following her into the kitchen. Summer stands behind the counter, looking into the apartment, frowning slightly. "Lacy ... has the flu."

"What?" I pull in my chin.

"I'm sorry!" she whispers, crossing her arms. "I didn't actually know until I came to open the door. I thought I heard her go out earlier, but I guess it was her coming home early because she was throwing up. If you want, we can reschedule. I don't want you to get sick by accident."

"That's all right," I say, glancing over at the bundle of blankets that was supposedly Summer's roommate. "I'm already here. If nothing else we can go walking somewhere."

"It's really snowy, I think we'd burn out before we were done, and then we'd be here again."

We'd already decided against a restaurant because we were talking about somewhat sensitive things. Fake or not, it felt better to do it in relative private.

Summer looks like she's thinking hard, crossing her arms, and biting her lip. Then she took a deep breath. "Lacy's going to wake up if we're out here, and I'd feel bad. If you want, we could ..." she trails off, as though she isn't entirely sure what to say.

"What?" I whisper, turning toward her.

"This is a suggestion. And honestly just a suggestion."

"What is it?" I ask.

She pauses for a moment longer and then nods over her shoulder. "We could go into ... my room? Please don't get the wrong idea. There's a couch and desk in there. It's comfortable, and more ... well, we won't disturb Lacy."

I think about this. "Sounds good. It's a good idea. No wrong ideas gotten."

I see the flash of a rather flustered smile from Summer, before she turns away and waves for me to follow her down the hallway.

I do. The hallway is dark, but as she opens the door to her room and we both step inside, I feel an immediate rush of peace.

It's hard to tell what exactly brings it on. It could be the perfectly neat surroundings with nothing out of place. It could be the fluffy queen bed along one wall or the equally fluffy couch along the opposite wall. It could be the framed photos and certificates hanging on the beige walls, adding to the air of order and calm.

Whatever it is, I follow Summer inside, shutting the door behind me. She motions for me to come to the desk, where she pulls out a high-end gaming chair and gestures for me to sit down, before moving to the couch to sit.

I walk over to the desk and sit down, jostling the mouse by accident.

The two desktop screens light up, and an image of her family comes up, as well as the login screen.

I study her family. Two brothers and one sister. Her mom and dad. Her mom is grinning widely in the photo, like she's extra, extra happy to be there. Her short curls—almost the same reddish brown as her daughter's, shot with grey—bounce around her head. Summer's father is on the stocky side, but there's a calmness about him that seems to diffuse into the room I'm sitting in, despite the fact he's not really here.

"Is this your family?" I ask, still studying their faces.

Summer stands up from the couch and comes to stand beside me. I'm not sure whether it's her personal scent or what she's put in her room, but warm vanilla tickles my senses, adding to the calm, comforting atmosphere.

"Yep," Summer says, standing closer to me than what's probably strictly necessary. I don't mind, though, and I don't move. "That's my dad, his name is Frank. I think he looks like one. That's my mom, Karma—don't ask. I have a theory about why she got named that, but it's weird enough you'll probably think it's a conspiracy."

I laugh, and she looks up at me with a smile. Her hair is in a ponytail today, her thick hair making it cascade like a waterfall around her shoulders. It's a good look.

Summer points to the woman who is probably her sister. "That's my sister Joan, or Joanie as everyone in our family calls her. She's four years older than me. Rhett's next, and he's two years older than me, and then that's Scottie. He's four years younger than me."

I smile down at her. "You're the dreaded middle child?"

Summer laughs and shrugs, looking up at me. "I have to live up to my reputation somehow. I was too busy being a gifted kid in high school to rebel much." She pauses, and frowns. "Trust me to get into an ethical fiasco. This tracks."

It's my turn to laugh. Stepping away from the computer, I cross over to the couch and settle down at one side. It rivals the therapy couch, both in terms of coziness, and also the fact it might be a rather undignified struggle to pull myself out of it. At least now it would be in relative privacy.

"Your family looks nice," I say, sitting back on the couch. "And that's a really nice set up. I know you code at home, do you game at all?"

Summer shakes her head. "I usually try not to be on the computer too much if I'm not working. Nothing against the computer or anything—obviously—but I'm just trying not to dry my eyes out."

"I feel it. Working on anything good? It sounded like you got your project done in time."

Summer exhales tiredly and comes and sits down by me. She flops down, drawing her feet up under her. "With a clearance of about a half an hour. I hate finishing that close to the wire. It doesn't feel professional to me."

I give her a sheepish grin. "Well, then, call me unprofessional, but I've worked down to the minute before. It got uploaded on time, though."

Summer laughs and leans her head on the back of the sofa. "And that's what counts, right? As long as it's uploaded at the end of the day, it doesn't matter much what else happens."

I nod. "Well, and nowadays I'm largely the front-facing part of our company."

"With a face like that?" Summer teases.

"Hey, I'll have you know someone called me "incredibly good looking" this week," I shot back. "You can't buy that kind of advertising."

Summer turns a healthy shade of pink. "That was ... that

was ... it was objectively speaking, Chase. I said that when I told you that. Anyone can see it."

"And we're both saying the same thing," I point out with a grin.

She scowls at me, but there's no real heat to it. She turns away, and I can see her fighting a smile.

"Actually," she says, "speaking of work ..."

Summer trails off, and I shift so I can see her better. "Yes?"

She looks at me, and then down at our therapy notebook, and then at her phone, and then back to me.

"Never mind."

"What?"

She shakes her head. "Never mind. Let's get to work."

I stare at her for a moment, not entirely sure if I should press the issue. I know that she works at the same company as Lacy, but I'm almost entirely in the programming-front-design part of technology, and she's in the behind-the-scenes, make-it-all-run-smoothly part of technology. There's some crossover, but she could hardly be asking for professional advice from me.

I can't guess what she's thinking, and so I move on. Andie gave her the assignment to tell me what she's feeling, and for me to honor that. I can't help her with problems that I don't know about.

To be perfectly honest, it might not even be a problem.

Time to let it go.

We start going through our goals. There are three questions that Andie left with us: 1) What are we trying to get out of our relationship? Specifically, our end goal. 2) What does our relationship mean to us now, versus what it meant when we first got together? 3) What are some shared experiences that we had at the beginning of the relationship that exemplify the goals we have for the relationship?

For any other couple, it would be simple enough work. For Summer and I, it's a lesson in storytelling.

It's a ridiculous amount of fun, and we soon lose ourselves in the narrative. It turns out we're both fans of foreign films—though generally different genres—and it's a little difficult to not put in too many cliches or plot twists. Realistically speaking, we're probably close enough to having the whole story without any fictional help.

After half an hour we've come up with answers to the first two questions. They boil down to:

1) Our goal is to have a positive, healthy relationship for both of us.
2) When we got together, our relationship was largely to have a relationship. Now we want it to mean supporting each other and helping each other become the best versions of ourselves.

Number three is turning out to be a little illusive, since we're still trying to base our answer on something real instead of a completely fictitious event. We simply haven't done a ton of things, and for it to be believable, we have to choose something meaningful.

Summer taps her pen against her lips as she thinks. She's doing this pouty thing with her bottom lip as she thinks which accentuates her rosebud mouth. It's rather distracting, and at the same time really fun to watch, even if it's not doing much for my ability to problem-solve.

"What if," Summer asks quietly, "We do something to fulfill the assignment?"

I pull myself back to the present. "Like what?"

She frowns. "I'm not—" Her words are cut off by a three-tone chirp, and she frowns at the phone on the small coffee table. Summer apologizes and reaches for the phone. Opening the notification, she stares at her phone for a long moment, her expression darkening. Then with an almost mechanical purposefulness, turns the sound off, and places the phone on the table, face down. Her countenance has sobered considerably, and she's staring down at the notebook in her lap with a heavy frown on her face.

"Summer?" I ask, tilting my head down to look at her. "Problem?"

She looks up, almost as though she's forgotten there's a man in her room. Then she swallows and looks around. "Sorry. It was a text from work."

From work? With that expression? "Everything okay? Do they need you to go in?" It's still snowing pretty hard, but I can drive her if she doesn't want to drive herself. And back, if I need to.

Summer shakes her head and looks up at me. "No, sorry. Nothing like that."

If not that, then what? "Anything I can help with? You look a little ..." 'Different' is the word that crosses my mind, but even if it is accurate, it is absolutely not the right word to use in this situation.

Summer shakes her head again and forcibly relaxes her shoulders. That was it. She had tensed up. She *is* worried about something. "Really, Chase," she says calmly. "Don't worry about it. It's nothing I can't handle."

I believe her, but it doesn't take away my concern. I know Summer is able to handle herself, but I don't think I've ever seen her respond like that before, and I literally have gone to therapy as a stranger with her. She was concerned then; I am willing to bet she's upset now.

Summer's quiet a moment longer, and then asks, "Do you think we could take a picture together?"

It's not what I expect to hear.

It's really not what I expect to hear.

"Why?" I ask. Then, realizing it might come off as rude, I shake my head. "Sorry, yeah, that's fine. But ... why?"

Summer sighs and leans her head back against the back of the couch. "It's going to sound a little silly."

I turn to face the same direction she is, so she doesn't feel like I'm staring at her. It's a legitimate concern at this point, because she's running that pen along the border of her lips again, and I'm not going to be able to concentrate on the problem if I have to watch.

You liiiiiiiike her, Avery's voice breaks into my thoughts. I push it away. Summer and I are connected in an oddly close way. I'm allowed to care.

"I'm good with silly," I say, breaking my own rule and turning to look at her as I talk. She doesn't look back at me, but she's staring down at her phone. Then she takes a deep breath.

"Okay. I have a coworker. He's really annoying. He's kind of sussed me out about the boyfriend thing, but it's more or less because I don't have a picture with you. He's also kind of getting after me because he doesn't believe I'm going to therapy."

I frown.

"Do you want me to talk to him?" I ask. It pops out, my voice deeper and more rumbly than I intend. Summer stares at me, eyes wide, like I've shocked her. *Way to not overstep, Chase.* "Uh, sorry," I say, running a hand over my head. "That's probably—I mean, it's probably a bit much."

Summer's expression softened, but she can't quite hide the smile growing on her face. "Just a little," she says, but she looks pleased. "I ... it's okay. I can handle him. In all reality, the picture would only be to get him off my back a bit, but if you're not comfortable with it, that's fine."

I frown a little. "Why wouldn't I be fine with it?"

"You want to have photographic evidence of the time you fake-dated someone?"

I shrug. "Why would I mind? There's nothing wrong with you. In fact, you're kind of awesome."

She looks at me, even more stunned than earlier.

"Objectively speaking, of course," I give her my best smile.

Summer scoffs and pushes me on my shoulder. "I knew that was going to come back and bite me."

I shrug with a smug grin on my face. "I didn't mind. Now, do you want your phone or mine? I will need copies of these for Avery."

"What kind of camera do you have on your phone?" she asks.

I have no clue. I don't actually use it much, unless I'm taking a picture of my dinner to show to Avery. Or rub it in when she misses a dinner because she's out with friends instead of hanging with her moldy older brother. I dig the phone out and hand it to Summer. She picks up her own phone and opens the phone apps on each.

"Hmm," she says, taking sample photos of her table. "I think mine is slightly better."

"Into photography?"

"Hmm? No. A little vain, though, especially if I'm going to be showing a picture of myself to Louis freaking Granger."

Ah-ha. I had a name. I'd have to talk to Lacy later.

Or not. I had to be respectful of Summer's space. Plus, with my luck, she'd probably reroute me back to Summer anyway.

But I could at least ask, right?

"Fair enough," I say. "So, what were you thinking with this one?"

Summer looks at me, at the space, and then up at her overhead light. "Well, we'll need to turn on a lamp or something, otherwise these'll all come out moody."

"Okay," I say, leaning over and turning on the lamp by Summer's desk.

"No, not that one," she says, standing.

I turn the lamp off.

Summer crosses the room, and flips on her bathroom light, her closet light, and the nightstand lamp.

"Hopefully this doesn't completely obliterate my power bill," she says under her breath. "This is the one time in my life I wish I had a ring light, but that's not going to happen."

She was treating this far more seriously than I had anticipated. The small kernel of nervousness that had sat in the husk of my psyche started to grow again.

"Summer, I'm sure it's fine." I reach for her hand and pull her gently to a stop. Summer stops, and looks down at me, biting her lip. "How about we take a couple of pictures and see where we're at after a couple of shots?"

Summer considers this, her eyebrows drawn together. Then she nods tentatively. "Okay."

I think for a moment. "Do you want to be taking pictures with me? We don't have to if you don't want to. I mean, I could probably show up at your work and it'll have pretty much the same effect."

"You will not do that," Summer says firmly. I blink in surprise. She shakes her head. "It's not just Louis. My assistant manager has sprung up with an unhealthy obsession with finding out everything there is to know about you. The only way I can make her not stalk your complete online presence is because she doesn't know your name or your face."

"And she would know both immediately if she saw me?" I ask.

"She's Lacy's assistant manager, too," she points out. "You're one of our clients. One of our more important clients, even, so ..." she trails off and squints a sort-of-apologetic look at me.

"Won't she see my face in the pictures?" I ask.

She hasn't thought of this, I can tell, and it's a little funny to watch her come to this realization.

"Confound it," she says, burying her head in her hands and sinking down onto the couch beside me.

I pat her shoulder. "Don't worry about it too much, Summer," I say cheerfully. "It would have to come out at some point. Your mom is going to want to see my face at some point as well. Plus, we can both confidently say I'm a catch. I won't give either of your parents a heart attack because I'm employed and successful, and you don't have to put a paper bag over my head, because I am objectively good-looking."

Summer turns to look at me. She's trying to look incredulous, I can tell, but she's way too close to laughter for that.

"You're smiling," I point out.

"I'm trying to be mad, but you're right, and it's annoying." She turns away, an incredible grin stretching across her face.

"It doesn't look like you're annoyed, Summer." I lean around to see her face.

"Well, I am." She turns back to me, managing to get the smile to drop off her face by forcing her eyebrows into a line.

"Are you?" I ask, leaning forward, my forearms resting on my thighs, getting as close as I dare. I'm still a respectable distance away, though. I know better than to push her too far all at once.

I don't expect her to lean in, too. She stops, less than a foot away from my face, squinting at me, like she's staring down a gunslinger. Still fighting to keep the corners of her mouth turned down, she shakes her head. "Don't push me, Merrill."

"Who am I pushing, Sunny?" I say, unable to keep the smirk off my face. It comes off significantly less breathless than I feel right now.

Summer rolls her eyes, and sits back, raising her eyebrows. The smile still dances around her lips. "Sunny, huh?"

"It fits," I shrug. "Problem?"

She shakes her head, her expression relaxed. "My dad calls me Sunshine. It's my middle name."

"I know," I say.

"How—oh, was that in the dossier I gave you?"

"Your rather incomplete file? Yes."

"How was it incomplete?"

"It didn't have your favorite restaurant in there," I point out. "Or your favorite things to do. Or the fact you drive a car older than most dinosaurs."

"Hey!" she says loudly, then glances toward the door. "Jennie is a classic. Also, she might hear you, so just ... keep it on the down low." Her expression turns into one of over-exaggerated concern, and I laugh. Then I shake my head.

"Let's take this picture, Sunny." I hold out my arm, and gesture for her to come closer. Still shaking her head at me, she comes close and tucks herself into my side.

And fits perfectly.

It almost makes my breath hitch, as she curls up into me, resting her head on my shoulder. Then I force myself to exhale, because Summer is definitely close enough to tell if I'm acting weird. Besides, why should it be weird? I cuddle. Or rather, historically I have cuddled. The fact that Amanda never quite fit so well or made my muscles relax quite so quickly doesn't have anything to do with anything.

"You're going to have to take the picture," Summer says softly. She's looking up at me, and I turn my head toward her.

But all this does is put me within three inches of her lips, and the weight of reality crashes down on me.

I don't know how, and I certainly don't know when it happened, but I am utterly attracted to this woman.

And that's a problem, because this relationship is one-hundred-percent fake.

Fake, fake, fake, the word bounces around my mind, even as I look down at those perfectly-kissable pink lips. *Fake, fake, fake.*

Avery's voice chimes in. *Chase and Summer, sitting in a tree, K-I-S-S-I-N-G.*

Thanks, Gills.

The voice of reason manages to make itself heard over the sudden din in my head. *Stop it, Merrill.*

"Why?" I ask, not sure whether I'm asking her or the little voice pinging around my mind.

"Because you have longer arms?" Summer says, apparently completely unaffected. "Unless you're okay with the fact that I'll probably end up cutting off half your face. Also, my hands are too small for my phone."

I blink.

She is unaffected. Because we are fake dating. None of this is real. I'm in breach of the agreement, pushing something on her she doesn't want.

Toxic, Amanda's little voice says smugly.

"You should get a little handle thing for the back of your phone," I say, trying to pretend my throat isn't suddenly dry.

Summer pulls a face. "I don't like how they look. Plus, I'm sure I'll forget it's there and end up breaking it."

I take the phone from her hands—are they always cold?—and look at the settings she has on, so I can fix them if I bump them. "Nah, they're pretty durable. Oh well, say cheese!"

Before Summer has a chance to pose or smile or do anything except look up, I take a picture high above our heads.

Summer's mouth opens in surprise, and she reaches up at the phone as I keep on taking pictures. "Chase, I didn't mean like that!"

I laugh and pull her close. She falls back against me, knocking us sideways on the couch so she's reclining against me. I snap another photo. "Every photoshoot needs a couple of candid shots. Otherwise, they all end up looking like school photos."

"Not all of them," Summer protests. "There's nothing wrong with a nice, professional photo."

"Except neither of us are professional photographers," I point out. Where she's settled against me, staring into my face, I can see the set of her jaw, and the tightness of her shoulders. I've had enough fun, time to give a little mercy. "Of course, there's nothing wrong with a nice serious photo."

Summer's shoulders relax, and she nods. "Good."

"What did you have in mind?" I ask.

"Well," she says, and she pauses, like she's trying to phrase her words properly.

"You can just say it, Summer," I say gently. "I promise my delicate sensibilities will not be offended by whatever you have in mind."

"I was thinking you could put your arm around me. Kind of like what you did before, but with less ... motion."

I gaze at her for a moment, drinking in her deep green eyes, and then dip my head in agreement. Sitting up, I put my arm around her shoulders. She slides into place, fitting perfectly, just like she did before.

I'm in such big trouble.

Still, commitment to the role, and all that. I pull on her shoulder, snugging her a bit closer to my side. I notice she turns into me, one arm sliding behind my back, and the other resting on my chest as her head leans against my shoulder. She's tall, and her head fits into the curve of my neck as we sit side by side.

She's close. I can tell now—the vanilla is coming from her.

Focus, Chase.

"Smile," I say quietly, looking up at the phone in my hand. I can feel Summer tilt her head and look more at the camera. When she looks into the lens, I take the picture.

It's a great photo. Of her. Of us.

There's a half moment of silence as we both look at the phone screen before Summer sits up. "I think that was a good one." Summer's voice is quiet. Easing away from me, she pushes herself to her feet, and pivots to face me. "Do you need anything? Water? Hot chocolate?"

I shake my head. "I'm fine." I wave her phone before she can turn away. "Can I text these to myself?"

Summer blinks and then nods. Walking forward, she unlocks her phone with facial ID and then walks out of the room.

For the barest of seconds, I'm tempted to look at the unread message from Louis Granger. I know better, and I am actually able to control my own impulses, so instead I open up my own text thread.

By the time Summer comes back into the room, I'm done sending the photos. I hand the phone back to Summer, and she looks at the screen.

She starts when she sees my one contribution to her phone. A picture of us now adorns the lock screen—the first one I took before Summer was ready, where she is reaching for the phone. The angle makes it look like she's reaching for the time. It fits perfectly, and she laughs, shaking her head.

I shrug. "It seems like you should have a picture of us on your lock screen. Y'know. Playing the part."

Summer is still shaking her head, a smile dancing on her lips. "Oh, I know you're right. But you have to pick one, too. For therapy."

I nod solemnly. "For therapy."

SUMMER

Chase leaves almost an hour later, after we finish our goal setting and write our journal entries. We put this event as our favorite relationship memory—which isn't too far off, if I'm honest.

I flop back on my bed, holding the therapy journal against my chest as I stare at the ceiling.

I'm in trouble.

Is it normal for it to feel so good when you lean into a guy? To feel small and feminine and protected? Half of me hopes it is normal, so I can write it off as having a perfectly normal afternoon with a man I enjoy spending time with.

But the other half is pretty sure it isn't.

And it's a problem. Because at no point did Chase sign up to actually get a relationship out of this. I would be in breach of contract, and that's not okay with me. He came to get therapy, and falling in love with him in the midst of all this wouldn't be fair to him. Sure, he wants to become a better partner, but shouldn't he be able to do that without interference from the peanut gallery?

It's me. I'm the peanut gallery.

It's not like I'd have any useful insights—I've never been in a relationship before.

The reality of it hurts, settling deep into my chest, and I know it's the truth behind my uncertainty.

I don't know whether what I'm feeling is really love, or whether it's because it's the first time I've ever spent this kind of time with a guy. Because it's somehow better than I expected, but I don't know whether I'm desperate or just naive.

Either way, I can't act on this for real. It's not fair to Chase, and it definitely wouldn't be acting within proper boundaries if I tried to do anything. Consent for men is just as important as consent for women, and anything else is simply ... taking advantage.

And I won't do that to him.

Because it's all an act on his part, and it needs to be an act on mine. Because this is temporary. Because this isn't real.

I get up and turn off all the lights in my room except for the one beside my bed. It's not quite bedtime yet—it's only about seven—but I intend to curl up in my nice warm bed and watch dramas until I fall asleep.

And I do exactly that for about four minutes, managing to settle on a drama in record time, until I hear Lacy gagging in the other room.

I get up to help my friend.

Chapter 13
The Fourth Appointment

CHASE

By the time Thursday lunchtime rolls around, I am pretty sure my phone is going to wear out from overuse. And not only because Summer and I are texting nonstop—which we totally are—but because the wonderful, silly photo where Summer is reaching for the phone is pretty much the only thing keeping me afloat right now.

Today has not been a good day. I was informed when I got in to work today that a prospective client had dropped through. Normally, it wouldn't be such a tragedy, but it was because of a mistake one of our representatives had made, rather than simply being a matter of going with a different company. One was business, the other was a potentially damaging incident. I had let Ed take care of it.

Then there's my car. It's icy outside, as is generally the case in February after two days of snowstorms, but playing bumper cars with an SUV sliding through a stop sign was not on my list for the day. We both came across all right with only a scratch or two, but the anxiety of watching the big vehicle glide gracefully out of control toward my car is proving a little bit difficult to throw off.

And then there's Amanda.

I frown as the thought surfaces, unwanted and uninvited, as I drive into the therapy parking lot. She'd texted me this morning. I cleared the notification before I had a chance to read the text, but it was following me around like a screaming monkey. Even after six months, even a reminder of her starts a tidal wave of her tirade, flooding my brain with everything I apparently put her through. It hurts. It hurts more than I thought it would this long since.

And, with Avery on a plane, I can't even call her about it.

I'm so sunk into my thoughts I almost don't notice that the Crown Victoria is already there.

Almost.

It's impossible to miss Summer. She's not loud or constantly demanding my attention, not like Amanda had been. She's simply herself, being herself, and it's like the first breath of air after being underwater too long.

She's still in her car, and I can see she's on her phone. As I grab my phone and key fob and stuff them in my pocket, I wonder what she does when she's not around me. Summer isn't super active on social media—not like Lacy is. I've checked. It's possible that she's a lurker. She's sent me plenty of funny videos and gifs, so she's definitely not ignorant about how it works, but it still doesn't answer my question.

I pause as I reach for the door handle. I'm wondering about Summer a lot, considering I'm not dating the woman. Except, aren't I? Fake dating is technically still dating. I want to walk the walk—I'm supposed to be a reformed boyfriend. Or at least in the process of reforming.

I leave the car, and walk over to Summer, who has noticed me, and is stuffing her phone into her purse. I open the door without any prompting, and she takes my hand, squeezing it in thanks as she stands up to her full height. She also gives me a dazzling smile, which I genuinely mirror as I take her car keys and lock the car for her.

"Thanks." She gestures with her chin toward the building. "Shall we?"

"Sure," I say, taking a deep breath. I subconsciously guide her forward by putting my hand at the small of her back. She gives me a small smile, and suddenly all I want to do is tell her about my absolutely awful day.

"How was your day?" Summer asks, and it's like life pounds down on my head. I have to physically stop for a moment, taking a deep, steadying breath. Summer turns back to me, and her expression changes to alarm. "Chase?" She reaches out, taking me by the arms. "You okay?"

I take a deep breath. "Yeah, sorry. It's been a day. I ..." Do I actually confide in her?

Yes. If nothing else, I know she's my friend. She'd care. Plus, she's capable of an excellent pep talk, which I could really use right about now. "Stuff—disappointing, hard stuff—happened at work, and then I got into a fender bender, and then Amanda texted me, and I've been in my head all day."

Summer studies my face carefully for a long moment without saying anything. Part of me wonders whether or not she's going to go into Protect Mode like she did last week, but her voice is gentle when she speaks. "First things first, are you all right physically? You didn't get whiplash or anything from the car accident?"

I shake my head. "He didn't hit me hard. We were both going slow. He was coming to a stop and hit ice."

She exhales in relief. Her hands slide down my arms and drop to her sides. I miss the contact immediately.

"Good. I mean, not that he hit you, but that you're okay." Summer frowns. "You said something happened at work?"

I press my lips together, trying to keep the frown from taking over my face. "We lost a pretty important account because of something we could have directly prevented. It was pretty bad."

"Was it you or someone else?"

"Someone else, but we're not a big company, and as CEO, I'm held responsible. Ed—Ed Victor, the Victor in Merrill and Victor—is taking care of it, but it's still a blow."

"Will it hurt the company permanently?"

"Hopefully not." It's not quite the truth, so I amend. "Probably not. It just feels different than if they were passing over our bid for some other reason."

Summer frowns in concentration. "I get it. One's rather subjective. The other one you can actually put a face to the name."

"Exactly." I sigh and rub my hand over my face. I look across the empty parking lot, grateful for the faux privacy.

"And ... Amanda?" Summer asks, her voice quiet. She sounds hesitant, but I'm not sure whether it's because she doesn't remember, or because she doesn't really want to know. She knows she's my ex, and she knows it ended badly.

"What did she say?" Summer's voice breaks through my runaway thoughts, and I force myself to concentrate. It's ridiculous. Any one of these things on their own would have been manageable. All three in a four-hour period was unfair.

"I don't know." I sigh. "I haven't read it yet."

Summer's eyebrows scrunch together. "You haven't?"

"No." I look around the parking lot again, not quite able to meet her eyes. "I'm not sure I want to know."

Summer snorts. "It's official, you have more self-control than I ever will."

When she sees my raised eyebrows, she explains. "Half of me would know to wait until it's a good time when I could process, but the actual physical notification would drive me insane. Don't you have a preview of your texts?"

"I cleared the notification on my lock screen before I could read it," I admit.

She shakes her head in wonder. "Mad respect, sir. The sheer knowledge would drive me insane before midday."

I can't help the huff of laughter. "Bold of you to assume it isn't. It *is* one of the three things that's bothering me today."

Summer smirks and folds her arms nonchalantly, her head tipping to the side. "As long as one of those things isn't me, I think we'll be able to make it through."

I look down at her, unable to keep the smile from my face. I'm not sure how she's done it, but it's easier to breathe now. She reaches out and runs one hand down my arm. She tips her head in the direction of the building. "You gonna be okay in there? I'm pretty sure we can reschedule if we have to."

I shake my head. "I'll be okay."

"Well then," she says, linking her arm through mine, "Shall we?"

As we walk into the building, I have a sneaking suspicion Summer is right—if she's with me, we'll be able to make it through.

Andie comes out swinging when we get inside. I've barely rested my behind in the ridiculously plush sofa when Andie gives us both a blinding smile. "So, what made you two choose each other?"

Summer's eyebrows lift microscopically. "What do you mean?"

Andie's only too happy to explain. "I'm talking specifics. When you met Chase, what convinced you that Chase was someone to take a chance on? Was it his looks? His sense of humor? You've talked about feeling like you needed to be in a relationship, but why with Chase?"

Andie then looks at me. "For you as well. You've talked about an ex before. Was Summer a rebound? Was it chemistry? Was it her smile? Walk me through this."

Summer and I glance at each other, and for some reason— maybe the pressure of earlier in the day, or even the little distance I now had from those awkward first meetings—the question strikes me as very funny. I make the mistake of smiling.

"Chase?" Andie says, leaning into view. "It looks like you know what you'd answer."

Oops. I open my mouth and laugh a little, embarrassed at being caught out. "It's ... well, it's not nothing. I guess it was Summer's tenacity. She's very straightforward. She's not in the habit of wasting anyone's time, and I guess it's why I felt comfortable saying yes."

We haven't talked about this specifically, but I feel confident she'll work with my answer. "I won't deny there was probably an element of rebound. Sorry," I look over at Summer, but she waves it off. "But there's something about her. It's like I have perfect license to be myself because she exists." I wonder if she knows how sincerely I mean every word I say. "I don't understand how or why, but it makes me want to be the best version of myself, because that's how I best fit with her. I haven't always understood it, but ... that's how I feel."

Summer's eyes are soft, and I feel the gentle pressure of her fingers as she touches my forearm, squeezing it briefly.

Andie doesn't speak while Summer gathers her thoughts. Summer's reddish-brown hair—straight today—drapes over one shoulder, as she thinks deeply. *Why am I holding my breath?*

"Chase gives me confidence," Summer says. "I don't like to admit it, but there are a lot of things I'm afraid of. Being old and alone is one of those things. When we first started therapy, I definitely jumped at the chance because I didn't think there was anyone else who would have me." She bites her lip as she thinks. *I can't quite look away from her.*

"But Chase ... he makes me feel wanted. He makes me feel like it's perfectly reasonable to wait in my car an extra ten seconds because he genuinely wants to open my door. He shows love like this to everyone. He's kind to servers. He treats his sister like a princess. And me?" She smiles. "I didn't choose him for the right reasons, but he's turned out to be so different from who I thought he would be." She laughs. "I guess I lucked out. I should cash in while I can, huh? There's no way I'll get this lucky again."

I stare at her, trying not to be utterly touched. I know she's faking it. I know it. But the smile on her face as she looks at me makes it hard to remember.

Andie laughs good-naturedly as well, but her expression softens as she looks between us, like she's almost relieved. A question I can't quite put into words prickles at the back of my brain. "Thank you for sharing. Now, taking what you've said into account, let's look at your goals. I'm excited to see what you came up with!"

We go over the goals and our journal entries. It's clear she's pleased with our progress. Honestly, I am as well. It feels natural, being with Summer, in a way I've never quite experienced before. Maybe it's because it's not real, the pressure is off. I don't feel like I have to impress her, I just have to *be*.

And yet, I do want to impress Summer. I want to be the best version of Chase Merrill I've ever been.

Andie continues the session, leading a couple more role-play conversations between Summer and I, and tells us to go over our goals together and make a couple of intermediate goals to help push toward them.

We stand up to go, Summer and I struggling a little bit to extricate ourselves from The Couch and laughing at ourselves a little as I push Summer out first before letting her help pull me to my feet. Andie is watching us fondly, and I suddenly know the question that's been dancing at the edge of my brain.

"Hey, Andie," I ask, helping Summer put on her coat. "You asked earlier about why we chose each other. Why was that? I mean, other than being a good therapy question?"

"What makes you think there was something extra?" Andie asks.

I shrug a little. "I don't know. You seem a little more happy than usual."

She smirks at me. "I am a naturally happy person. I guess it was in response to what I'd noticed during your first appointment. Most couples when they're having troubles don't touch each other, but you two were possibly the worst case I'd ever seen. In fact, when you first came in, I could have sworn you two didn't know each other at all." My stomach drops, but thankfully Andie can't actually read my thoughts. "Ever since then, you two still don't touch that much, but it's gotten better bit by bit. I guess these questions are me trying to help you remember why you started dating in the first place."

I try to keep my expression neutral. Glancing over at Summer, I can see that her cheeks are a little flushed.

"That's understandable." I laugh a little. "Well, it's working. And speaking of work, I should probably get Summer on her way. We've taken a little extra time today."

"For sure." Andie looks between the two of us. "We meet in two weeks?"

"Yes," Summer says quickly.

"Well, then," Andie says. "I'll see you two then!"

It's quiet as we walk out to the car. Summer is biting her lip and hugging herself before we even get to Jennie. She looks half nervous and half deep in thought. I think I know what she's thinking about. At least, I do if she's thinking about what I'm thinking about as well.

"I think," she says at last, "we got lucky in there."

I lean up against the Crown Victoria and raise my eyebrows.

"Lucky?" I ask. "She pegged us."

Summer nods, lips pursed unhappily. "You're not wrong. But it sounded like she was at least trying to talk herself out of her suspicions." She's still biting her lip. "We should probably do something about it."

I turn to her, not quite believing what I'm hearing. I mean, Summer isn't against touching at all, but we are a long, long way from being two people in love. I mean, if the people around you aren't at least faintly nauseated, are you even dating?

Apparently, I'm wrong.

At least we were supposed to be having problems. Back then, at least. Come to think of it, we should probably plan something to have friction over. We're supposed to have been dating poorly over the past six months. Is five—has it only been five?—weeks since we started therapy supposed to be so immediately effective?

"Chase?"

I'm lost in my thoughts, and jump slightly before I turn to Summer, who's still staring thoughtfully across the parking lot at the therapy building.

"Hmm?" I ask.

"What if we practiced?"

I'm stuck in my thoughts. I don't think she means practicing having fights. If our fake history shows anything, it proves we'd do fine at it. Real life? Well, it might actually take some work.

"I'm sorry, I was thinking. Practiced what?" I ask.

Summer looks up at me with her eyebrows raised but then bites her lip again and faces the parking lot. "Physical affection."

I nearly choke on my own spit. "What?" Good heavens, I already know I'm attracted to this woman. This is just unfair.

Summer shrugs but doesn't look over at me. "I'm not going to lie, I have significantly less dating experience than you. It might be worth it to," she closes her eyes, and I'm willing to bet she's a little mortified, "practice being physically affectionate. To the level of people who are dating."

I wonder if she knows how much she already touches me. It's never been inappropriate or even uncomfortable, but it's happened more than once where she's linked her arm through mine, apparently without noticing. Even earlier, before our appointment, she'd taken me gently by the shoulders. She's definitely not as touchy-feely as I am—I'm not an octopus, but I am a hugger—but she's not repressed or anything.

Maybe that's the point she's making.

"Is it something you're comfortable doing?" I ask. "I'm not about to make you do anything you aren't one hundred percent on board with."

"No, no," she says, finally looking up at me, though a faint tinge of pink is definitely blossoming across her cheeks. "I'm sure. I'm okay with it, I promise. Like I said, though, you've had more experience dating, so you'll know better than I do what Andie will be looking for."

I turn toward Summer, folding my arms. Her expression falters. "Do you ... You don't want to do this with me." It has turned into a statement.

I think carefully about what I'm about to say. Do I have a problem with "practicing" with Summer? No. Absolutely not, in fact. But is it more than we have to do in order to get by? Yes.

"You know that we can get by without it, right?" I ask quietly. "Like, you realize that she thinks that we're a couple on the rocks, and we're breaking up at the end of this."

The words fall like a massive oak between us, and she looks down, swallowing hard. I have to say it, though. I have to remind myself that in a few short weeks, my time with Summer will come to an end. I don't want it to—I feel like my relationship with Summer is already one of the best of my life, which is actually rather embarrassing—but the point of this is only to trick the therapist into thinking we're dating, not to pass ourselves off as a healthy dating couple.

"I know," Summer says quietly, her eyes looking anywhere but mine. "And I know we're breaking up at the end of this. But even if this is going to end with us breaking up, I want to be able to tell her if I run into her on the street we tried our best. I know it's silly and unnecessary, but she's putting a lot of work into this. I guess it feels less like lying if we're actually putting effort into it." She takes a deep breath. "But, if you're not comfortable with it, that's that, end of discussion. Consent is important on both sides. I'll keep it in mind for the future."

"I'm not saying no," I say, bending my head to look her more directly in the face. At first, she looks away more, and then what I've said registers in her head.

She pivots to face me. "What?"

"Summer, I need you to understand two very important things. If what you're saying is right, and I have more relationship experience than you, the last thing I want to do is to rush you into something before you're ready, even if it's only practice. It's not fair to you, and it won't be fun.

"The second thing is we both know I'm more physically affectionate than you. It's not a judgement, it's just fact. What I find normal with someone else might not be our normal, and that's fine. It's our relationship." Fake relationship.

Summer bites her bottom lip once more—which is something that I need her to stop doing, particularly while we're talking about physical affection—but it's clear that she's giving it serious thought.

"I understand," she finally says. "I'll tell you what—during all of this, I will be extra careful to let you know how I'm feeling. We do have different backgrounds, but you're also my friend. I trust you to look after me, and I know you well enough to know if I am good about communication, you will respond accordingly. We're both adults. We both know our limits. All I want to know is how to do it convincingly. For therapy."

Cool relief washes over me, and I can't help the smile spreading across my face. "All right, then. For therapy."

The smile that's been absent since we left the office starts to grow across Summer's face. "Awesome. So, we have a couple of dates for assignments. I bet we could do a bit of crossover, right?"

"Sure," I say. "Saturday night, my place?"

Her eyes shoot up but there's only surprise there, not incredulity. "Really?"

"Really," I say, reaching out and unclipping Jennie's key from the outside of Summer's purse. "I'm not practicing in public."

For a split second, Summer's expression is completely, hilariously shocked, and then she mock-scowls at me. "Is flirting part of the practice?"

I nod solemnly. "Everyone outside of our relationship must be as uncomfortable as possible."

Summer snorts as I unlock her car and open the door. "And I bet you're not opposed to some impromptu kissing as well?" She's challenging me, and I smile, leaning on top of her car door, hoping she can't hear the sudden thudding of my heart.

"Volunteering?"

Summer shrugs nonchalantly with one shoulder. "Anything for my therapist." She slides elegantly into the vehicle.

She hasn't said no. Laughing to cover my sudden breathlessness, I tell her to text me when she gets to work, and promise I'll do the same. I shut the door and watch as she drives away.

My phone pings as I slide into my car. I look at the notification.

Amanda Rowland.

I clear it without looking at the text and start my car.

SUMMER

I'm about halfway to work when my mom calls. Pushing the cassette receiver into the dashboard, I listen as Jennie pretends that she's compatible with twenty-first century technology. Once the speakers pick up the dulcet tone of Lacy saying,

"Summer, your mother is calling" over and over again, I pick it up.

"Hi, Mom," I say. "Sorry I didn't pick up right away—I'm driving."

"Oh!" she says, like she's kind of surprised that I know how. No worries, Mom. I've only been doing it for half my life. "I'm sorry, do you need to talk later?"

And have it hanging over my head all day? No, thank you. "No, it's fine. I have you on speaker phone."

"... Can Jennie do that, sweetie?"

I sigh. "Yes, Mom. They've got all sorts of compatibility stuff nowadays. But never mind that, how are you? How's Dad?"

"Hi, Sunshine!" Dad calls from the background.

"Hi, Dad! Are you two on speakerphone?"

"Yes, sweetie." Mom's voice is as businesslike as it ever gets. "I just wanted to remind you your father and I are going to California this weekend to visit Scottie and Rhett, in case you tried to drop by."

I probably would have, seeing how it was the Sunday we usually had our family dinners. Thankfully, I did actually read the family texts and already knew about the plans. "Thanks for the reminder."

"Of course. You know ..." she says, "with all the therapy you've been doing, I was wondering if you could bring ... oh what's his name again? Your boyfriend, I mean?"

"Chase?" I say blankly and then realize my error almost immediately. *Backpedal, Summer!* "I mean, what?"

"Chase?" Mom says, sounding like I've given her the Crown Jewels. In her mind, I probably have. "You know, I'd just love to meet him and have you tell me how therapy is going."

"It's going fine," I say, suddenly wanting to hang up as

quickly as possible. "You know, Mom, I don't know how he would feel about meeting everyone. It's a lot and—"

"Oh, come on, sweetie. You keep putting me off like this and I'll have to assume the man doesn't exist."

She just has to put it like that.

Freaking Karma.

"... I'll have to ask."

"Please do, sweetie," Mom sounds unbelievably smug. I've lost this round, and we both know it. "I know your father and I would love to meet him."

I almost nod, then I realize she can't see me. "I'll do my best to get him there."

"Love you, sweetheart!"

"Love you, Mom," I say dully. "Love you, Dad. Have fun in California."

"Bye, Sunshine," Dad says.

Mom hangs up, leaving me with the consequences of my own actions.

Great googly moogly.

Yet another consequence rears its ugly head as I push the gear shift into park at my work. A text from Louis. This is just getting better and better.

I consider ignoring it. The problem with Louis is there could be something important in the middle of whatever he's complaining about next. On Saturday, when I was working with Chase, he'd sent a message that pretty much said I should be working overtime or I wasn't dedicated enough to be a team lead, but he also noted that we had an early-morning team lead meeting on Monday I'd forgotten about. I can't avoid his texts, but interacting with him is getting hard. I open the text.

Louis Granger: You going to get back on time today? By the way, how's the squeeze? Still fictional?

I resist the urge to throw my phone across the car. Jennie can probably take it, but my screen wouldn't hold up so well. Instead, I pull up the picture where Chase and I are cuddling on the couch, and with no small amount of glee, send the picture.

Me: About as fictional as you are. Walking into the building now.

Five minutes early, as a matter of fact. And while I get to see the sour, I-had-a-big-piece-of-humble pie expression on Louis's face as I walk by his desk, I can't shake the feeling that things have started to go too far.

Chapter 14
The Lesson

SUMMER

When I first started this whole fiasco, I honestly thought I had only lied to my family. It turns out, without a doubt, I am a big ol' liar.

Not necessarily on purpose, mind you, but when St. Peter at the Pearly Gates reads the tally on my lies of "omission" I will be first on the elevator south, as it were.

The reason? Despite reassurances to the contrary, I *have* lied to Chase. And it's been on purpose.

Call it a pride thing—yet another reason for the swift trip to a warm, unpleasant destination—but I guess I didn't want to admit that I haven't dated anyone. And, since I'm not one to make out with random people, it means I haven't kissed anyone either.

It's not because I don't want to date, or I had some secret past trauma that made me feel like I'm unworthy of love, I was just ... busy. I was doing extracurricular stuff all through high school, I went to school to actually study, and when I came back to Utah after college to work, life took over immediately.

It's not that I don't know how to talk to people or anything. But anything beyond that, anything closer, never happened.

Not that I necessarily feel ashamed about all of this. It's just I feel like I've given Chase the impression that I have had boyfriends, or at the very least I've experienced some sort of relationship. Lying to him makes me feel worse than if I'd endured the initial embarrassment of telling him that I've been single since the day I was born.

But that's not the only thing I'm worried about. What if I don't ... like it? Human contact, I mean. Like it's fun and fine to be handed in and out of cars and generally being treated like a princess, but what if that's all I'm comfortable with? What if I actually don't like being hugged? I mean, it's never been the case, and there's been more than once that I've practically jumped on Lacy at home because I've wanted a hug, but WHAT IF.

Maybe I can fake it.

Great googly moogly. I hope I can fake it. For therapy.

It's five thirty. It's almost time to head to Chase's for dinner. I've dressed, done my makeup, chosen a different dress, redone my makeup, put my hair up, taken my hair down, and revolved through every single one of my eighteen winter coats—I like having options, even in the winter—and I'm almost out of energy.

I hear the door open. It must be Lacy. I sit up.

Lacy. Lacy knows. Lacy will know what to do.

I open the door to my room and step out into the hallway. Lacy is there, and so is Renner, with his black hair and his super blue eyes. I don't need him, I need Lacy.

"Lacy," I hiss from where I stand.

She looked up sharply, like she's not expecting me.

Right. The hall light isn't on. Neither is my room light. The sun's already gone down. I'm shrouded in darkness. I am Summer the Single Hallway Gremlin.

Man, I hope this isn't an omen.

"Summer?" Lacy says hesitantly. "Everything okay?"

No. The answer is no. Emphatically no, actually.

"Uh, Renner? One sec," Lacy says, hustling across the room faster than I think is possible.

Did I say that out loud?

It doesn't matter. My answer is the same.

Lacy flicks on the hall light. I blink hard at the sudden brightness, and Lacy grabs my arm and pulls me back into my room. She turns on the overhead light and studies me from head to foot.

"On a scale of one to ten, where are you right now?" She's still looking at me uncomfortably close. "I haven't seen you lurking in the dark since your mom signed you up for that dating app. Now. Where are you at?"

"About a four—five. A five," I grumble, still blinking against the sudden light.

Lacy raises her eyebrows.

"A seven," I admit. "But in my defense, I didn't turn the lights off, I just didn't turn them on. It was ... nice."

Lacy crosses her arms and tilts her head at me expectantly. She wants me to keep talking. Like I can help it. I don't even pause for breath. The whole inconvenient truth spills out all over the place until I'm a little out of breath.

"What do I do?" I ask, a little desperately.

Lacy doesn't even bat an eye.

"Do you like Chase?"

My brain, which has been spinning for the last four hours, grinds to a sudden halt. How did she find out? I just barely found out, a week or two ago, and have mercilessly been trying to suppress it ever since. I can't admit to anything, it would only make everything more complicated.

And lie again? Good freaking grief.

"I—well—I mean, I like him in a perfectly normal way for the relationship we have." Plausible deniability. Nice.

Lacy rolls her eyes. "I mean, you enjoy being around him, yes? In general?"

I have misread the situation.

"Yes," I say meekly.

"And you trust him?"

"Yes," I say, even more meekly. But sincerely. Lacy knows me enough to know that.

Lacy studies me, then looks down at the sheer amount of clothes I have pulled from my closet and strewn all over the floor and an expression of compassion rolls over her face. She takes me by the elbow and pulls me over to sit on the bed. "Summer, tell me this, are you nervous about this because you don't want to do it, or are you nervous because you're actually excited, and you don't know how to express it?"

My mouth drops open. "I—I—"

"You don't have to answer." Lacy's voice is gentle. "But think about it. As for what you said about Chase not knowing that you've ever been in a relationship, why not tell him?"

"Because he thinks I have been? And he already knows I've lied to my mother for years. If he's found out I lied about this, then he's never going to trust me ever again." I flop back on the bed. "How often do you have to lie before it becomes a pathological problem?"

Lacy thinks about this. "Did you tell him, or did he assume?"

I think about it. "He assumed, I think. But I may have accidentally agreed to something in conjunction to that."

Lacy rolls her eyes again. "Summer, you're overthinking it.

So, what if he's assumed something else? You're thirty-three, it's a reasonable assumption. But if you trust him, maybe try to trust him with an explanation? The fact you want to tell him, and the fact I, y'know, actually *know* you reassures me you are not a pathological liar."

I squint up at her. "How do you know I know I'm not lying to you?"

She pats the back of my hand. "You're not that great at lying. You always end up spilling your guts."

I shoot to a sitting position. "I do not."

"Your mother doesn't count, Summer. That's a survival tactic."

I frown. I will neither confirm nor deny whether she has a point. "Whatever."

Lacy sighs a little and then stands. "I don't think your problem is with the practice. You would have never suggested it if you didn't want to do it. I think your problem is you feel like you lied to Chase."

Was she a therapist in another life? Probably. With my karma, almost definitely.

And she was right. Probably.

"So, what was the advice your therapist gave you? Way back at the beginning of things?

"Communicate?" Give him something to work with.

Lacy nods. "Communicate. I think you'll be pleasantly surprised by how he takes it."

I mull it over, not completely convinced, but reassured she doesn't tell me to ghost him or something. That's not what I want to do. I only ... need to communicate.

Sigh.

Lacy glances out into the hallway, and I realize as much fun as it probably is talking to me, she probably wants to get back to her boyfriend. Not that she wouldn't help me if I asked, but I'm supposed to be leaving soon anyway.

"Having a night in?" I ask.

"Since you're not going to be here, yes," Lacy says with a smirk as she gets to the door. "And yes, we will probably be making out, so don't come back early."

I check my watch, grimace, and stand. Definitely time for me to go.

... That's not necessarily related to what Lacy has said. "Wish me luck."

Lacy leans back into the room and winks at me. "If it goes poorly, just jump straight to kissing."

I blush to the roots of my hair. "Lacy!"

She shrugs, unbothered. "Worked for me. Have a nice evening, Summer!"

Fifteen minutes later, exactly one minute and thirty-seven seconds before six pm, I exit my Crown Victoria after the shortest drive of my entire life. I've never prayed that Jennie would break down before, but Jennie has never run smoother than the drive over here.

I thought I could at least count on rush-hour traffic, but I forgot it was Saturday.

Now, standing on the street, looking up at his house, I am coming to the realization that Chase has money. His company is a very successful one, but I didn't know he was on the level of buy-your-own-English-townhouse-lookalike money. I didn't even know that these existed in Utah Valley.

Low-key, I want one.

As much as I feel like I'm about to face a firing squad, I am feeling better after talking with Lacy. I mean, what's the worst thing that could happen? Chase calling the whole thing off because I'm some sort of weird psycho who couldn't get into a relationship because she was too busy and totally hasn't kissed anyone and then lied about it?

Yeah.

Well, I mean the Yellowstone volcano could erupt, but maybe it would be a blessing.

Snap out of it. The worst he could do is call it off. What's more likely to happen is we'll talk about it ... and maybe call it off.

But we are going to talk about it. But if there was one thing I am not going to do, it's bring it up right out of the gate. I am a normal human and can pick my time. I mean, it isn't pressing down on me so heavily I can't wait and will blurt it out the minute my foot passes over the threshold.

And I'm right.

I wait for both feet to pass the threshold.

"Um, Chase?" I try not to gawk up at his twenty-foot-high entry ceiling as he takes my coat.

"Yeah?" he says, hanging the coat up on the peg, and pulling out a pair of slippers for me. I slide my feet out of my boots and into the cozy, fuzzy lined slippers.

"I have something to confess."

"Oh?" he says, motioning me further into the house. His hand presses against my lower back to guide me forward, but for once I resist the motion.

"Maybe it would be better here." My voice lowers unconsciously, and he turns back.

His eyebrows go up, and then he furrows his forehead. "Everything okay?"

"Um ... sort of. But I think I might have ... well, it was an accident, but I think ... I ... lied to you." My voice kind of drops off at the end, and I'm staring down at the cleanest wood floors I've ever seen in my life outside of Tokyo. Does this man dust mop constantly?

I don't think I deserve him. I don't think I've even seen a dust mop.

The Dust Mop Owner looks at me in confusion. "You've what?"

There's a surprising lack of incredulity in his voice. It occurs to me he might not have heard me. I now have to repeat my confession. There's some sort of idiom for that. Haste makes waste is the one that comes to mind, but for some reason, I don't think that's it.

Or it could be.

Better to jump in with both feet. I close my eyes and wrestle the words out, trying to pretend I'm not blushing from the crown of my head to my pinkie toes. I'm pretty sure even my hair is getting redder. "I mean ... I think you might be under the wrong impression that I've ... been in a relationship before."

Chase looks at me, his expression softening into something resembling ... relief? "You haven't?"

I shake my head. "No."

He blinks a couple of times at the mortification in my voice. "Um, okay?"

It begins to dawn on me that he doesn't seem as worried about this as I am.

"I ... you've said, or rather implied a couple times you thought I have been, and considering we're practicing things, if I don't know how to do something, or if I look uncomfortable, I'm really not, I'm just inexperienced, and so you can ignore me and it'll be—"

"Summer?" Chase's voice is soft, and he's craning his head

a little to look down at me. He's got a funny little smile on his face that makes me want to smile back, but I don't know if I'm emotionally ready yet.

"Yeah?"

"Thank you for telling me."

"You're welcome." It feels lame, but it's all I've got.

He seems to study me for a long moment, probably wondering if my skin will ever return to its original color—the answer is probably, but I won't take bets—and then says, "Let's go into the kitchen to talk."

Honestly, I expected more of a reaction, but I'm not going to complain if this is it. Chase taking my single-tude in stride.

If I think we're done talking about this, however, I am sadly mistaken. I shuffle into the kitchen, trying not to gawk at the beautiful white and grey kitchen. He's already started to prepare the food and picks up a black waist apron as he walks past the island.

"You had me worried," Chase says, walking over to the sink where a pile of vegetables is waiting.

"Oh?" I swallow.

"Yeah, I thought you were going to tell me you're actually dating someone else." He glances back over his shoulder. After Chase finishes rinsing the vegetables, he brings them over to the island where I'm sitting. "This is more manageable. I have a couple questions though."

"Oh?" I say, my voice dropping with dread.

Chase looks like he's trying to hide a smile. He's failing, but weirdly it makes me feel better. If he's smiling, I'm not about to get the third degree, right?

Right?

Then the smile drops off his face. "First and foremost, in the spirit of making sure we're on the same page, are you worried about me crossing some sort of line?" His voice is frank and surprisingly refreshing.

"Oh! Absolutely not," I exclaim, shaking my head. "If I was worried, I wouldn't have come. Or suggested it for that matter."

Chase nods, like it makes sense. "Okay. Second question: Have you felt uncomfortable at any point since we met with the amount of touching that we do? Like, linking arms, me touching your back to guide you somewhere, that kind of thing?"

I shake my head. That wasn't the same thing, was it? "No, that's been fine." Besides, hadn't I been the instigator of some of that?

Huh. Maybe I was better at it than I thought.

Chase nods once, with finality. "Okay. We'll start from there and feel it out. Please keep giving me feedback, though. If for some reason it doesn't feel right or if you don't like something, let me know asap. I'm not interested in doing anything we won't both enjoy."

I mirror his motion, dropping my chin into a nod once. "Okay."

"Good."

"Awesome."

"Fantastic," Chase responds, his smile returning. "Well, I was hoping for some help in cooking dinner tonight. Interested?"

And in an instant, the tension in my chest seems to fizzle out. He wants to make sure I'm comfortable. He cares about me.

Or he doesn't want to be accidentally committing assault, the unimpressed part of my brain chips in. *But yes, it assures his green flag status.*

"Sure am!" I say, pushing away my thoughts. "I'll have you

know I am accomplished at more than just ordering things off a menu."

"Oh really?" Chase says with a bright smile. He hands me a waist apron like his, only mine is white. "Awesome. You can start by chopping those veggies."

We fall into an easy routine after that. He's an accomplished cook, but I'm far from inexperienced myself, and we find ourselves maneuvering around each other like we've had years of practice. As we make the hearty stew, every so often Chase will lean over my shoulder to take a look at my progress. It's all he does. He doesn't put a hand on my waist or even stand close enough to touch. He's simply close.

And frankly, I'd like him to break the barrier already. I'm ready for it now. I'm not going to freak out.

But I get the feeling he's waiting for something. What it is, I have no idea, but that's definitely the vibe.

We make it through making the stew, leaving it to simmer on the stove, before moving on to dessert. It's then that I get my bright idea. If we're going to practice, we need to actually practice, and that means actual, honest-to-goodness contact.

So, I start. Touching his arm or his back as I maneuver around him where he stands at the stove, creating the filling for the little tarts we're making. I clear the counter of all the dinner prep dishes, and make sure I rinse the dishes as I put them in the sink. Then, I begin to make the pastry, something I've done a million times before, but which always takes a little care.

The smell of sugar and berries fills the air as I combine the ingredients and begin to roll the dough out. Behind me, Chase finishes the filling and puts it into the refrigerator to cool. As he passes, I feel the gentle pressure of his hand on my shoulder, keeping me where I am.

Why do I feel like I've won?

Victory is not short lived. He comes back to me, looking

over my shoulder, putting his hands on either side of me as he looks down at my work.

"Flaky crust?" he asks. He's not pressed up against me by any scope of the imagination, but I can still feel the rumble of his deep voice against my back.

"Just like my momma taught me," I say with a smile. "Problem?"

"None whatsoever. It can be a bit temperamental."

I shrug and turn my head so it's inclined toward him. "Worst case scenario, we can eat the filling plain?"

Chase pushes off the counter to stand up straight. "I like the way you think, Sunny."

I turn around and smile at him. "Check the stew, would you? I'm getting hungry."

Chase grins and mock salutes. "Your wish is my command. While you finish the crust, I'll set the table."

"Sounds good to me," I respond. "Oh, hey, did we have any plans for after dinner? I got banished from my house. Lacy and Renner are having a night in. It's not Netflix and chill, but it's ... probably not appropriate for kids under the age of thirteen." I say, and then add under my breath, "Or thirty-three."

Chase snorts. "Point taken." He nods toward the front of the house. The lights are off, but I can see the silhouette of a staircase and an entertainment center. "I've got a lot of movies. How about we pick one after dinner?"

"Sounds good." In short order, the dough is rolled out and cut, the tarts are assembled, the table is set, and we sit down to eat.

The stew is to die for, and the perfect thing for a midwinter night like tonight. He even has some crusty bread to dip in it, and before I know it—with only a brief interlude where the timer for dessert dings and Chase presses me gently back into my seat with a hand on my shoulder so he can take care of it—almost the entire pot is gone.

"Sir," I say, leaning back in my chair with a second trimester food baby, "it is a very good thing we are not in a real relationship, otherwise I would quite possibly be the size of Violet Beauregard from *Willy Wonka and the Chocolate Factory*, pre-deflation."

Chase laughs and leans back with a contented sigh and a smile. "One almost doesn't need tarts, do they? More for me, I guess."

I raise my eyebrows. "I didn't say that."

He raises one eyebrow challengingly. I'm jealous. My eyebrows don't have the power to move independently. I fold my arms and lift my chin. "Dessert is a different stomach, my friend. If I was limited by what I could eat at dinner, there would be a whole lot of desserts cruelly left untasted."

"Dessert junkie?"

"Connoisseur sounds kinder."

"Fair," Chase says. And so, we eat dessert.

The tarts—with cherries, blueberries and blackberries—are delicious, especially with an added dollop of whipped cream, and it isn't long before Chase turns on the lights to his living room. Almost the entire right side of the room is covered with ten-foot-high shelves. Books, movies, even board games are neatly organized on each of the shelves. It is pretty much eye candy, and I can't help my slow stroll as I feast my eyes on the beautifully-curated collection.

He reads more science fiction and non-fiction than I do, I notice right off the bat, but our movie tastes seem to be fairly well aligned.

"I'm going to have to come back when I can really look through all of these," I say in awe, looking up at the higher shelves out of reach. The only thing I don't see is a rolling ladder, which seems like an oversight. "You have a beautiful collection."

"Thank you," Chase says, stepping up beside me so our shoulders are touching. "I used to have a rolling ladder, but it's getting repaired right now."

I blink. "Used to?"

Chase shrugs. "Avery was playing Belle on it around Christmas time. We're still not sure how it happened, but it swung off the railing on the top and sent her head over heels into the kitchen.

I wince. "Was she okay?"

"Miraculously, nary a scratch, aside from a bruise on her knee where she hit the floor," Chase says, shaking his head. "Though, I attribute her survival to the snowman onesie she was wearing at the time. The stuffing provided some padding." He looks around at the wooden floors to make his point.

I try to imagine Avery pulling off something like that and found that I absolutely could. "Lucky."

"No kidding," Chase agrees, walking to the end of the shelves. "Anyway, the carpenter is fixing the ladder and reinforcing it so it won't come off the railing next time. He's thinking he'll be done by the end of March. In the meantime, I get to manage this." He pulls out a three-step stepladder and shakes it open. "It's not particularly elegant, but it gets the job done. Good thing you're tall, otherwise I don't think this would work."

I laugh. "I could always sit on your shoulders."

Chase thinks about that for longer than I'm comfortable with.

"Um, that was a joke," I say.

"How come?"

"Uh, because no one has picked me up since I topped five foot six?"

Chase looks at me quizzically. "Don't you have an older brother?"

"He's my height. Also, he chooses life."

"Ahhh," Chase says with understanding. "You don't want to be picked up."

"No, thank you," I say. "The last thing I want to do is to throw some poor gentleman's back out. It's a mercy call."

Chase thinks about this, then looks up at the bookshelf, and then back to me. "You're, what, five-foot-ten?"

"Yeah, give or take a quarter of an inch," I say suspiciously. "Why?"

He looks away from the shelves and saunters off. "No reason. Pick a movie."

I do.

He's surprised.

"You know that's a horror movie, right?" he asks a couple minutes later when I show him the DVD case.

I nod. "When Lacy and I were both single, we'd have Horror Movie Fridays. Basically, it was a contest to see whether or not we could scare the other. We prefer suspense over gore, but this one looks pretty good."

He looks it over. "Oh, *Wait Until Dark* is a good one for suspense. Have you seen it before?"

"No," I say. "Have you?"

"Once or twice," Chase confirms. "If you like suspense, you're going to love this one."

Perfect.

We settle down on the couch. Chase has apparently caught onto the fact that I like cozy things and has laid a sherpa blanket over my side of the couch.

I settle down into the couch cushions. Chase goes to put the movie into the DVD player, and I examine the case. It's made in 1967. How scary can this actually be?

I voice the question out loud and Chase looks back at me with a faintly incredulous look on his face. On one hand, it's kind of encouraging, meaning I'm probably in for a good show. On the other hand ... Well, if it scared Chase, it means one of two things: he's either a scaredy cat, or I'm about to get schooled.

He gets the DVD in the player and makes his way back to the couch. He takes one look at me, curled up against the armrest, and lifts his eyebrows. "Were we going to practice?" he asks. There's a definite smile on his face, so I know he's teasing, but the man has a point.

"Sorry," I say with a smile. "Going into Movies With Lacy Mode."

Chase gives me a full smile, and my heart stutters. "Well, I'm not Lacy."

No, he isn't. And this was either going to be a top-tier movie experience, or I was about to make an utter fool of myself.

And considering I was me, and this was a horror movie ... both were a strong possibility. Chase sits down on the couch, right by the imaginary center line. The couch itself is very nice. It rivals the couch at therapy in terms of softness, though this one does have the edge, considering I don't have to jump three times in order to get out of it.

Then Chase lifts up his arm. "C'mere."

I wouldn't classify myself as particularly obedient, but considering our agreement, and it's Chase that's asking, it's not a hard thing to scoot closer to him. He's warm and solid and about four steps up from the arm rest.

Actually, probably five, but I haven't done much research into the matter, and unlike mathematical theorems, I don't mind the prospect.

But it would probably help if I could relax.

I'm trying, but there's something holding my neck muscles hostage and making my breathing all funky and borderline asthmatic. It's the weirdest thing. I definitely enjoy the closeness—I'm honest enough and sure enough to acknowledge that —but ... what?

"Summer?" Chase asks, his voice quiet. He hasn't started the movie. Maybe if he does, I'll be able to adjust without him noticing. "You okay?"

Well, snap.

"Yeah, I'm fine," I say, pretending my voice hasn't gone up an octave, still trying to convince my shoulder muscles that they aren't made of concrete, and that it's really not necessary to touch my ears on both sides. This is ridiculous. I genuinely like this, what's the problem?

Chase doesn't speak for a minute, but doesn't look down at me either. He's probably giving me a chance to keep my composure, and it's appreciated. Finally, he speaks. It's about what I expect.

"I don't want to ... I don't know," he starts again. "I don't want to say I don't believe you, but you don't look like you feel very comfortable. Do you want me to move away?"

"No," I say quickly.

He does look down now, and concern is clear on his face. I shake my head. "Honestly, I don't mind being here."

"Would you mind talking me through it?"

"Uh, if I can?" I say, looking around. The sight of the dark brown wood and the texture of the fuzzy rug under my feet helps clear my head a little. "I think ... I think it's new."

"New?"

"Yeah. Remember, I haven't done this before?"

Chase nods, and briefly I wonder if he's forgotten. It's more likely to acknowledge what I said, but it makes me feel a little better that I've done well enough today he's forgotten I'm a total newbie.

But it's not only the newness of it. Because I've cuddled with Lacy—especially during scary movies and her various breakups—and it didn't feel like this. Granted, Lacy is also not a good-looking man—or rather, a man, since she is good-looking —nor has she held me quite like how Chase is practically cradling me now.

But it's not that I don't like it.

What is this?

Am I worried *he* isn't going to like it? That seems closer, but not quite ... Oh.

"I think," I say, my throat a little dry, and my gaze anywhere but him. I pinch my eyes shut. "I think it's because I like it. A lot. And it's not real."

Chase's expression flickers and he frowns. "Could you walk me through that a little more?"

I take a deep breath. "So, I'm not sure if I should like it?"

He thinks about it seriously. It's actually kind of nice. He's listening carefully to what I'm saying and thinking about his response.

And his last girlfriend called him toxic? I'm starting to form an opinion of Amanda, and it's not a good one. Blind, shallow, and a criminal class of moron come to mind.

"Let me ask you this," Chase finally says, turning toward me. He hasn't moved his arm, and it puts us nearly nose to nose. My breath is squeezing again, but it's different. For one, it is not nearly as unpleasant as before. For another, I can actually breathe fine, but my breath keeps hitching unless I focus on lengthening my breaths. "You enjoy sitting close to Lacy during movies, right?"

"Uh-huh," I say. We've been likened to a pile of kittens by Renner before.

"So," he says softly. "We're friends, too, right?"

"Uh-huh," I repeat breathlessly, trying to sound convincing. I'd give it a fifty-fifty chance.

"I know what we're in for," he says with a slight smile. Then he leans forward until our foreheads are nearly touching. "I'm not going to take it wrong. You don't need it, but you have my permission to enjoy yourself."

My breathing's just about shot, and my heart rate could rival a hummingbird's but somehow my shoulders have relaxed. I force my head to nod and look down from where I am clearly staring at his lips. It's not on purpose—they're right there in my eyeline. *Friends, friends, friends, friends, friends, friends.* "Sorry," I mumble, as much for my insecurity as for the lip-ogling.

Chase turns to face forward, apparently not having noticed the lip thing, scooting a little closer to me in the same motion, and it's like he releases me from a spell. I lean into his side. I enjoy it. He gave me permission. "You don't have to be," he says with a smile. "Thank you for looking out for me." He then looks at me wonderingly. "Now close your eyes."

I look up at him, pulling in my chin. I'm pretty sure it gives me the appearance of an approximately three-hundred-year-old turtle, but it's a chance I'm willing to take. Because we're friends, right? I'd be comfortable having Lacy see me as a turtle. "Why?"

"Because the DVD menu has spoilers, and I'm not spoiling your first watch of this. Eyes. Close 'em."

I comply, facing forward as he turns the TV on and the plunky, discordant music begins. There's a moment where Chase presumably flicks through the menu and presses play.

"Open your eyes," he says, and I do, and the movie begins. It sucks me in immediately.

Turns out, Chase is a whole lot more comforting than Lacy is during horror movies. Lacy is maybe five foot five inches on a good day. Something about Chase's six-foot-two frame lends me absolute security as poor Susy tries to navigate everything that's happening to her. I can feel the suspense through every part of me and even though I'm wondering in the back of my mind if I should really practice so wholeheartedly, I move closer and closer to the solid wall of man to my left. Soon, my blanket is up around my chin, my knees are to my chest, and if I could physically be any closer to Chase, I would have moved that bit closer.

Even with the suspense, though, I can't ignore the fact that Chase smells better than any man who has ever worn a scent, and the subtle strength I can feel in the arm around my shoulders grounds me. I know I'm safe, even with all the terror on screen.

None of that, however, prepares me for the jump scene. In the infrequent flashes of light, seeing the villain so suddenly elicits a very real scream out of me, and I make a leap of my own, straight into Chase's arms.

I say 'leap.' I will be honest: I throw the blanket over my head and hedgehog-roll forward into his lap.

It doesn't really work. I'm way too tall for it, but it doesn't stop him from catching me and pulling me into his arms—and lap—with less effort than I expected it to. As I pull the blanket from my face, desperately needing to see what happens next, I wind my arms around Chase's shoulders, pressing my head against his as I watch with one eye open.

I am ridiculously glad the hall light is still on behind us, and as the movie ends, I sit there, arms wrapped tightly around him. He's holding me in place, one of his hands at my waist and the other gently rubbing my shoulder.

"You gonna be okay there, Sunny?" he whispers in my ear.

"I'm thinking about it," I say, my face still buried in his

shoulder. "You were right. It's scary." I pull my head back. "Why did we watch this at night?"

He's trying to hide a smile, and it's not working very well. "This was your idea."

"I know, I know," I say, burrowing my face in his shoulder. "I'm just going through all the requisite regret that needs to follow watching a horror film."

"You know," Chase says, his voice rumbling through me in a way that is not at all unpleasant, "I have a feeling it's very fun to be around you in October. Do you ever go to haunted houses?"

I pull back and give him a disdainful look. "Of course."

"Do you like them?"

"... I like going to them with people," I offer. "What about you?"

He smiles up at me. "I like going to them with people," he says, repeating my own words, inflection included. We sit there for a long moment, not saying anything. I study his face. He's got smile lines by his eyes, which are a gorgeous mixture of green and brown. I don't know whether I haven't looked closely enough, or whether I didn't simply appreciate them enough before.

He has some scruff. I could feel the scrape of it on my cheek when I'd buried my head in his shoulder. Now, I wonder what it would feel like on my fingertips, but I'm not quite brave enough to reach up and find out.

Chase is holding my gaze with a soft expression, as though he's trying to read my thoughts. I don't know if I want him to. They're not exactly what a friend would think.

"Well," he says finally. "We got a little further into practice than I anticipated we would."

I look around. I'm still in his lap, arms around his neck, pressing a little closer than absolutely necessary. The adrenaline from the movie has mostly worn off, but my heart is still pounding a little heavier than normal.

Me of four hours ago would be horrified. Or in awe, I'm not sure which. And it's that thought that makes me snort and lean my head down onto his shoulder again.

"Great googly moogly," I laugh, shaking my head. "You're going to think I'm a hussy."

"I like to think of it as naturally inclined to physical contact," Chase says with a laugh.

I can't help the giggles, as they're well and truly established now, and I lean back. Chase lets me go, and I flop back on his comfy couch. I put an arm over my eyes and laugh until I can't anymore, the adrenaline from the movie, and whatever I'm feeling here with Chase proving a heady combination. He sits there with my legs across his lap, laughing with me until the giggles abate.

When they finally die down, he looks down at me and says, "So, I can just let you get to Jennie on your own then?"

I pick up my head and glare at him. "You knew exactly what was in that movie when you showed it to me. I demand an escort to my car. If I'm feeling insecure, I might demand that you follow me home, too."

Chase fights a smile and nods seriously. "If that's what you need, Summer, I'd be happy to."

I sit up. "What, really?"

"Don't look so surprised. I'm supposed to be your boyfriend."

I squint at him. "Yeah, but Lacy knows that you're not really my boyfriend."

Chase squints back. "Yeah, but the fear that I inadvertently caused is real."

I assume a nonchalant expression. "It wasn't that bad."

"The somersault into my lap says something different."

It was a hedgehog roll, but I didn't have the dignity to correct him. "It ... might have been intense in the moment." I cast my eyes across the room. "And the moments since."

Chase smiles and reaches out, taking my hand. "I'll take you out to your car, Sunny. And if you need me to follow you home, I will."

He says it so sincerely that it's really hard not to be touched. I shouldn't be, but I still am, and I smile at him. "That's okay. On the 'follow me home' part. I'm not leaving this house without you." Then I realize how that sounds. "You know what I mean."

"I do," Chase says, "but I do expect you to text me when you get home."

"I always text you when I get home." I squeeze his hand to punctuate my point.

He squeezes back, and the warmth pushes back against the tension. "Good. Then keep it up."

I mock salute with my free hand. "Yes, sir."

It takes us another minute to stand up and make it to the entryway, but we eventually get there. It's about eleven o'clock now, and while I've been here, snow has started to fall, leaving Jennie under her very own fluffy blanket. Chase insists on cleaning Jennie off before I can leave the house, so I put on my coat, scarf and boots while I wait. The quiet of the house slightly creeps me out—nothing can be truly creepy while I can still smell the berry tart filling—and I open my phone.

To six messages from Louis, each more insistent and annoyed than the last, until the last where he seems to explode.

Louis Granger: Where is the YellowPlay file?

Louis Granger: Summer, where is the YellowPlay file?

Louis Granger: Where is it? This is important!

Louis Granger: SUMMER ANSWER ME
WHERE IS THE FILE.

Louis Granger: Are you seriously ignoring
me? The Assistant Manager will hear about
this first thing Monday morning. I knew you
were too irresponsible to be a team lead.
What was she thinking?

Louis Granger: Fine, take the day off, you
lazy—

I stare at the text message, suddenly feeling lightheaded and unsure. For all he'd been doing, Louis had never called me names before. He'd never sworn at me.

And now he'd done both.

This had gone too far.

Chase opens the door right then and sees me looking down at my phone. He stills when he sees my expression.

"Summer? You okay?"

I look up at him. For the briefest moments, I think about handing the phone to Chase and showing him what Louis has written. And then, in the next second, I'm reminded Chase isn't actually my boyfriend. "Uh, yeah." I slip the phone into my pocket. "Sorry. Got a message from Louis. He's being needy again."

Chase nods, most of the unease dropping from his face. A small smile climbs his cheeks. "Maybe you should use some of your therapy-trained assertiveness and tell him to get off your back."

Because that would make things better?

I override the grimace with a smile. I'm too tired to think about this anyway. "I probably should, but I am tired."

Chase opens his arms. Without so much as a second thought, I step close, sliding my arms around his waist. It's like his arm around my shoulders times a thousand. Chase hugs with his whole heart, like he's offering a Chase-sized shelter from the world, trying to block out all the bad things. And it almost works.

"You going to be okay?" he whispers into my ear.

I'm not sure, but for the moment, he can't see my face. "Yeah, I think so." Then, because my voice was too soft to be convincing. I lean back my head so I can see him. "If I can't sleep, I'm texting you all night."

He grins, looking down at me. He probably only thinks I'm out of sorts because of the movie. Good. It's better than involving him in this. "I'll look forward to it. Now, come on. Jennie should be defrosted by now. She seemed to be heating up when I turned the car on."

I grimace comically. "Hope so."

We head outside and stop by the car. Everything is hushed and quiet, muffled by the white fluffy flakes as they drift around us. Beside us, Jennie purrs comfortably as she idles, waiting patiently to take me home.

All of a sudden, it's a little difficult to leave. Hedgehog-rolling aside, this was a genuinely fun evening. It might even be safe to say I don't want it to end.

But I already have my shoes and coat on, I'm already by my car, and Chase isn't my boyfriend.

And so, I smile up at him and step in once more. It's selfish of me, but that first hug felt so good I have to see if it was just the shock of the text or something more.

And it's something more. His strong arms around my shoulders, his delicious warmth, and the subtle beating of his heart wrap around me, and I find it a little difficult to let go.

And that's when I do let go. Because he's not really my

boyfriend, and I think I might be making things harder on myself. I step away and look up at him. "You still good to go to my parents' house for dinner next week?"

He runs his hands down my arms, gripping my hands. I'm wearing gloves, but they're still freezing in his warm palms. "I wouldn't miss it for the world. Good night, Summer." He opens the door to my car.

"Good night, Chase," I whisper, and I sit down inside.

Chapter 15
The Dinner Pt. 1

SUMMER

I've decided I'm not going to panic about the dinner with my family. It's not going to do any good, and I am exhausted. After I got home from the movie, I totally slept with my bathroom light on, texting Chase at intervals whenever I woke up. He'd always answer within a couple minutes or so. I'm still not sure whether or not he stayed awake all night as well, or if he'd turned off his Do Not Disturb function.

I'm still not sure because he won't tell me.

We've seen each other almost every evening since. Usually, I go over to his house and we make dinner, but last night—Saturday night—Lacy and Renner had gone out so I invited Chase over to our apartment and we watched a movie.

It wasn't a horror movie. I've learned my lesson. Not that the cuddling afterwards was a bad thing, but when I close my eyes, I can still see the jump scene in Technicolor.

I've learned a couple of things since then, the main one being that Chase is a cuddle-bug. No, Chase invented cuddle-bugging. It's never too much, and never unwanted, but if he can, I'm pretty sure his natural habitat is touching another person. I'm still getting used to it, but it's like I'm getting used to wearing a favorite ring or necklace.

In fact, I'm getting a little worried about how quickly I've adapted to this. I've tried to keep front and center in my mind the fact that this is all fake, and he's not my boyfriend. But when I'm sitting on the couch snuggled securely in Chase's arms, listening to him pretend he's not humming along to Cinderella as he plays with my hair, it's a little hard to remember this isn't my future, and I don't get to experience this for the rest of my life.

But I need to keep strong, otherwise I'm in a world of hurt later on. Because although I'm definitely catching feelings, I don't think Chase is.

My evidence: Chase is a very nice person.

That's not all. I have more.

Item one: The car door thing. He's explained how his father drilled into him to open the door for any woman, old person, or child. I have seen him do this.

Item two: He's naturally kind. He sent sports drinks, cans of chicken soup, and saltines via a delivery service when Lacy was still feeling sick the Monday after we took our picture. He also sent a vitamin supplement in the same package for me to make sure I didn't get sick, but the majority of the package was for Lacy.

Item three, and probably most importantly, he's physically affectionate to everyone. We've run into friends of his when we've been out, and he's constantly touching their shoulders and slapping their backs. His sister is the same story. Every time he sees her—we went out to dinner with her again on Tuesday—he always picks her up and hugs her. It's always completely appropriate, but I'm not the only one he touches.

Which means I've got to get a hold of myself. I think we're

genuinely friends, but it's not okay if I assume it's any more than that.

And all the while I need to pretend to everyone else everything is the complete opposite and we're falling madly in love.

It's exhausting. It would be exhausting if that was the only thing I was dealing with.

But then there's Louis.

After I'd gotten home the night he'd sent me those texts, I'd responded to him, letting him know in as professional terms as possible that what he'd sent to me was inappropriate. The YellowPlay project was over, and it had been completed to the satisfaction of the client. There was no reason he needed to poke through it.

This last week hasn't been pleasant. The texts have been almost relentless. He hasn't gone to Ana yet, but neither have I. I don't know how to tell her about this without it becoming a he-said-she-said scenario, but I know now I can't handle this by myself. I'll have to tell her eventually, and knowing Louis, I realize the minute I do, I will rain fire and brimstone down on my head. I don't have the strength yet.

I haven't told Chase, either. I want to, but while I'm not necessarily worried he'll do anything physical to Louis, I'm worried he might talk to Lacy, which would put the whole matter completely out of my hands. She would tear up the workplace and possibly Louis himself, and neither she nor I need the manslaughter charges. I know I need to do this myself, but it's hard to figure out how to address it the right way.

So, I'm still thinking about it. I somehow make it through the whole week and nearly the whole weekend and now I'm sitting on my bed, wishing that, rather than going to face my mother, I get to curl up in bed and watch a movie, eking out every last bit of my weekend before I have to face Louis again tomorrow.

But then I'd miss out on Chase time. Even if it's with my family, that's the last thing I want to do. Therefore, I'm dressed in a nice Sunday shirt and skirt combo, waiting for Chase to come pick me up. We figured it would make the best impression on my mom if Chase drove us. It's also currently colder than it has been all year. In the parking garage at work, or under my canopy at home, I feel like Jennie has a reasonable chance of starting, but sitting outside my mom's house on the street, I'm a little concerned.

My cell phone buzzes, and it's Chase.

Chase: At the door.

Me: Aren't you supposed to honk from the parking lot?

Chase: I feel like the spirit of my father would descend from the sky to completely school me.

Me: Isn't your dad still alive?

Chase: And thus, the severity.

I snort, grab my purse and coat off of the bed beside me, and head toward the door. I slip my coat on as I go and then throw the front door open.

"You know, we could blow this off and go make snow angels or something," I say, half serious.

Chase grins, and grabs my hand, pulling me to him. I step into his embrace, closing my eyes as I lay my head on his shoulder. My muscles relax as he rocks me slowly from side to side, filled with a comforting warmth. I am in so much trouble.

"So you've said," he says, his voice rumbling in my ear. "And said, and said, and said."

I shrug, the movement muted by his arms. "It's called fair warning."

"They really can't be that bad," he insists. "Besides, you get to see your dad, right?"

I should never have told him all this personal information. I lean back and scrunch my nose. "I feel like you're using me against me."

He draws his eyebrows together. "How's that work?"

I try to pull an answer from the air. "It just does."

"Fair enough. Well," he says, gripping me tighter, and reaching out to close the door. It's only barely out of reach, so he grabs me a little tighter and pushes me backward to grab the handle. It knocks me off balance and I grip him tighter out of self-preservation.

"Chase!" I gasp.

He chuckles as the door swings closed, the keypad beeping to tell me it's locked, and then he steps backward, pulling me back onto my feet. He reaches up, running his hand over the back of my head as he presses his forehead to mine.

"I've got you, Summer," he whispers, the warm air from his breath blossoming across my cheeks.

He's so close, and my cheeks flush as his words sink into my brain. I know they're true—I would never doubt him—but with him so close, with his lips so close, all I want to do is let my eyes close and see what he would do.

But Chase has got my back, and so he never would. He doesn't think of me that way, and it's probably a good thing. I drag my miserable little kissing monster back into the cage in my brain and straighten in his arms. Ours is not a relationship of impromptu kisses. We are not really a relationship of kissing at all.

We're really not in a relationship.

"I know you do," I say lightly against the pang of the statement. "But I am way too big for you to be throwing around like that. You'll throw your back out, and then I'll have to pay for worker's compensation or something."

Chase snorts and pulls himself to his full height, tweaking my nose. "If you think you're big enough to throw out my back, you have another thing coming, Sunny."

"Oh really?" I ask. Then I freeze. That sounds way too much like a challenge. A strange light ignites in Chase's eyes, and I back away toward the stairs. "That's not a challenge, Chase."

"Oh really?" he says, repeating my words with a smile that is far too big.

"It's not a challenge!" I shriek, and book it down the stairs.

Wearing boots without a heel today was a very good choice. It almost made me fast enough to make it to the car before he caught up. The next thing I know, two strong arms come around my waist, lifting me with seemingly no effort.

For a moment, it feels like I'm flying, and then I shriek involuntarily, and twist, sending us both off balance into the deep snow piled by the walk. I land half on and half off Chase, accidentally catching his stomach with my elbow. I can hear the air leave his lungs loudly, only drowned out by my gasp of horror.

"Chase!" I say, spinning to face him, and only managing to trip myself up in my coat, and landing fully on top of him instead.

I'm normally better than this, I promise.

I know I've hurt him, but he's laughing by the time my inner ear has regained function.

"Hey, look, Summer!" he wheezes. "We made snow angels!"

It takes me a second to realize exactly what he's talking

about—namely my half-attempt at a diversionary tactic—and I practically sob in relief.

"This wasn't what I had in mind," I mumble, pushing myself up, so I'm in a half-push-up position over him.

He's laying there, still laughing like a madman, when he suddenly quiets, a mischievous smile on his face. "I would like to submit to the court that my back is completely fine right now. My solar plexus on the other hand ..."

My head drops. I can't laugh about it. "I'm sorry, Chase."

He sits up carefully, making sure he doesn't bonk heads with me, and puts his finger under my chin, guiding me to look up at him. "I'm fine."

"I clearly heard me line driving the breath out of you."

Chase tries to hide his grin. "I think you mean pile drive, but you also don't mean pile drive. I think that was actually a classic Wrestling Diving Elbow Drop. Don't quote me. I didn't wrestle."

"Chase, I'm so sorry."

"No, no," he says, standing up, and then offering his hand to me. "This is a good thing."

"What?" I say, taking his hand and climbing to my feet. I shake out my skirt with one hand while Chase leads me back to the sidewalk.

"Yeah. I have absolute confidence you could defend yourself against pretty much anyone."

I drop his hand and glare. "Chase."

He puts up his hands. "I'm serious. And for the record, I'm sorry for picking you up without your permission."

I pause for a long time. The truth of it? Except for the dive into the snow, it wasn't terrible. In fact, it kind of felt like I was ... flying. And even the snow would have been fine if I hadn't hurt Chase. "It's okay," I finally said. "I'm sorry for Flying Elbow Diving or whatever it was on you."

He smiles and then offers his hand. "Shall we go to dinner?"

I smile in return. "For the sake of our safety, maybe we'd better."

CHASE

We're almost to the house when Summer repeats the same caution she's repeated constantly over the last week.

"I know I've said this before, but please don't feel like we have to stay very long. I know Mom and Aunt Zen can be a lot, but don't let them overwhelm you."

I look over at her, the streetlights illuminating her beautiful face in short bursts of light as we draw near to the house. "I know, Summer," I say with a soft smile.

I park the car in front of Summer's parents' house, right behind a garishly green Hummer, and I quickly exit the car and step around the vehicle to hand her out. It's freezing outside, but I don't want to go into this without giving her one last assurance. Instead of dropping my hand, I pull Summer into my arms, and whisper into her ear.

"This is good practice for work—getting to know people I haven't met and I'm unsure whether I'll get along with them." I lean back to look down at her. The dim light of the streetlamp deepens the shadows but doesn't diminish anything about Summer's sweet face.

I think it's safe to say that I have it bad. I care about this woman far, far more than anyone in a fake relationship should.

I absolutely turned my phone off 'Do Not Disturb' the night we watched *Wait Until Dark*, I absolutely want to make a good impression on her parents, and I absolutely know if this girl wanted to make this relationship a real one, I would jump in with both feet.

And it worries me.

I'm in recovery. I'm beginning to realize I wasn't the entire problem when it came to me and Amanda, but it's hard to deny things weren't exactly healthy there. Whether it started that way or was simply the result of two people not quite meant to be together, I'm not sure, but I need to figure it out before I commit for real to anyone.

But now, knowing Summer, holding Summer, meeting Summer's parents, being involved with her life, it's hard to remember that. I want her to succeed. I want her to be confident. I want her to have a good relationship with her parents. I want Louis Granger to leave her alone.

"Are you sure?" Summer whispers.

For a second I think she's asking about Louis. Then I realize she's talking about her family. Eh, the answer's the same. "Absolutely."

I look up at the house. I notice someone with gray, curly hair in the front window, hands cupped around their eyes as they look out toward us.

Time to make our entrance, then.

"We should go in," I say.

Summer stiffens. She's really nervous, and there's not much I can do about it. Well, nothing but be loving to her.

That's not the hard part.

I take her hand, giving it a gentle squeeze. "Buck up, Sunny," I say with a grin. "I'm right here. Let's do this."

Chapter 16
The Dinner Pt. 2

SUMMER

MOM OPENS THE DOOR PRACTICALLY BEFORE WE MAKE IT onto the top step. Her curly brown hair surrounds her head like a halo, identifying her as the patron saint of homemaking and getting up in my business, and her face splits into an enormous grin as she looks in between the two of us.

"Summer!" she shrieks, holding her arms out to me like I didn't see her two weeks ago. I smile uneasily and step into her arms. She gives me a brief, tight hug and then releases me to look up at the man I brought with me. "And you must be Chase. Oh, come here, pumpkin, let me look at you."

Chase looks at me with an expression just short of uncertainty as Mom grabs him by the arm and yanks him bodily into the house. She looks him up and down, like I've brought home a prize steed instead of a boyfriend.

"Oh, sweetie," she says to me, as though Chase can't hear. "I'm so glad you brought home a man taller than you. You're so tall yourself. I was worried everyone was intimidated."

I bury my head in my hands, and mumble. "Thanks,

Mom." When I look up, Chase is hiding a smile. That is, until Mom looks up at him, and he chooses to widen it.

"I grew this tall specifically for Summer," he says with a grin. "It's nice to meet you, Mrs. Weathers."

Mom's mouth drops into an 'O'. "Oh, dear, I've totally forgotten to introduce myself. How rude of me."

I don't mention how she just did a full-body assessment on the man I brought home.

"No problem," Chase holds out his hand. "Chase Merrill."

"Karma Weathers." Mom ignores his hands and pulls him in for a hug.

For a second, there's a slight look of shock on Chase's face as he bends down. Panic jolts through me. This is it. This is when he realizes it's not worth it and runs for the hills. But then, glancing at me as he half-hunches over my five-foot-four mother, he gives me a reassuring smile and gives me a subtle thumbs up behind her back.

And drops his hand immediately as Joan walks in. I stare at my older sister as she takes in the man Mom is attempting to smother. Of course, Mom would invite her.

Of course, if Joanie's here, that means—

"Well, well, well, look who's here." Aunt Zen's voice is almost a drawl, and I look toward the doorway to the den, half-expecting her to be wearing a gun belt and a ten-gallon cowboy hat. "You must be Summer's boyfriend."

I am suddenly worried. Mom is one of the nicest people on the planet. I'm pretty sure she would have tried to rehabilitate Stalin. But Zen ...

Zen is the reason why Chase is standing in my living room, being accidentally objectified by Mom. She is literally the reason why we are in therapy. She is also a type of protective that neither of my parents are. You have to earn her trust, and I have put Chase in an extremely disadvantaged position.

I swear, after all of this I'm never lying ever again.

Mom releases Chase, and Chase reaches out to shake Zen's hand. I resist the urge to tackle the older woman to keep her at bay. She only *looks* seventy.

"You must be Aunt Zen."

"Sure am," she says, taking his hand delicately. I notice that Chase matches her grip strength and silently approve of the move. If there's one way to get in Zen's good graces, it's to be polite and professional. It's only been recently she's been working at the therapy center a couple of days a week, and it's because she got tired of being a high-powered businesswoman for an international company. Only the highest levels of professionalism will impress her.

Chase has a better chance than I'm giving him credit for.

Still, Zen is still staring him down by the time Dad walks in, looking around the room with interest.

"Did I hear my Sunshine walk in?" he asks.

I smile—my first genuine smile since I crossed the threshold—and walk to him, holding out my arms. "Dad."

Dad laughs and hugs me back. Then, he says quietly, "We've been on pins and needles all day. Your mom could barely sit still in church she wanted to see your boyfriend so bad."

I also could hardly sit still in church, but not for the same reason. Guilt and impending doom, with a nice sprinkle of Eternal Judgement, has a way of doing that to you.

"We don't need to make such a big deal over it," I say with an uncomfortable laugh. "He's a normal—" I break off. Chase is human, yes, but normal? I look up at him where he's fielding questions from Zen. As he does, he catches my eye and smiles at me and then turns his attention back to Zen. "Well, he's Chase."

"I can see that," Dad says with a smile. Smiling, he puts an arm around my shoulders and directs me toward the kitchen. Yes, I leave Chase behind. But he's doing well so far, and if nothing else, I have absolute confidence he can beat Zen in a fistfight. Once we're in the brightly lit kitchen, Dad turns to me, snitching a celery stick off the veggie tray waiting there.

"And how's my little girl?"

The smile on my lips is more genuine than I expect as I grab a carrot. "Better than I have been."

He shifts. Dad isn't one to beat around the bush, but he's also not one to press me on sensitive topics. To be fair, he's never had to before.

"And therapy? Is it ... helping?"

I look up at him, the smile fading with the change of topic. Shame floods through me. Dad's the most trusting man on the planet. I've never lied to him before, and every time I have to do it, I hate myself a little more. But it would also be a lie to say the therapy hadn't done anything at all.

"Yeah, Dad," I say quietly. "I think it is."

"Is he treating you right?"

I reach out for another carrot. I want to tell him. I want to tell him everything. But would he feel betrayed when he found out he was worrying about a situation that doesn't exist? I have only myself to blame.

"Dad—" I take a deep breath. "I just want you to know that he's never been purposefully mean or anything. We've been working on communication, and our goals. Ways to be good together, and not just on our own. It hasn't all been Chase. It's been me, too. I'm getting better, too." And one day I'll be able to tell you everything.

Dad puts his arm around me and tucks me into his side for a brief hug. "Well, I can't say I thought anything was wrong with you before, but I'm glad you feel like it's doing good. I guess everyone can improve in one way or another. Even me."

He says it with a twinkle in his eye, and I gasp in mock shock. "What? You?"

He laughs and pats me on my shoulder. "Even me. Well, I suppose I should go introduce myself."

We both look toward the knot of people in the living room. Chase's head is bent toward Mom, clearly listening to something she has to say. Joanie is standing beside her, arms folded across her chest. She's not exactly frowning, but I know my older sister well enough that I know she is not happy.

Dad walks toward the front room, and I take a couple of steps to follow, pausing in the doorway, listening to Mom.

"And I was just telling Joanie the other day that I am *so* glad Summer has found someone. We were quite worried about her, you know. Joanie was married years ago, and we've only ever wanted the same for Summer."

"Uh, Mom!" I start from the doorway as Joanie breaks in.

"Mom, Summer and Chase are only dating. Don't jump the gun."

"Oh, I guess you're right," Mom says, throwing her hands up in the air. "I guess I'm just excited to meet you."

"And I'm excited to meet you." Chase doesn't seem discomfited at all by Mom's insinuation, if anything he sounds reassuring. It's Chase all over, and I relax back into the door frame, smiling. After a minute, I back into the kitchen, letting the swinging door close, and start putting the food on the table. I didn't have to, of course, but it would help dinner progress faster, which in turn would help us leave faster, too.

"Bold of you to abandon your boyfriend with Mom the Unfiltered."

I look back to see Joanie standing by the door to the living room, her arms folded. I turn back to where I'm placing salad on the table.

"I'm sure Chase can handle it. He handles working with

me on a regular basis." I mean it as a joke, but Joanie's expression turns more serious.

"You shouldn't feel like a burden, Summer."

I stop where I'm standing, halfway between the table and the counter, utterly concerned. "What?"

Joanie takes a step toward me. "I'm serious. If he's making you feel like you're unimportant or lesser in any way, you need to run. Now."

"I—" I'm staring, but I can't help it. Joanie and I don't have this type of relationship. We're the send-a-card-on-birthday type of sisters. Not ... this. Not a single word comes to my mind. "I don't feel like that." I'm shocked enough that it doesn't sound very sure, and Joanie pounces on it.

"Summer, listen to me. I know that you've been single for a while, and Mom probably—scratch that, *definitely*—hasn't been helping, but I'm telling you, it's not worth it to be around someone who makes you feel unimportant or badly about yourself."

"Joanie—"

"And I know you're in therapy, and that's all very well and good, but I've *been* there, Summer. I've been with a guy that made me question everything, who straight up messed with my brain, and I don't want you to even get near that. I don't want you to question whether or not you're worth his time. I don't want you to feel like it's a burden for someone to love you. That kind of behavior is toxic, and it's harder than *anything* to come back from."

She has a point, I know that. I'm hearing it with my ears, but my mind is spinning. I can only think of Chase, and his hugs and his way of making me feel more important than anyone else in the room.

Toxic.

If there is one truth in this world, Chase is not toxic.

"How could you even think that Chase is capable of doing something like that to me?" The words are out of my mouth before I really think about them, and for a terrible moment, I wonder if I've given the game away. And then I realize I don't care. "Chase? Really?"

Joanie is frowning now, her arms crossed tightly across her chest. "'Really?' Summer, all I've ever heard about this guy is that he always puts himself first, and how unhappy you are. He's never taken time out for you, you're always complaining about how he makes decisions for you—How in the world am I supposed to believe he's anything else?"

Her voice is loud, and the meaning pounds down on my head. I want to fight. I want to tell her that she's wrong, and that if she knew Chase as well as I did that there's no way that she would ever say something like that about him ever again.

But then I realize: She doesn't. Joanie doesn't know Chase. She hasn't been to therapy with him, and every single thing she knows about my 'boyfriend' is a lie that I have told to either feel included or purposefully be left out. It's been hurting her.

And now it's hurting Chase.

I'm suddenly exhausted. I want to go home, where I can live with the consequences of my own terrible actions in private misery. But that's not an option right now. Maybe I can at least give Chase and Joanie a fighting chance. "We're working hard, Joanie. I fell in love with him for a reason."

Joanie's frown doesn't go away, but it changes from anger to pleading. "Sometimes that's not enough, Summer. He has to want to be with you, too. Otherwise, it's not fair."

I'm about to respond when the kitchen door swings open. Dad's there, and looks between the two of us with a worried expression on his face. I wonder how much he's heard.

But he doesn't say anything, just looks between me and my

older sister, and asks us if we'll finish moving the food over to the table.

Joanie and I obey Dad, not looking at each other as we cross from the kitchen to the dining room over and over again.

In the silence, I can hear Mom chattering excitedly to Chase. The guilt stabs deeper and deeper. She's so happy right now. About Chase. About me.

Joanie was married years ago, and we've only ever wanted the same for Summer.

My eyes sting, and I have to clear my throat to keep them from overflowing.

He has to want to be with you, too.

The pain in my chest is twisting harder and harder. I know it's true, and I know what I have to do.

I just want to do it less and less.

"—And this is the kitchen and dining room!" Mom's voice practically booms across the silent kitchen, and I turn to see her, Chase, and Zen. Chase's eyes sweep the room and land on me.

His expression changes. His eyebrows draw together and he shifts, as though he's about to come to me. His eyes dart from Dad to Joanie, and then back at me, a question meant only for me appearing on his face. I'm frozen. If I try to talk, I might realistically burst into tears. But I can't honestly wave him off. I don't want to.

And then he comes to me. Smiling at Mom and making a comment about how beautiful the room is, he crosses the room and puts his arm around my shoulders, gently pulling me into his side.

It's casual, natural even, but my world rocks beneath my feet as it stops spinning. I lean my head on his shoulder as I wind an arm around his waist. Part of the weight shifts in my chest, and the tears stop threatening.

Just like that.

Great googly moogly. I'm in trouble.

But his arm is secure around my shoulders, like he's sheltering me from not only my family's judgmental stares, but also the weight of my own guilt.

It almost works.

I listen to my mom excitedly telling Chase about our homemade kitchen table—Dad made it—and the dishes that we were using—Joanie made them—before she realizes that all the food is on the table, and we're ready to eat.

She quickly arranges us with me and Chase on the near side of the table, her and Zen on the other side with Joanie and Dad on the ends. I don't think she draws breath for a full thirty minutes, with the exception of saying grace, until Zen takes a chance and pours Mom some water. While Mom takes a sip, Zen asks Chase regular questions. College. Work. Questions about how we met show up, and instead of cutting in, I listen to Chase, too. I trust him.

I trust him.

I am so far gone.

We have to break up in two weeks. I should be looking for ways to drive wedges in between us. I should be looking for his faults and making it more believable that we'd go our separate ways.

Only, the more I think about it, the more I think about *him*, the more I absolutely don't want to do that.

"You know," Zen says from across the table. "I'm really impressed with the two of you."

Her statement yanks me out of my thoughts and snaps my head in her direction.

Chase is already paying attention, and smiles at Zen. "Oh?" Reaching under the table, he slides his fingers down my arm and captures my hand in his, interlacing our fingers. I look down, then at him, and he sends me a smile I can't help but return.

Zen sees it, and nods, her silver-gray curls bouncing with the motion. "Summer wasn't very happy with you earlier this year."

The table goes absolutely silent. I'm eighty-two percent sure my heart has stopped beating.

This is worse than the intervention.

"Auntie!" I protest, but Chase gently squeezes my hand under the table.

"Don't I know it," Chase says quietly, looking around the table. "The first couple of therapy sessions were rough." Out of the corner of my eye, I can see Joanie shift in her seat. She doesn't look happy, but I can tell that she's listening.

Please see Chase, not the 'boyfriend,' I pray.

"I will admit I didn't have a lot of hope for you two," Zen says. "And although I'm surprised, I'm glad to see the two of you turning things around. It's rare to see a relationship recover so well."

Chase nods self-deprecatingly. "I'm surprised she gave me another chance. It's amazing to me how well a relationship can work out when both people are willing to work at it. We had a long talk about it a couple of weeks ago about what we really want out of a relationship that opened my eyes about her. We haven't stopped, and the longer we talk about it, the more I realize I can't imagine my life without Summer."

I look up at him, half in awe at how sincere he sounds, and wishing with everything in me what he said was true.

The rest of the dinner goes comparatively normally. Zen's words seem to break the ice, and even Joanie's expression has softened somewhat on the opposite end of the table. She even manages to find it in her heart to ask Chase a couple of benign questions of her own.

And then it's time to leave.

Chapter 17
The Talk

CHASE

SUMMER IS EXHAUSTED. I CAN TELL BY THE SET OF HER shoulders and the half-smile as we turn away from waving in front of the car. I open the door, and hand her in, and then take my time walking around the car. I can't give her more than about ten seconds before she'll wonder why I'm taking so long, but after the chaos and noise that is her mother's house, I know she needs a moment of quiet.

I don't mind it. Karma Weathers is a force to be reckoned with—to say nothing of her older sister—but I've dealt with all sorts of people on the job. Micromanagers, manipulators, even just very focused people who have A Timeline. Karma, for all her intensity—and an itty-bitty bit of meddling—is a normal person who loves her children and wants to be involved, even as they go and live their adult lives. She might be overstepping, but it comes from a good place.

I'm trying not to be jealous. My mother is loving, in her way, but it was as though the day I moved out of the house I was no longer her child. The day Avery moved out was the day I effectively ceased to exist. Now I have a quarterly call when they come back to the United States to make sure their house is still standing, and even that is five minutes or less—the adult equivalent to a pat on the head.

I've been outside been more than ten seconds, and I slide into the car a little guiltily.

Summer *has* noticed, and her eyebrows lift. She doesn't ask if everything is okay, though. I suspect she's thinking I need a moment alone after the vibrant chaos of the Weathers family. I don't think she would ever guess I want more.

"I had fun today," I say, turning the car on and pulling away, making sure Summer's seat warmer is on.

"Really?" Summer's voice is so incredulous that I chuckle. Summer's expression turns from worry to incredulity, which she quickly rearranges into a rather unconvinced nod. "I'm glad. They can be ... a lot."

"It's definitely an experience. Your family is a lot different than mine," I say with a smile. "But I enjoyed myself."

Summer grimaces. "I thought Zen and Joanie were going to gang up and shank you."

I laugh. "Zen does come on a little strong, doesn't she?" It's teasing, but I can tell Summer knows.

"Not just her. Joanie looked at you like you were the devil incarnate until you explained you were taking therapy seriously."

"Exactly what I would expect from a good older sibling. To be perfectly honest, I've been that person for Avery a time or two."

I say it to make Summer smile, but her gaze has drifted out the window, and it reminds me of the look on her face when I had walked into the kitchen. I'd never seen Summer look like that before. We'd only known each other for five weeks or so, but I'd seen anger, frustration, embarrassment, joy, and fear all written clearly on her face. Her expressions were possibly the most honest part of her, and most of the time it was fun to watch her thoughts play out. But I could have sworn that she had been about to cry when I walked in.

Andie had told me to listen, but it's not always about Summer's words. She's still hurting, and I need to know why.

"What were you and Joan talking about before we came into the kitchen?" The question hangs in the air between us like a slowly deflating helium balloon.

Summer doesn't look away from the window immediately, but then her chin drops, and she studies her hands in her lap.

"She wanted to make sure I don't feel like a burden in this relationship. And to make sure that I'm not the only one who wants it."

I know the criticism isn't about me—it literally couldn't have been—but it does sting a little. I wait to speak. I know Summer isn't done.

"Joanie ... is different from me. She didn't have any problems getting dates in high school or college, and enjoyed going on dates in general, but that meant she also met guys that weren't good to her. One guy in particular ... he was a lot harder to shake. She got out, but ... I don't blame her for what she said to me. I really don't. You're just not the person I complained about to her. And hearing her talk like that and having you in her mind ... it hurt. Lying hurts. I'm so sick of it."

Summer's staring straight ahead at the road, but in the light of the streetlamp and stoplights, I can see an extra shimmer of moisture in her eyes.

I reach out and take her hand.

"Have you considered telling Joanie the truth?"

Summer lets out a shaky breath and laughs. "No. Joanie would go straight to Mom. It's juvenile to call her a tattle tale, but even Dad has said that sometimes it feels like there's an echo in the house with the two of them. If I don't want it to get back to Mom, I can't tell Joanie.

"Maybe it would be different if ... I don't know. With Mom it always feels like the reward for something is the quest toward the next big thing. We'd celebrate graduations and have dinners, but the questions were always 'so what's next.' At my master's party, my mom asked me flat-out when I was planning on finding someone and getting married."

I listen, just taking it in, the only sound other than Summer's voice the quiet shushing of the slush under the tires. When Summer doesn't continue, I mull her words around in my brain.

"This is just a question," I say, "and there's no judgement either way, but have you talked to your mom about any of this?"

Summer shakes her head. "No."

"Why?"

"I don't know whether that type of feedback would be appreciated." Summer's voice is quiet. "It feels different when it's a parent. How are you supposed to guide a person that's guided you your whole life?"

I think about that. "I don't know that there's an easy answer to that. But she is human. It's possible that she doesn't know she's doing it."

Summer's frown lessens a little at that. "I guess."

"What I know, Summer," I say, squeezing her hand, "is that your mother does love you. Really. From my experience, if someone doesn't care, there's silence. It doesn't mean her way of showing it is what you need, or even good, but it's something."

There's silence in the car. "From your experience?" Summer's voice is tentative, and she squeezes my hand.

I take a deep breath. "My parents' relationship with me is

very different from you and yours. It's something that I've had to come to terms with, too."

"I'm sorry."

"It'll be all right," I tell her with a smile. "I promise."

Summer gives me a half-smile and as the silence carries on, less painful now, Summer keeps on holding my hand and looks out the window. It's a clear night for once, and I can see stars peeking through the darkness above while we drive a little ways out of the city, even with the light pollution. An idea pops into my brain.

"Hey, Summer?"

"Hmm?" she responds, her voice a little distracted.

"Have you ever gone stargazing?" I ask.

She lifts her head from the window and looks back at me. "Not, like, officially. Why?"

I smile, the beginnings of a plan percolating in my brain. "We should go sometime."

Summer smiles. "I'd like that."

The rest of the ride is silent, but relaxed. At one point, Summer gets a text message, but she doesn't touch her phone. I can understand the sentiment. When we arrive at Summer's apartment, I get out, too, and pull her into my arms. I don't want to leave, not until Summer feels more like herself.

"You gonna be okay?" I ask, my breath billowing out in the cold winter air.

She heaves a sigh and then answers. "Yes. It's really nothing I haven't dealt with before. Except it involves you. I guess I'm feeling a bit protective, considering you're only under fire because I dragged you into it."

"I seem to remember volunteering," I say thoughtfully, and Summer laughs.

"I remember Lacy press-ganging you."

"Nah, I wanted the therapy."

"Still worth it?" She tips her head back to look at me.

"Of course." It takes everything in me not to close the short distance between us and press a kiss to her lips, but I know better. There are some lines a fake relationship shouldn't cross. Not if I want my sanity at the end of all of this.

Summer's still looking up at me, her eyes still a little sad, a small line of worry between her eyebrows.

"How about you?"

She smiles, but it doesn't change the look in her eyes, or smooth that little line. "Absolutely."

Not therapy then. Maybe it's still her family. "Are you sure you're going to be okay?"

I surprise a little laugh out of her. "Yes, why?"

I keep one arm wrapped around her but bring the other up to touch the little line between her eyebrows. "You look a little worried still."

Summer bites her lip and looks down. "Oh." She turns her head, surveying the parking lot. "Work ... it's been a little rough lately."

I frown. "Is it Louis again?"

She sighs heavily. "Yeah."

I can feel my frown deepening. "Is there anything I can do to help?"

Summer's arms tighten around my waist, and to my surprise the worry line disappears. She looks back up at me. "Honestly, I don't know."

"Will you tell me if you think of anything I can do?" I ask, studying her.

Her eyes trail over my face, and there's the hint of a smile around her lips. "I will."

"Good." I pull her into me and hold her tightly for a moment longer before dropping a kiss onto her cheek.

Her eyes follow me as I step back. Her smile hasn't disappeared. If anything, it's grown.

"Everything is going to be all right," I tell her, believing every word.

"Promise?" she says, stepping up onto the sidewalk.

"Promise. Now go inside before you freeze."

Her smile broadens into a grin. "Goodnight, Chase."

"Goodnight, Summer."

The warmth I feel only lasts as I watch until Summer enters her apartment, and I sit down in my car. Instinctively, I reach out for my phone and check my messages. There's one unread message, and I click it, wondering if it's Summer facetiously texting me that she got home safe.

It's not.

> Amanda: Chase, please respond. I know I made a mistake, and I'm sorry. I just want to talk.

I stare down at the text. For a second, I feel angry, wondering if she's crawling back to me because her relationship had inevitably failed. Then it fades away, and I sit there in my car, wondering what she's expecting of me now.

A relationship? Do I have any feelings left for Amanda?

I don't.

Part of me wonders whether it's because of my infatuation with Summer, but I realize the real truth quickly. It's Amanda's words about me that have haunted me all this time, not grief. Amanda made her choices, and with them killed any chance of a future reconciliatory relationship stone dead.

I back the car out and start the drive home, calling Avery over speaker phone.

She picks up. "You've reached Avery, Master of the Universe, to whom can I direct your call?"

I smirk. "Uh, yes. I'd like to talk to the Relationship Advisor, please?"

She snaps to her serious mode so quickly that I'm left a little stunned. "Oh. My. Goodness. Are you in love with Summer? Have you kissed her yet? Actually, don't tell me, I don't really need to know. That would be weird. Tell me all."

"It's not about Summer, Gills."

There's silence.

"You haven't ruined a super good thing, have you?"

I have to think for a moment to realize what she means. "I haven't broken up with Summer." You have to actually be dating someone to break up with them.

"Uh, okay? Who else could you be possibly talking about?"

"Amanda texted me."

Avery's tone is anything but happy. "Did you tell her to throw herself into the sun?"

"No, I haven't responded at all."

"Good. Run for the hills. Change your name. You know, if you marry Summer, it's become a thing now for the groom to change their last name."

"Gills, if it gets that bad, I'll probably just do it on my own." Fake dating is hard enough. Fake marriage sounds like a nightmare.

"Eh. It's an option. So, what did she say? You're not tempted to try anything with her, are you?"

Cheat on my fake girlfriend with my terrible ex-girlfriend. "Nice to know what you think of my sanity."

"I don't know what you want from me, Chase."

Hearing my own name rocks me back into reality. "I guess I

just want to make sure ..." I trail off. I know my answer. I'm not being unfair to Amanda. We gave it a good try, and it absolutely didn't turn out well. It's time to be clear and communicate well.

"You know what, actually I think I'm good," I say.

Avery snorts. "So glad I could help." She pauses, and her voice is softer when she speaks. "Chase, you're okay, right?"

"Yeah, I am." I look around the car, and out the window. "I, uh, met Summer's parents tonight."

"Oh? Good or bad?"

"Good. Her mom is thrilled. I think a little too thrilled."

"Ooh," Avery says, "You charmer, you."

I bark out a laugh. "Nah, I think it's more to do with them being happy for Summer. I'm just a nice byproduct for not being a creeper."

"Oh." Avery sounds intrigued, and with a start I remember I haven't told her about fake dating or therapy. "Protective?"

"Her sister is. Not too bad, though. It sounds like she's had some stuff happen in her life, too."

"Fair."

"Do you think Summer will ever be able to meet our parents?" The words are out of my mouth before I can really think about them. If I did think about them, the answer is probably no. Summer and I only have two therapy appointments left, and then we part ways. In order to meet my parents, we'll have to wait until they're in the country or go to them. That'll take longer than we have.

The stabbing in my chest tells me how I really feel about that.

"Probably," Avery says, her voice a little distant. "It'll depend on timing."

"Yeah." I sigh a little as I pull into my neighborhood. "Well. I'm almost home, and then I need to head to bed. Love you, Gills."

"Love you, Morkie. Don't do anything I wouldn't do." Her voice drops to a whisper. "I would tell your ex to take a hike."

I laugh. "Fair enough. Bye."

She echoes me, and hangs up so I don't have to, just as I pull into my garage. I grab my phone and open it, looking down at Amanda's message.

We're done. And I'm not going to drag it out for her.

Me: No, thanks.

Chapter 18
The Fifth Appointment

SUMMER

CHASE IS WAITING FOR ME WHEN I PULL INTO THERAPY ON Thursday. I probably shouldn't feel quite so happy—I was at his house until almost midnight the night before—but my heart seems to pick up the pace when I see him leaning against the side of his car.

Things have been better since Sunday. I have completely and utterly convinced my family that not only are Chase and I dating, but we're on the road to recovery. Even Joanie seems to be coming around, and we've been texting back and forth.

It does nothing to help with the guilt. I'm still lying to everyone. But it's only for a couple more weeks. Then Chase and I will break up and this unfortunate chapter can fade into the hidden annals of my history.

Which would be fine, except I have to break up with Chase.

He pops Jennie's door open, pulling me into an embrace as I stand, and I close my eyes as he enfolds me in his arms, wanting to stay there forever.

Unfortunately, I'm a little late today, and so we hustle into the building, hand in hand. Andie the Therapist takes one look at our joined hands and gives us what is quite possibly the largest smile she's ever given us.

At the beginning of all of this, I might have minded. Today, I get to be the girl who's holding Chase's hand and let the rest of life sink more into the background.

Andie takes our couple's journal, and runs through all the entries we've written over the past two weeks. I haven't noticed before right this second, but the entries are getting longer, and I notice Andie smiling as she glances through one of them. I wonder which one. I've read all of them, of course. That was part of the assignment, to write about our experiences and share them with each other.

It's changed me. I've never been much into journaling—scheduling is different—but doing this, it's changed how I look at a relationship. The two perspectives. The two intertwined lives.

It's not been a perfect experiment. Chase and I are still two different people with two perspectives, but it's been nice to see that even if we disagree on some things, it doesn't have to affect our relationship. I'm allowed to be myself and love him at the same time.

Love him.

Be careful, Summer, the little voice in my head tells me. It's become quieter over the last couple of weeks. I don't know whether it's a good or bad thing.

Chase's knee bumps mine. I look up at him, and he raises his eyebrows, silently asking what's wrong. I smile at him and shake my head. I'm fine. Just thinking. He seems to understand, and he squeezes my hand.

My heart flutters, and I squeeze his fingers in return.

"Well," Andie says, smiling between the two of us. "It seems like you guys have made a lot of progress since the last appointment a couple of weeks ago. How are the two of you feeling about things?"

Chase has an unconscious smile that sends butterflies through my stomach. "Well," he says, "I have this sneaking suspicion I love my girlfriend."

It's fake, and I know it is, but I can't help returning his smile.

Andie grins. "Well, that's a good sign. Tell me more."

Chase sighs happily, settling back in the sofa with his arm touching mine. He thinks for a long moment. "It's hard to explain. I feel ... safe. In a lot of the previous relationships I've had, I feel like I've needed to keep constant contact, basically chasing them around to make sure they know I exist and that I care. Weirdly, I think I text Summer more than any of them, but it doesn't seem forced. I spend more time having fun with her than worrying about whether or not she is thinking about me. I know she's committed, and it's ... comforting."

I look up at him, recognizing the statement for what it is. After that day in the car when he told me about Amanda and everything she'd said to him, I've tried to watch my words. Not that I've really wanted to say anything remotely similar, but it made me conscious of what I say, and my expectations of him. He's human, but he's wonderful. It isn't hard.

How blind was Amanda that she couldn't see that? How self-centered did a girl have to be to take a person like Chase and everything that was good and gentle about him and turn it into an insecurity. How dare she?

One thing was for sure: I never wanted to meet her, because if I did, I might shortly be served with an assault charge.

"And you, Summer?" Andie says, breaking me out of my less-than-ladylike thoughts. She must have sensed that I'd briefly checked out, because she gives me a smile and says, "How have the last two weeks been for you?"

The last two weeks. Full of Chase hugs, handholding, and spending time with one of the best men in the universe. I can't keep the smile from my face as I sigh, a little wistfully. "It's been great. I agree with Chase. It's been ..." I trail off, suddenly feeling the weight of this particular admission. "It's been what I need. Chase is always willing to stop and listen in the middle of whatever we're doing. He's never laughed or made light of something that's important to me, and he's always there for me. It's been ... what I need." It feels a little lame to end it like that, but it's deeply sincere.

Andie seems to understand and looks between the two of us with a big smile. "I'm so glad. For both of you. Now, today I wanted to talk a little bit more about approaching and building intimacy between the two of you."

Chase stiffens beside me, and we both glance at each other.

"Um," I say, if only so Chase won't have to.

Andie smiles but shakes your head. "I remember your questionnaires, and how you both indicated that you're waiting for marriage for that type of intimacy. It's a very good sign to be united on that front, since sometimes that can cause undue stress in a relationship if someone feels pressured or ignored.

"That being said, today is the first day I've seen the two of you holding hands, and I feel like this might be something we can build on to help you deepen your relationship, especially since now you're definitely enjoying a greater depth of emotional connection."

Chase makes a choking sort of sound in his throat, and he looks up at Andie like he's suddenly experiencing acute appendicitis. "Andie, I ..." he closes his eyes. "I know I like the idea behind this plan, but Summer isn't as fond of physical contact as I am. The last thing that I want to do is accept a challenge that will make her uncomfortable in any way."

I'm blushing. I know I am. But even while my heart absolutely floods with love for this man sitting beside me, and I turn lobster-red out of low-key mortification, I have to open my mouth.

"But I'm not the only one in this relationship, Chase," I whisper. "And you love it."

His shoulder, which was tense, turns to absolute stone.

He turns to me, his eyebrows nearly touching in concern. "Summer, you—"

"Chase, I'm sorry for interrupting, but ..." I take a deep breath. "You're right. I don't automatically reach out to people physically, and frankly rather hate the idea of some random guy throwing his arm around my shoulders." I put my hand on his knee. "But you're not a random guy. You're my boyfriend. From you ..." I feel my face reach Firetruck Red and press my lips together. "From you I don't mind. In fact ... I like it."

Is it possible to die from blushing too hard? Every part of me is flushing red. Even my hands are more pink than they were a moment ago. Thank goodness he still sees this as a fake relationship. I can't even imagine what I would do if I had to confess, knowing that it was for real.

Chase is looking at me with utter disbelief, and I can see in his eyes we are absolutely going to talk about this later, but I break eye contact with him and turn back to Andie.

"What did you have in mind?" I am probably approaching beetroot purple by now.

Andie's expression has softened into a deep smile, and she looks at Chase. "Well, this part will be up to you. Since I'm not with you every minute of every day, I don't know your personal limits, but stick to things you enjoy and work up from there. If you need ideas, or if you don't know where to begin, start by giving each other a kiss hello and goodbye. Make sure you give each other at least a one-minute hug every day, or if you're apart on business or can't see each other in person, speak to each other voice to voice once a day. I still want you to have dedicated date nights to go do things, but I'd also recommend cuddling two to three times a week.

"Like I said, all of these things are suggestions. They're not meant to be an exhaustive list of everything you can or should do, but I think they should give you a good foundation."

I nod, my mind buzzing.

She said to kiss Chase.

It's not like I haven't thought about it. A lot. Especially after spending most evenings with him. If we were in an actual relationship, it probably would have happened by now, but Chase is too respectful, and I've been way too shy—and respectful of his boundaries—to expect it.

Also, I've never kissed anyone. And I don't know how to hide that.

Chase already knows, I remind myself.

"How does that sound, at least to start?" Andie asks, looking between the two of us. "Do you have any questions?"

None I dared ask. One did not ask your relationship therapist—particularly the one who thinks that I've been dating my proposed kissing partner for the last six months or so—exactly how one kisses someone.

Good grief.

Was I going to have to ask Lacy?

Great googly moogly.

I'd never hear the end of it.

But I'm not trying to avoid kissing Chase. That's not it at all.

Will Chase be able to tell how much I want to do this? Goodness gracious, how did consent figure in all of this?

Cuddling was one thing—friends cuddled—but kissing would be walking off the plank of our friend-ship into the shark infested waters of absolute confusion.

Except I wasn't confused. I knew how I felt about Chase.

Which was probably the biggest problem of them all.

"No," I say quietly, and sounding far less panicked than the inside of my brain, "I have no questions."

"I think I'm good." Chase is studying me.

Andie looks between the two of us brightly. "Awesome! Well, on that note ..."

The rest of the session is remarkably normal. So normal in fact, that I almost forget the conversation we had at the beginning of the session until Chase takes my hand to walk out of the session.

Just his gentle touch on my bare skin, and the zinging energy that follows my arm all the way up to my heart, brings the entire situation back to the forefront of my mind.

Chase isn't exactly smiling as we walk back out to the cars, and as we reach Jennie, he turns around to look at me. For a minute, I think he looks angry, until I realize it's deep concern turning his whole face to stone.

"Summer," His voice is deep, and he steps close.

"Yes?"

"You don't have to do this." He says it more fervently than I've ever heard him say anything. "I won't—I would never make you—" Chase's cheeks are flushed, and he can't quite look at me, and my heart sinks as I realize what he wants to say to me.

"You don't want to kiss me, do you?"

Chase is looking down, but his head jerks up so fast that I

feel the air move. "What? No, that's not what I meant. Not at all."

I frown, my disappointment freezing in anticipation. "Then what do you mean?"

"I mean I'm serious, Summer. The first time I put my arm around you, it felt like you turned to brick. I know ..." He closes his eyes briefly, a cloud of condensation puffing out of his mouth as he sighs, apparently dissatisfied with the way he's expressing himself. "I know you haven't been kissed before. I don't want to ruin that experience for you. I don't want even the slightest bit of awkwardness between us or, or obligation to be attached to it in the least. You deserve more than that."

I'm staring up at him in awe. I'm pretty sure that my mouth is actually dangling open as my brain blankly fizzles out, trying to come up with some sort of response that isn't a) attacking him with a kiss of my own, b) confessing my undying love, or c) simply outright proposing.

There isn't a woman alive that deserves this man, and he's the only one that I'd ever want kissing me.

And I don't know how to express that in words. So, I step forward toward him, until we're almost chest to chest.

As I do, the words spring into my mind, and I look up at him. "I know you too well to feel obligated to do anything, Chase," I whisper. "And I've hedgehog-rolled into your lap way too many times to feel awkward around you."

His expression softens. "I just ..."

"I know." For some reason, now that Andie isn't here, it feels less awkward. Less forced.

And then I look over Chase's shoulder and notice a little figure in one of the windows. I don't have to see the knitted sweater with alpacas on it to know it's Andie. Chase notices her, too.

"Chase," I say, looking at him, with an encouraging smile. "I trust you. Kiss me. For therapy."

He looks down at me for a long moment, looking completely floored. Then, slowly, almost tentatively, he takes a step forward. We're chest to chest, and he reaches up, taking my shoulders gently.

I tilt my face toward his. My heart is starting to pound, but I don't move a muscle, feeling like if I do, Chase will run for the hills and leave me standing here, Andie or no Andie.

He starts to dip his head toward mine. He's so close now. I've never been this close to anyone else. Not like this. His eyes don't leave mine, and he pauses, a hair's breadth away.

Then he smiles. "For therapy."

Relief blossoms in my heart. My eyes drift closed, and then his lips are warm and gentle against mine. My heart, already thudding against the inside of my chest, seems to skip a beat, and I lean into him, gently pinching his coat in my fingers to keep my balance.

I'm finding I like kissing. Specifically, I like kissing Chase. I like it a lot.

And then he steps away.

His head is still bowed toward me when I open my eyes, and I take a deep breath to try to come back to reality. For a moment, I'm worried that he didn't like it. I mean, I am a novice. Did I even do anything? I did kiss back—I think. What if I did it wrong? I'm in touch enough with the world to know there's technique involved.

I never thought I'd regret not making out with random people in high school.

But then Chase smiles down at me. And it's a real smile.

"Still okay?" he asks.

I give him a large, genuine grin. "Perfectly."

But then we don't say anything more. I don't know if there's much more to say. So, in the quiet of the parking lot, Chase opens the door of my Crown Victoria.

"Text me when you get to work," he says, once I'm seated. He's still holding onto my hand.

I squeeze his fingers. "I will. Drive safe."

"I will," he says. And then he closes the door.

Normally Chase waits for me to drive away, but he has a meeting today. As I watch him drive out of the parking lot, I press my fingers to my lips, unable to keep the smile taking over my face at bay. I'm grinning so wide it feels like my face is going to split in half.

And then, like a landslide, part of my joy breaks away, my heart breaking a little. It's not real. And we have only one more appointment before it's over.

I bounce my hand off of Jennie's steering wheel a couple of times as I try to find the balance between the two emotions. I don't want it to be over. I never want to let go of Chase. Maybe there's something that I can do. Something to keep us from breaking up. Something that I could say to convince him to want me for real.

I need him.

Because I'm starting to realize life without Chase in it looks really, really bleak.

Chapter 19
The Plan

CHASE

When Summer arrives Wednesday night, I can tell she's had a really difficult day. She knocks twice and lets herself in, as is now our custom, but when she gets to the kitchen, her shoulders are slumped, there are bags under her eyes, and she is walking slowly in her fluffy cabin socks.

I can tell she's stopped by her house, given she's in an oversized hoodie and sweats and is holding her slouchy bag. Her hair is even up in a topknot, which I have been informed would only be shown to me under the direst of circumstances.

For a split second, I wonder whether I should ask if it was a bad day. But I can read the room. I open my arms. "Hug or hot chocolate first?"

She drops her bag and shuffles into my arms without saying anything. I wrap my arms around her, tucking my head against hers. As I sway from side to side, I murmur in her ear. "What's going on?"

Summer heaves a big sigh, and shakes her head, burrowing her head further into my shoulder. Her arms are tight around me, and I feel like she needs my comfort more than she needs me to press the issue.

Part of me is wondering whether it's the right thing to do. I think I know at least part of the problem—Louis, aka the majority of Summer's problems since I've known her—but it could be her family. I don't know how much I should press. On the one hand, she's entitled to tell me whatever she wants. On the other hand, I don't want her to bear it alone, especially if I can help.

Bit by bit, Summer relaxes her grip, until she's leaning against me, her breathing long and deep.

"Did you fall asleep?" I cradle the back of her head with one of my hands. My voice is gentle, and I can feel her shoulders shake with a small huff of laughter.

"No." She leans her head back to look up at me. "But I'm tempted. It's been a day."

I frown. "I'm sorry."

She shakes her head reassuringly. "Not your fault."

I nod in agreement. "You're right. But I do care. I hope you know you can tell me about it if you need to."

Summer nods, her eyes far away. It makes my chest ache. I know that she's stressed, and I wish I could take it all away.

I reach up and cradle her face. "By the way," I say, my voice dropping into a whisper. "I forgot to say hello."

Summer's green eyes flick up to mine, and she finally smiles. I return the smile, leaning in until we're almost touching. "This is hello," I whisper, and press my lips to hers.

I can feel her smile against my mouth, and I let my eyes drift closed. Summer's vanilla scent wafts over me, and it takes all of my willpower to remember to pull back. Of all the things I don't need to keep myself from getting attached to Summer Weathers, it's being able to kiss her at least twice a day. It's a heady sensation, and for all her inexperience, she's taken to it in a way that is simply not fair.

Summer follows me as I straighten to break the kiss, rising to her tiptoes before our lips part. I'm tempted to dive back in, if only for the sake of comforting her, but I need to retain some semblance of self-control. Summer and I aren't actually in a relationship. I don't want to step over some boundary on accident because I've misread a signal. I look down at Summer to read her expression, but rather than looking me in the eye, she turns her head and rests it against my shoulder, looking out into the kitchen. Then she stills.

"Chase?"

"Hmm?"

"What's that?" She nods toward the counter, and I look, having completely forgotten anything that is not Summer. What meets my gaze is a large bouquet of red roses, tied with a deep red ribbon, and resting in a glass vase.

"Hmm? Oh, those are for you."

"Me?" Her voice is mostly disbelieving, and she looks up at me. "Really?"

"Well," I say, in the most conversational tone I can muster. "I was thinking about it the other day. We met for the first time in early February. That technically means I was your fake boyfriend over Valentine's."

"It's March."

"I didn't get you anything."

"So?"

"So," I continue, "That is a black mark on my record. I've always gotten my girlfriend something for Valentine's Day, and I refuse to besmirch my own good name."

Summer snorts. "You didn't have to, though. We were on the outs back then. It makes sense."

"It does, but now we're not on the outs, I think it's probably important to make up for it. That way you can send your mom and Ana a picture to show I'm not a complete jerk. You could probably send one to Joanie and Louis if you really want to."

Summer raises her eyebrows. "I'm pretty sure you're out of Mom's black books. Ana was thrilled with the pictures I showed her last week, and I think Joanie would rather die than get another picture from me." Then she smiles up at me. "But thank you. They're absolutely gorgeous. I love them."

I note she leaves Louis out completely, and I'm willing to let the matter drop. Surprisingly, Summer isn't. She begins to help me prepare dinner, unpacking the gnocchi for the creamy soup. She's just opened the package, when out of the corner of my eye, I see her shoulders drop.

"Chase, I'm going to tell you something, and I need you to not overreact."

My head whips around so fast I nearly burn myself on the pot of water on the stove. I barely manage to stop myself from peppering her with questions. Instead, I take a deep, subtle breath and say, "That's a bit of a loaded request. I'll do my best." She nods, but I'm not quite done as I turn back to the water. "The way you said that makes me worry, though."

Out of the corner of my eye, she nods. "Me, too."

"Okay," I say, turning around and folding my arms. "What's going on, Summer?"

She turns around, her arms crossing as well. She's not angry, I can tell right off the bat, but she is struggling to find words. And so, I wait for her. I know she's looking for the right way to express how she's feeling, but it's hard not to elbow my way in and start asking questions, or to gather her in my arms and tell her not to worry about it.

Finally, she begins.

"You know how I became a team lead at the beginning of the year?"

"Yes, I do."

"Well, I've told you about Louis. He's one of the other team leads. He's really good at his job, and for the most part, he's a good worker and at least a decent leader. I used to be on his team, and he was always really good to us, and kept us focused and motivated.

"After I became a team lead, it's kind of ... changed. At first, it was like he thought I didn't deserve the job, or like I couldn't do it, but he wouldn't actually say it out loud. He trained me as a team lead, so it was normal for him to check my work before submitting projects and things, but that training ended at the end of January. But he hasn't stopped. He keeps searching through my project files, leaving me comments, texting me on the weekends—even if I'm up-to-date on my projects—and insinuating that because I'm not consumed by work, I'm not dedicated enough to be a team lead.

"A couple of weeks ago ..." She looks down at her hands, and swallows. Then she takes a deep breath and continues. "The night we watched *Wait Until Dark*, he texted me, wanting to know where one of my team's files was. I can only guess he wanted to review it, but I didn't see the text because I was watching the movie with you. He told me I was too lazy to be a team lead and he was going to talk about it with Ana. Then he swore at me."

She's still looking down. "He didn't tell Ana, but it's gotten worse since then. It's never been out loud or over professional channels, but he texts me constantly. It just ..." She trails off. Her gaze never clears the height of the counter. "I ... I don't—" her voice breaks, and she squeezes her eyes shut. I push myself off the counter to enfold her in my arms, but she takes my hand before I can step any closer.

Anger is pounding through me to the beat of my heart, and

all I want to do is text Lacy and get Louis's house address. He can't text if I break both of his thumbs, now, can he?

This is probably what Summer means by overreacting. I take a deep breath, trying to temper the fury that's blasting through me. "Summer ... do you want me to do anything about this?" My voice is nearly breathless, but it's better than heading for the garage and zooming away for some vigilante justice.

Not while she's watching, anyway.

"No," she says quietly. Her eyes flick up to mine. "Not right now, anyway. I'll let you know if it changes."

I squeeze her hand and take another deep breath. "You can't let him keep on harassing you like this."

She opens her mouth to protest, and I shake my head. "No, Summer. This is harassment. Whether it's at work or on your personal device, he is overstepping good professional behavior. Actually, *any* good behavior. Normal people don't go around cussing out their coworkers."

She presses her lips together. "No, I know. I'm going to talk to the assistant manager about it—Ana will be able to tell me what to do about it, I think—but I still don't know how to ask. I mean, what if she can't do anything, and it only makes things worse?" Her voice is small, and she rubs her forehead.

I do step closer this time, leaning back against the counter beside her. Reaching out, I pull her into my side. She turns into me, and I fold her into my arms, letting her fully lean against me.

"If you don't do anything, nothing's going to change," I tell her softly. "I know you want to keep everyone's dignity intact, and say things in the right way, but sometimes the only right way to say something is to tell the truth. Louis has destroyed his own reputation. The only thing you're doing right now is trying to maintain the status quo."

"But what if it gets out and I'm just that one kid who can't take it?"

"Summer," I tilt her chin toward me. "You shouldn't have to take it in the first place. This is not a matter of you whining. This is a matter of you having the right to work without being harassed. Maybe it's time to tell Ana what you're feeling. Give her a bit of knowledge to work with. If Louis is willing to go this far with you, statistics say you're not the first."

Summer shivers in nervousness and buries her head into my shoulder. "Easier said than done."

I close my eyes and hold her tight. Pressing my face into her hair, I can't help but leave a gentle kiss to the side of her head. "If anyone can do it, you can. You're tougher than anyone thinks. Blow him away."

I look down at her, and I can see she's smiling.

SUMMER

I feel like my shoulders are relaxing for the first time in years. After dinner—creamy gnocchi soup is always a winner—we curl up on the couch for an action movie. It's an old favorite of both of ours, and that makes it fun. My head is in Chase's lap, and he's playing with my hair.

My relaxing shoulders probably have everything to do with Chase's ministrations, but I'm feeling a little lighter anyway. Simply hearing Chase tell me that what Louis is doing is wrong is a relief in and of itself. And his belief in me? It actually makes me think that I can report Louis *and* that it'll turn out okay.

I never thought I had trouble standing up for myself. I'm pretty chill about most things, but when I have a preference, I can talk about it. I guess I've never had someone actively trying to hurt me. It's a whole different experience.

Chase smooths my hair and catches a longer strand, his fingers brushing across my forehead as he gently pushes it away from my face. "Hey, Summer?"

I turn my head and look up at him. "Yeah?"

"You're off this weekend, right?"

"Yeah. We don't have any projects due, and we're up-to-date everywhere else. How come?"

"Do you want to go stargazing?"

I sit up, turning to him on the couch. He follows me with his eyes. "Really?" My voice comes out a little too earnest, and I pinch my lips together.

Chase puts his arm along the back of the couch, running his thumb over my shoulder. "Yeah. I have a friend with a cabin up on the mountain. He keeps his road in good condition, and it's supposed to be clear on Friday and Saturday."

"Will it be cold?"

"Yeah, but I was going to rent a truck to get up there anyway. I figured we could put a whole bunch of blankets in the back. It'd be more comfortable than chairs."

I think about the idea of spending time with Chase under the stars and can't help the smile growing across my cheeks. "Would this be our date?" I ask, my voice dropping. I don't know why I'm feeling so bashful now. We've kissed, for crying out loud. But this feels different somehow. It feels ... personal.

"Yes." He lifts his arm and I scoot myself closer, resting my head against his shoulder. The rumble of his deep voice is soothing. "It'll also be a good chance to cuddle as well."

I grin and lean my head back. "I'll look forward to it."

At the end of the night, it's hard to say goodbye to Chase. At least, I note as I drive away, leaving him waving on the sidewalk, I get a goodbye kiss. It was wonderful—I'm pretty sure it's physically impossible for a Chase kiss to be anything but—but I can't deny that I wish it was a little ... longer.

I blush furiously, even sitting by myself in the car, unable to stop grinning. I needed a reality check. Chase was being a perfect gentleman, especially considering he was really doing this as a favor to me and my therapist.

As I drive through the nearly empty streets, I let myself imagine what it would be like to kiss him for as long as I want to, and then I feel a little ashamed. It's not fair to Chase if I'm not as committed to keeping our limits as he is. He's already doing more for me than any one person ever has done, and it's like a slap in the face if I can't support him, too.

At least I know I can trust him. Boyfriend or not, I am completely safe with him. Not only that, it really feels like I've known him forever.

It's going to be so hard when all of this ends. It almost feels unfair—to learn what kind of love I could have, only for it to be completely one-sided. Then again, what's the old saying? It's better to have loved and lost than to never have loved at all?

It's hard to believe I could ever love someone else how I love Chase. I have a long life ahead of me, but if this is the only chance I get to love someone like this, I'm glad I get to have it.

Chapter 20
The Mountain

CHASE

I'M VIBRATING WITH EXCITEMENT BY THE TIME FRIDAY night rolls around. The sun is starting to lean heavily toward the horizon by the time I roll up in front of Summer's apartment, but she's already ready for me, her overnight bag over one shoulder, reddish brown hair wrapped into a braid and peeking out from under her oversized beanie.

In fact, Summer is bundled up like the world's most adorable, most fluffy snowman, and I can't help but smile as she practically waddles toward me. I hop out, running around the car in order to beat her to opening the door. She's not exactly the fastest land mammal on the planet in her snowsuit, but she gives it a good shot, laughing when I get there before her.

Taking her cold cheeks in my hands and wondering how long she'd been out there waiting for me, I whisper, "This is hello."

The kiss is sweet and wonderful, and altogether too short. But, not wanting to overstay my welcome in the name of therapy, I step back and open the doors for her.

"You can hop in," I tell her, stepping toward the sidewalk in order to grab her little overnight bag, trying not to notice the absolute mound of blankets she piles into the back seat of the truck. I've also brought a mound, but it's relatively hidden in the bed of the truck. My friend Jack is letting me borrow said vehicle. It has a truck bed cover, so I can keep everything clean and dry.

"That's okay," she says, her voice straining a touch, "I figure if I bring it, I should be responsible for it."

"Ahhh," I say in understanding. Then, stepping up behind her to help shove the tsunami of cozy apparatus into the truck, I lean down and whisper in her ear. "Does that mean I'm responsible for you?"

She turns around, bringing us chest to chest. Or rather, as close as her parka will allow. For a moment, I'm expecting her to be a little nervous at the closeness. Summer of a month ago would have been. But the Summer of now is more accustomed to my presence. She lets her eyes drift over my face and then smiles. "Well, I hope so. It's not like I've gone camping since I was sixteen."

I take a half step forward, putting my arms around Summer and pulling her close, partially deflating the parka. "Your mom didn't like camping?"

"My mom has been the church camp director for the last twenty-five years," Summer says evenly. "My dad could not be paid to sleep in a tent. Guess which parent I take after."

I snort and pull her a little closer. Summer lets her head lean against my shoulder. "How was work?" I ask.

She sighs, and her shoulders droop a little bit. "It could be better. I'm starting to compile everything so if nothing else, I have a record of it. But I didn't have time to talk with Ana about it today—one of my teammates was out so I did some of their work on top of mine to keep the project from getting behind."

I open my mouth and then close it. I know from coworker

and classmates' experiences that abuse is hard in any scenario, but even more tricky when your livelihood is messed up in the mix. I want to give Summer the space to work it out her way. But what if she doesn't? At what point can I—or should I—step in?

And what right do I have to do that in the first place? I'm not actually her boyfriend. Stepping in might shatter the trust we do have, and I'm not willing to give everything up simply to make myself feel better, especially if she's still willing and able to handle it on her own.

"I just worry," I say quietly, laying my head on hers.

Summer squeezes my torso a little tighter. "I know. I'm sorry."

"You don't have to be sorry. It's my privilege." Even if it's temporary.

We stay in each other's arms for a moment longer.

Summer leans her head back. "Thank you."

"Of course," I say, looking down at her and trying to resist the urge to kiss her. To distract myself I smile and let her go. "We should probably hit the road before too long."

Summer smirks. "Wouldn't want to miss the stars."

I laugh. It'll be clear all night. Still, we're both excited, and it only takes me and Summer a minute to finish getting all her stuff situated in the truck. Then we're headed southwest to Provo Canyon toward Vivian Park.

We're technically headed past the park, near South Fork Park, where another friend of mine has a cabin. I'm glad it's March. There'll still be snow up there, but the weather has been good the last couple of days, otherwise it would be crazy difficult to get up there. After seeing how excited Summer is, the last thing I want to do is disappoint her. I've already been up once today to make sure the cabin is clean and to set every-thing up.

One upside of living near the mountains, I guess. Even a little stargazing is only a half hour away. We don't technically have to visit a cabin to do it—just about anywhere where the light pollution doesn't reach us should be amazing—but not having to drive back in the middle of the night will be a plus.

Summer's smile is enormous when we get to the cabin—an elegant log A-frame, with huge windows facing into the valley. There's plenty of parking out front, perfect for stargazing. Lights from the neighbors won't be a problem—the nearest is nearly a mile away. Even the lights from the city are blocked by the mountains.

We go inside. Summer takes her stuff to one of the two bedrooms—the other of which I will be occupying for the night —and then comes out to help with dinner, the snowsuit shed for comfy sweats, her favorite gray hoodie, and the thickest, fuzziest cabin socks I've ever seen.

She grins at my quizzical look and shrugs. "I've never worn cabin socks in a cabin before. I wanted to do it justice." She turns on her woolen heel, her ponytail swinging behind her, and I can't help but grin.

It's nearly completely dark by the time we're ready to eat, and by the time we're done with our pasta, it is well and truly night outside.

"So," I say, putting the last of the dishes in the dishwasher. "I know you've brought a lot of blankets."

Summer lifts her eyebrows, wiping the last bit of the table. "I get cold." She says it nonchalantly and I nod knowingly, hiding my smile.

"Of course. Well, for your comfort this evening, I have completely packed the bed of my friend's truck with as many blankets as I could buy, borrow, or steal. You are welcome to bring yours out, or we could pile them on your bed for later when you inevitably get cold in the middle of the night."

Summer crosses the kitchen in a flash, sliding across the wood floor the last couple of steps with her cabin socks, swinging the rag at me with a big smile. I dodge. "Hey!" she says with a laugh. "I resemble that remark." Then she fixes me with a half-serious look. "So, I've been around all types. When you say you've 'completely packed' the bed of the truck, that means ...?"

"There's a literal foot of bedding in there," I clarify. "Seriously, if we're in the middle of them, we won't feel the cold or the truck bed."

Summer's eyebrows lift, and she leans back against the counter. "You took this rather seriously, didn't you?"

I don't even have to think about it, also leaning against the counter, a little further down. "You were excited about this. If I failed it would have been a black mark on my boyfriend record."

For a second, I'm a little worried Summer will point out I'm not her boyfriend for real at all, but her expression doesn't even flicker. "Well," she draws out the word, straightening and stepping closer to me. "We can't have that."

"Of course not," I say, turning and taking my own step forward.

She shakes her head, her smile widening. "Absolutely not."

I take one more step toward her and put my hands on her shoulders. I study her face, wondering what she's thinking with that impish smile dancing on her lips and that twinkle in her eyes. I'd better be careful. There's something in that look that makes me want to kiss her more than ever, and not our customary two-second peck.

"We should get dressed up, and head out," I say, my voice quieter and deeper than I intend.

Summer smiles, and nods, her head still tilted up towards mine. "Sounds good to me."

Neither of us move, before I take a deep breath and step away, hoping she doesn't notice the way I've been holding my breath. She doesn't seem to, and she quickly goes back to her room to put her snowsuit back on.

It takes us another twenty minutes to actually get out to the back of the truck. We have to turn out all the lights in the cabin and then clip the truck bed cover up so it won't fall on us while we're laying there, then actually get into the bed itself, leaving our boots on the tailgate.

"I have this terrible feeling it's going to feel absolutely frigid to put those back on," Summer says as she bundles down into the blankets. Then, approximately ninety-seven percent covered by said blankets, she sighs. "I'm pretty sure this is the comfiest thing I have ever laid down on."

I snort and scoot in beside her, moving close to make sure we share the pocket of warmth we're creating. "Don't fall asleep," I warn.

Her eyes pop open, barely visible in the blackness. "Oh? Why?" Her voice has a definite tenor of humor in it, and I debate not answering her just to see what she'll come up with.

"It'd defeat the point of bringing you out here," I say, settling down on my back, and looking up at the stars.

"Oh." She turns back toward the sky. "I thought you were going to say that you'd leave me out here, or the people you stole these blankets from will come and steal them back."

"I'd never leave you out here," I counter. "Andie would not approve. And saying I stole these would be like saying Joanie lent you a blanket and you took it."

Summer lifts up her head again. "These are Avery's?"

"Less than half," I say defensively. She turns her head in my direction. I shrug. "I might have gone on a shopping spree. Blanket shopping is fun. It's like the possibilities are endless."

Summer laughs. "And this is why I like you."

I laugh, but my heart stutters. I know that's not what she means, but it doesn't stop me from feeling like I've been launched onto cloud nine. Summer likes me.

"Nothing beats floating in a puffy, blankety cloud," I say, trying to keep the smugness out of my voice. This was a little ridiculous. She said she liked my blanket hoarding abilities. Was that even something to be proud of?

If Summer likes it ...

I shut the little voice down. This is not helping. *Think of something else, Merrill.*

"So," I say. "You're going to have to walk me through this stargazing thing. I've never been before."

Summer laughs. "Well, you know I haven't been either."

"Do you know the stars, though?"

"A bit," Summer admits. "Though it's mostly from going to the planetarium as often as I could as a kid. And as a teenager. And as an adult. Every so often when I was in college we'd go to the beach at night, but that was more so my friends could relax and listen to the waves than actual stargazing."

I suspect she's being humble. "So ... what's that one, then?" I manage to free my far hand from the mounds of blankets and point up at the sky. It's not exactly random, but pretty close.

"That one ..." Summer draws out the word as she thinks. "Is the constellation of Ursa Major."

I frown. "Um."

"Ursa Major means Great Bear."

I frown up toward the heavens. "I don't see anything close to a bear up there."

She smiles, and I feel her shift a little closer to me. Then, she points up at the sky. "It's part of the Big Dipper."

I look over at her, only a few inches away and shake my head. "Wait, where's the Big Dipper? I'm confused."

She laughs. "Scoot closer, I'll show you."

And she does. Somehow, I see the box of dim stars, and then she tells me about the Underground Railroad, and how they'd use it for navigation. She shows me how to use it to find the North Star. She shows me Orion, and Auriga, and Mars. She shows me Sirius, and Canis Major, and a dozen other things, until I'm in utter awe at the expanse I see in front of me.

Silence lapses between us, and for a long time we simply lay there, looking up at the heavens. It's the oddest feeling. Since breaking up with Amanda, I've felt like a walking disaster, like not only am I broken, but I'm going to stumble around making everything worse for everyone.

Shattered.

Toxic.

Small.

But now, here with Summer, staring up at the night sky, where I should feel the smallest I've ever felt in my entire life, I have never felt less tiny or unimportant. I feel seen. I feel understood. I feel loved.

Maybe that's not how she intends it. In fact, it's almost certainly not, but the love I feel for the woman looking at the stars with me is anything but insignificant or small.

I'm not a stranger to asking questions, but suddenly I want to know everything about her. Everything that makes her happy, or sad, or scared. I want to know what her fears are and make her feel safe. I want to know what her dreams are and make every single one of them come true.

I haven't felt like this about anyone else, and as frightening as that is, there's something about Summer that makes me more grateful than terrified. I can love people. I can connect. And it's beautiful.

At some point we start to talk. Most of it isn't significant stuff. I ask Summer what her favorite memory from being on the beach in Georgia is. She asks me what it's like running a company. I ask her the weirdest fact she knows. She asks me if I ever wanted to do something else with my life.

"Well," I say, thinking about it. "At one point I actually wanted to be a dog walker."

"What?"

"I was about ten," I admitted. "I think it was right before my dad got his first at-home computer. After that, I was hooked."

"Video games?" she asks lightly.

"I played a few, but they stress me out," I laugh. "No, I liked looking at all the graphics and screensavers."

Her head whips in my direction. "You were a screensaver kid? I was a screensaver kid! Dad's always had computers around, more as a hobby than anything else. I was always wondering how they worked. That's when my mom found a programming camp. I've been tinkering with computers ever since."

I grin and turn back to the sky. I almost miss Summer's quiet, sad statement. "I've missed out on a lot because of it."

I turn my head to look at her, and quiet falls between us. It's heavy, and I can almost hear Summer's thoughts.

Almost.

"Talk to me, Summer," I whisper.

She inhales, and it's a little shaky, and I can't help but reach out to her, turning onto my side and scooting a little closer in the darkness.

"I guess," she says, "it's the whole life truth that if you choose to do something, you choose not to do something else. It's not that I'm not happy—I promise. But there are some times I wish I'd chosen something else."

"Like what?" I ask.

"Like a relationship. Like a family." She's staring up at the star-strewn sky, but she angles her head to rest against my shoulder. "My mom's wrong, you know. She thinks I've been so preoccupied with my work and career that being a wife and a mother never even crossed my mind. The truth is I can't stop thinking about it. About how much I want it."

"But?"

"But it's not only my choice, is it? First there has to be a guy —which, given my profession isn't hard, but it hasn't clicked. Then there has to be mutual attraction, and I have the worst timing ever."

"You don't," I protest.

"No, really, I do." There's laughter in her voice, but it's self-deprecating. "Looking back over my life, I can definitely see how some guys across my lifetime have been interested, but so far, it's taken an average of four to ten years for it to really sink in and have me realize it. Obliviousness, thy name is Summer."

I laugh softly. "I wouldn't despair too much, Summer. Wasn't there a study at some point where people were asked if someone else were flirting with them, and were right less than fifty percent of the time?"

"Sounds about right," Summer grumbles. "For me, at least."

I lean my head against hers. Her skin is cool. We'll have to go in soon. "Well, speaking as a serial dater, I'm not sure if you've missed much."

"Apart from all the experience?" Summer asks. "And the feeling of belonging?"

"And the disappointment, and the confusion, and the misunderstandings?" I counter. "Dating is as much of a mixed bag as the people involved in it are. Do you know what I think?"

"What?" she asks.

"I think you want to be cherished," I say. "I think you want someone who will make you feel utterly wanted."

"I said that in therapy," she says quietly.

"And I agree with your self-assessment," I respond. "You want what a relationship should be, and I think that's a very special thing. I don't think many people can put it into words."

Summer looks up at me, and although it's dark, I can see the glimmer in her eyes. "I've had a long time to think about it."

"I know," I whisper, running a finger down her cheek. I don't know how she's waited this long. Summer is gorgeous, warm, and utterly wonderful. She's got so much love to give, and it is an absolute testament to the incredible lunacy of the male gender that this woman is still single.

But then, if someone had taken her, we never would have met. And even the thought of that makes me cold and breathless.

I need her.

I need Summer.

"Summer." My voice rumbles in my chest.

"Yes?" she whispers.

"May I kiss you?" I ask, my own whisper feeling altogether too loud in the silence. "Not a hello kiss. Not a goodbye kiss." I'm not sure how to explain in good taste that if she gives me permission, this will not be a grandmotherly peck.

Summer understands. "I'm not sure how," she admits, her voice even softer than before.

It's so vulnerable. So trusting. I don't deserve Summer.

"May I teach you?" I murmur. I'm frozen, wanting her to know how captivating she is, but refusing to let myself move an inch until she gives me wholehearted permission. I will not break her trust.

"Yes." The word is stronger than I anticipate. The knot in my chest releases, and my muscles relax. Lowering my head to hers, I press a kiss to her cool lips. I didn't realize she was so cold. I lift my head slightly to switch angles, and when she moves with me, we bump noses.

I pull back with a breath of laughter, but I can feel her stiffen. She scoots to a sitting position, still swathed in blankets, and I follow. She takes a deep breath.

"Sorry," she whispers. I sit up as well, putting my arm around her.

"Nothing to forgive. It's part of the experience," I whisper, pulling her closer. "Trust me."

"I do." She closes her eyes as I brush another kiss across her lips. Cradling her cold cheeks in my hands, I press kisses to the corner of her mouth, her top lip and bottom lip. After a moment, she kisses me back, as though she's feeling it out. Trying her hand at it.

She's a natural.

As I press another longer kiss to her lips, she sighs deeply and then grips my coat with her gloved fingers. "Chase," she whispers against my lips. It's half murmur and half plea and that's all I need. Encircling her in my arms, I deepen the kiss.

Suddenly, her shoulders tighten, and her hands grab fistfuls of parka.

I can't help the sudden stab of disappointment, but I'm not about to fail her now. I pull back and gently release her. "I'm sorry," I whisper, mortified. What a way of taking my own desires and overriding what she was telling me. But for the life of me, I thought she was okay with it.

"No." She shakes her head. "I'm sorry."

"I shouldn't have assumed it was okay." I'm probably babbling, but I don't care. Anything to make sure she's not self-conscious about keeping her boundaries. "I should have asked if you wanted to take it to another level. It's not what everyone likes—"

"Chase, that is *not* the problem," Summer says. She's holding her hands to her cheeks. Is she—is she blushing? It's too dark to tell for sure, but I'd bet money on it.

It takes me a minute to wrap my head around her words. Finally, my heart still hammering in my chest, I say, "What?"

"Chase, I think I'm taking advantage of you." Her words are breathless.

Her? Taking advantage of me?

"What?" It's a little too vehement, and I back off. "I'm sorry. Could you explain that to me?"

Summer shakes her head and buries her head in her gloved hands. "Liking the kissing or the—the techniques isn't the problem. I'm ... really, really enjoying it, and I feel like I'm taking advantage of you again."

She's enjoying it. She's enjoying it and she doesn't want to take advantage of me.

I shouldn't laugh. I really shouldn't, but I can't help it. It's small, but the huff is obvious in the silence. "Summer," I say, putting my arm around her again, "You aren't taking advantage of me. I started it. Kissing is meant to be enjoyed. If you like it, it means I'm doing a good job." Summer's shoulders relax, and I pull her closer, looking into her eyes. "No apologies necessary." I wait for a moment, before looking into her eyes and asking, "Do you want to continue?"

In response, she leans into me, her lips finding mine. It feels different this time, and it occurs to me that Summer has never kissed me before. I've always initiated each kiss. But now Summer is in control, and she seems born to it. She wraps her arms around my neck, pulling me close. My eyes drift closed, and I hold onto her for dear life, giving her as good as she's giving me. Summer is physically smaller than I am, but somehow, she is holding me, supporting me. It's like she's gained confidence, and it's everything I've ever needed.

The night blurs by, and by the time we head indoors, I am simultaneously too warm and too cold. As we quietly walk to our separate rooms, Summer smiles at me with lips that have obviously been thoroughly kissed. I don't dare kiss her good-night but instead pull into her a long hug.

"Goodnight, Sunny," I whisper.

"Goodnight, Chase," she responds, pressing her face into my shoulder.

And then we part ways. I lay in bed for a long time, reliving the evening, wondering how I'm possibly going to survive without Summer.

Chapter 21
The Coworker

SUMMER

I am addicted to Chase Merrill. I've been trying to deny it for the last four days, but considering I've seen him every day since then, my weak internal ponderings are too little too late. At least if I'd recognized it earlier, I would have had the desire to do something about it, but now it's more or less a lost cause.

I'm so much of a lost cause I can almost forget this is probably our last date before our therapy appointment tomorrow. Chase can't meet up tonight because he has a meeting with a couple of overseas clients, and even though I have hobbies, part of me wonders whether I could at least hang out with him at the office until he finishes.

But I've never actually breached his office, and I don't think the last night we have together is the best time to do that—particularly since I don't know if it's allowed anyway, security-wise.

But now I'm back at the first coffee shop we met at, and I've gotten here first for once. Getting out of my car by myself, I walk over to the front overhang, and wait for him there, watching the gentle snow shower. I watch the big fluffy flakes fall, grateful the storm had waited until after Saturday.

Saturday.

I can't help the smile that crosses my cheeks. Unconsciously, my hand rises to my lips, and I can still remember the feeling of Chase's lips on mine. Part of me is still a little worried I've taken advantage of him, but he certainly showed as much enthusiasm as I did.

If it was anyone other than Chase, I might have even been a little worried about their motivations. But this is Chase. We both know what we're in for, and let's face it, it was a great journal entry. Andie will be thrilled.

It doesn't take away from the fact I desperately wish it was real, but even if it's not romantically, I know Chase has my back.

I stamp my feet—which are encased in my three-inch battle heels—trying to warm them, wishing I'd worn something different. I plan on going to go see Ana today about Louis. I still feel uneasy about this whole thing, but I know Chase is right—what Louis is doing isn't right, and if he's willing to go this far with me, I'm probably not the first to be affected by him.

That being said, these battle-heel-encased feet are currently freezing, and I idly wonder whether or not I should have waited for Chase in the car.

I've no sooner thought this, when Louis Granger steps out of the coffee shop.

I *definitely* should have waited for Chase in the car. I'm already going to confront Ana about him at work, why can't I avoid him here as well? Maybe he hasn't seen me. If I turned my back ... I would still be the only person standing here under the eaves of the coffee shop, instead of doing the sensible thing and heading inside.

And, before I can make any sort of decision one way or the

other, he looks up and sees me. His almost-handsome face twists into a sneer, and he sidles up to me.

"Well, well, well, if it isn't Miss Truant."

I've been putting up with this for close to a month. I've received his texts, listened to all his under-the-breath comments, and put up with passive-aggressive notes on projects he shouldn't even be looking at. It's different in person. Outside of work. And it's suddenly very, very difficult to not give him a piece of my mind.

"Oh, Louis," I say, trying to give the impression I hadn't seen or heard him. "You're on your way out. Have a good lunch."

"On your way to meet the boyfriend, are you?"

I pause as I step past him. He hasn't moved, and I take two slow steps back. For some reason I don't want to turn my back on him. Not because I'm worried he'll hurt me, but for some reason, it feels like I'm backing down, and I don't want to do that anymore.

"As a matter of fact, yes," I say evenly.

"Nice to know your dedication to work comes first."

"Yes, well, even I have to eat." I say it before I can help it. It's suddenly so ridiculous and infuriating. *Even I have to eat.* Of course I do. And I have a right to have feelings for someone. I have a right to be treated well. I have a right to be viewed as a professional, and no lowlife like Louis Granger has the right to change that.

"Maybe someone so new at their job wouldn't understand, but I worked through every lunch for the first year as a team lead in order to make sure my team was performing up to standard," he says, glaring at me.

"Well," I say quietly. "That was your choice."

"That's the expectation," he snaps. "And if you think Ana

doesn't notice and judge you for your lack of dedication to their work, then you've—"

"I'll have you know I spoke to Ana at the beginning of this, and she encouraged me not to take overtime as much as possible," I say calmly. "My work schedule, and the way I manage my time are none of your business. Neither is my personal life, nor how I spend my time outside of work. I have the good fortune to have someone who cares deeply about me, who I like to spend time with, and I will continue to choose to spend that time with him. If there is a time when I need to work overtime, I will take it and be dutiful, but you have no say over when that happens. You have no say over me, and you have no right to insult me or call me names if I make different choices than you."

"If that's the way you feel about it, you shouldn't have become a team lead. The company needs people who are dedicated, willing to put in the long hours to get things done." Louis steps forward. I hold my ground.

"I complete my work on time," I say, sharper than before. "My team is ahead of schedule, and our error occurrence rate is lower than yours. Don't think I haven't noticed you accessing things after hours. Everything is logged, Louis. I can see what you've looked through and your 'adjustments.' After the incident with YellowPlay and Jack, I got suspicious and I looked through the program. His name wasn't on those adjustments, Louis. You were the last person to log on there."

Louis blanches and then reddens. I've made him well and truly angry now. Part of me wants to retreat, but part of me hears Chase's words in the back of my head.

Blow him away.

Yes, sir.

"Are you threatening me?" Louis demands.

"No," I say, my voice quieting. "I'm informing you I have

seen your involvement, and when I come back from lunch today, I will be reporting you, your actions, and your abuse to Ana. I'm done with this. I'm done with you."

Louis growls and steps forward. "You'd better watch what you say to me, or you'll regret it."

I step forward once. Because of my battle heels, I'm looking down at him, feeling every inch the professional I know I am. "Bring it on," I say mildly.

He doesn't have a ready response, staring at me for a long, stunned moment. Then he swears at me. And then swears at me again. I stand there, unmoved, frowning down at him, daring him to make a move. Then he glances over my shoulder, and Louis Granger goes white.

CHASE

It's not every day I walk up to a situation where a man is actively abusing my girlfriend. I stand a little ways down the sidewalk, watching the situation carefully, making sure Summer isn't in any physical danger. Although, with the way she's laying into him, I wouldn't put it past her to deck him if he makes a move.

And then Louis sees me. I know in a moment that he recognizes me—his face goes white, and the foul curse he's spitting at Summer dies mid-breath. I raise my eyebrows, not moving, not speaking. I'm absolutely sure Summer doesn't need me to stand up to him, but I think Louis needs to know Summer isn't the only person who knows about him.

It takes Louis three full seconds to get his act together. Snapping his mouth shut, he turns on his heel and storms away, his face turning a deep shade of red.

Summer stands there, watching him get in his car and driving away, still unaware of my presence. She heaves a big sigh.

It's time to announce myself. "I want to clap," I say, not moving toward her. "But I don't know if it's appropriate in a public venue."

Summer turns around, her loose hair swishing around her shoulders as she turns. There's an instant where I can see the stress and the hardness Louis's encounter has brought up, but it melts away as she sees me, and she smiles.

I know two things. One: I love Summer Weathers, and Two: Boss Chick looks good on her. Most everything does, but the confidence in her eyes is downright stunning.

She walks up the sidewalk toward me, slowly, almost as though she's exhausted. When she meets me, she slides her arms around me, relaxing into me.

"Are you all right?" I ask.

"Yes," she says into my shoulder. She's shaking a little, and I don't think it's from the cold.

"Are you sure?"

"Yes. Being brave is tiring. Being brave and kind of angry is even more tiring."

I tighten my hold around her. "I'm proud of you. Confronting him is the first step."

She sighs. "Ana will hear about this before I get back."

I still. "Do you have the proof you need?"

Summer nods into my shoulder. "I have copies of everything. Printouts, digital copies, saved copies. He can't go into the system and change things—he's key logged when he accesses anything. Frankly, I'm kind of shocked he didn't think of it."

I'm proud of her. "Good thought on backing it up."

She nods. We're silent for a few moments, before she asks in a quiet voice. "Why me?"

I think about it. "I don't know. He probably thought you were vulnerable. Boy, was he wrong."

Summer shakes her head. "I was at the beginning of this. I was new to the position. He knew I was lying about the boyfriend somehow. I was vulnerable."

I frown, not liking that answer. Today is me and Summer's last full day together. What will happen to her after tomorrow? Is she going to become vulnerable again? What if someone tries to do this again?

"At least I know what to do now," she whispers. "Because of you." Then she pulls back, looking up at me. She's closer to me than before because of those high heels, and I am here for it. She gives me a small half-smile and says, "This is hello." And then she leans forward and kisses me. Then, after our customary far-too-short two seconds, she pulls back. Looking me in the eyes, she says seriously, "And this is thank you."

Her lips meet mine, and I close my eyes, relishing the sensation. I wind my hand underneath her hair, cradling the back of her head, pulling her ever closer as I kiss her in return.

Finally, after what is probably too long on a public sidewalk, I lean back, breaking the kiss. "This is the best reward I've ever gotten for just standing around."

Summer shakes her head. "You've supported me since the beginning of this. I wouldn't have done it if you hadn't told me to report it. It's taken me a bit of time to get there, but this confidence is in good part because of you."

I shrug. "Still, the best reward for—"

She laughs and leans in, kissing me again.

After another moment, we realize we should probably go in and get some food before our respective lunch breaks run out. We talk about Lacy, Summer's parents, Avery, even Joanie. But nothing about work. Nothing about the future. It's setting in that this is the last time I'm going to be able to sit across from her and listen to her little anecdotes and watch her eyes light up.

Part of me wants to ask her not to end it. I know there's no one else in the picture—we'll both be single after this, and we've both enjoyed our time together.

But I shove the thought down. I came into this to get therapy, and I have. That's all Summer expects of me. We've had fun, and I know we're good friends now, but if I suggest a relationship now, I feel like it would be betraying her trust. Like doing a bait and switch with boyfriends and relationships. Crossing a line that should not be crossed.

And so, the lunch date passes far too quickly, and finally we have to say our goodbyes. We walk outside, and I place a lingering kiss on her lips, running my hand over her hair, before cradling her face in my hands.

"Do you need me to go to work with you?" I ask, completely serious.

She shakes her head. "I'm pretty sure Louis is crazy, but he's not physical violence crazy. Especially not at work."

I frown. I'm not so sure, but she's right. He's more inclined to words and sabotage. Like that's so much better.

"Well, then," I say quietly. "Be brave. I'll be there in a moment if you need me. Just call."

Summer presses her lips to mine. I hold her there, taking her in—her scent, her taste, her touch.

And then Summer pulls away. "I will," she says. "I promise."

SUMMER

I stride into work with my head held high. I don't go to my workspace, beelining straight toward Ana's office. She's just getting to her own door, apparently only having gotten back from lunch as well. She looks surprised at my appearance.

"Ana?" I say quietly. "We need to talk."

I show her everything. The text messages, the notes, the logs. She pulls up the data entry in the files, and everything is still there. Ana tries to call Louis's desk, but he doesn't pick up.

Pat, a member of Louis's team, pops his head out of his office. "Hey, Ana, do you need something from Louis? He hasn't come back from lunch yet."

Ana frowns. "Didn't he leave like two hours ago?"

Pat nods, but shrugs. "I haven't heard anything. I guess something came up?"

Ana's frown doesn't ease, and she looks down at everything. "Do you have printouts of everything?"

I nod. "With time stamps."

"Get me the physical copies and also send them to me by email. I'll look into this."

Something in my chest eases, and my throat tightens. Suddenly, it's a little hard to keep tears from welling up. "Thank you."

Ana looks at me, all good humor in her face long since gone. "Thank you for coming forward. This isn't the first time this has happened."

Chapter 22
The Sixth Appointment

CHASE

I'm early to therapy, and I don't know why.

It's been a strangely normal day. Nothing's gone wrong. In fact, things are going very well. I've even gone so far as texting Avery to that effect.

> Avery: Bold of you to invoke Murphy's Law. You realize that everything's going to hit the fan after lunch, right?

I think about that. I'm standing outside my car, waiting for Summer to arrive. It's almost warm outside, and I'm enjoying the feeling of the sun on my face. It flies in the face of what's going to happen today, and how Avery is absolutely right.

> Me: I'll take my chances.

> Avery: Bold. Very bold.

There's a long moment of silence, where I'm just listening to the birds singing and the cars driving by on the freeway. The calm is hitting my soul just right, and I don't know why. I know what will happen later today, but I don't want to think about it.

Avery: You seem happier.

Me: Uh, thanks?

Avery: Summer has been good for you.

I look down at the text, feeling the simultaneous joy and twisting pain in my chest. I can't think about what comes after lunch.

Me: I think I love her.

I brace myself waiting for Avery's response. She's most likely going to go into raptures.

She surprises me.

Avery: Are you going to tell her?

I stare at the text.

Me: I don't know. It's complicated.

Avery: Why?

I don't have an answer to that. Not one that I can tell Avery.

Chase: I don't know.

Summer drives into the parking lot, Jennie complaining as she comes, distracting me from my phone. Shaking off the conversation, I smile as the red Crown Victoria comes to a stop a couple of spots away, and jog over to open the door for her.

Summer's smile is wide as she meets my eyes, and more relaxed than I've seen it in weeks. A knot in my chest relaxes. I already know she's met with Ana, her assistant manager—Summer called me last night about their meeting—but seeing it in her face releases tension I didn't know I'd taken on.

I open the door and offer my hand. Summer takes it, standing up and stepping close to me.

I give her a grin, meant only for her. "This is hello," I murmur, and press a kiss to her lips.

We've graduated from the two-second kisses of before. It's probably not what either of us would normally do in a parking lot, but it's almost empty, there's a good chance our therapist is watching, and I don't know if I'll get another hello kiss from Summer.

Because today's the last day of therapy. Our final appointment.

Part of me is ecstatic. We've done it. We've fooled the therapist. I was able to go to therapy. I have made the best of friends in Summer.

No, I've fallen in love with Summer.

If it were any other circumstances, I would broach the topic. What if we didn't break up? What if we ... kept on dating? But it never seems right.

There's a couple of reasons. Despite having progressed to the point where I don't think I'm toxic anymore—not perfect, just not unrepentantly terrible—I'm a little worried I only think that way because of Summer. What if I spend time away from her and date other women and fall into the same old habits? Or, we *are* going to a relationship therapist. What if the reason why I fell for Summer in the first place is because the therapist convinced me I was in love?

Or even worse—we've been very close physically. What if I've fallen in love with her because she was the one I was hugging and kissing? Physical attraction isn't going to make a relationship work. What if I've fooled myself, and she's unaffected? She knew what we were getting into. She's probably better at keeping her brain compartmentalized.

On the other hand, would Summer tell me if she wanted more? She's been so worried about my consent with everything in this relationship, from cuddling to kissing, what if she's afraid to even ask for a real relationship?

And yet ... I'm not convinced. Part of me whispers I could be right, there could be something real, something *permanent* between us, but there's enough serious doubt there to keep my mouth shut. No matter how much I want to ask.

So instead, I focus on right now, where I'm standing here, Summer in my arms. I know that by the end of today I will not have this. I will focus on nothing but her.

I finally pull back, but I don't loosen my hold. Summer rocks back on her heels, a large smile on her face. I trace my thumb along the edge of her bottom lip.

"You look happier today," I note.

Summer tips her head to the side. "I talked to Ana yesterday after we got back from lunch, and we've spent most of the time since then gathering my case. We talked to HR this morning. And Louis."

I frowned. "How did he take it?"

"About how you'd expect. It's not ... it's not looking good for him." She looks faintly troubled, and I duck my head to look at her more clearly.

"Why don't you sound happy about that?" I ask.

Summer sighs and shrugs. "I didn't go into this to get him fired. I only wanted him to leave me alone. The way he's acting after all of this came out, he's just making it worse."

Something tickles in the back of my brain at that, but I'm too focused on Summer to know exactly what it is.

"Well, it sounds like he's making his choices," I say. "There's nothing you can do to change that. If you could, you wouldn't be in the middle of all of this."

Summer pulls a face. "No joke. He did try to blame it on me. He was calling me all sorts of stuff." She must feel my shoulders and arms tightening with anger, and she smiles. "Like I said, he's not making it any better for himself. Actually, the best part of today was when Ana trotted out my team statistics versus his since I started, and I've been outperforming him. I didn't even know. I wasn't doing it for something like that—I was just doing my job."

I grin and lean into Summer, pressing a kiss to her forehead. "Good girl. Way to stick it to him."

She relaxes in my arms. "It's even more obvious because he's been going in after hours and putting bugs into the programs on purpose. They think he was trying to make me want to leave. Or get fired."

"Are they firing him?"

"I don't know," she says, not moving. "It's not my decision, and I'm not going to put that on my shoulders. He is a good worker. He does know what he's doing. But he's also made his own choices, and that's not my responsibility."

I hug her a little closer to me, bending down and pressing a kiss to her cheek. "That's my girl."

We stay in each other's arms until it's time to go in. We both seem oddly reluctant today, like we know when we walk out of that building in an hour, everything will be different. At this point I don't even know if it'll be for the better. We haven't talked about it, but I wonder if I'll even see her after this. She probably doesn't want to hang around the guy who practically begged to go to therapy with her.

Even if she did, would I want to if we weren't in a relationship? Could I handle just being friends with her?

The not-so-distant memory of her kiss floods through me as I look down at her, and I know it's impossible. I love this woman, and if I cannot be with her, I must stay as far away as I can.

Which means today is goodbye.

Summer takes my hand and walks with me across the parking lot. She doesn't seem to be affected by any of this—further proof this is the best decision. She talks about Lacy and her dad, and how she's going to try this new little taqueria that opened up further south in the valley. I answer as casually as I can, trying to match her enthusiasm, and probably failing miserably.

"How's everything with Amanda?" she finally asks. Ah, the only thing—other than our imminent separation—I didn't really want to talk about. Then again, this is Summer. If anyone will understand, it'll be her.

"She's messaged again, after I told her I didn't want to talk about it." I look around the parking lot as we near the door. "I'm debating answering her for a second time."

"Do you think it'll help from a closure standpoint?" Summer asks, stopping before we reach the entrance.

"I don't know," I say honestly. "I don't know if it'll help or dredge up things that I'd rather not think about or experience again."

"That makes sense." Summer takes a deep breath of the cold, outdoor air and shrugs. "Well, that's ultimately up to you. Not every relationship has proper closure, does it?"

It's like it's the death knell of our relationship, but I can't let her see. I won't let her see the twisted mess of what's left of my heart. "You're right. I'll probably journal about it. See what I come up with."

Summer looks contemplative. "You know, I don't know how you'd feel about this, but I bet Andie could find you a regular therapist. You know, if you feel like you need one after this. I'm thinking about it myself."

I lift my eyebrows. "Really?"

Summer hums. "I'm finding there's some stuff I could benefit from working through. It's not that I'm suffering or anything, but ..."

"Tools in the toolbox?" I finish.

Summer smiles gently. "Yeah."

I reach out, running my hand down her arm. *Please read my mind and know how much I care for you. If you're scared, please believe in me. Please,* I plead in my head, *I don't want to say goodbye.*

But Summer is no more of a mind reader than I am, and we finally make our way into the building.

Andie, like always, is thrilled to see us. "Oh, look at you two, my two favorite patients on their last day."

Summer and I exchange looks. Summer's smile looks bright, but I feel like mine's as brittle and fake as a frozen plastic flamingo.

"Here we are!" Summer says.

Andie beckons us into her office, and just like the other appointments, we hand over the journals. She glances through our entries, smiling at a couple of remarks—she's too far away for me to read what part she's at, but if I was a betting man, I would bet she's reading our cabin entry. I believe the exact verbiage is "We kissed. A lot ;-)."

After the journal entries, she does a bit more follow up. It all feels so normal. I want to take the therapist by the shoulders and say, 'You're supposed to be a professional, can't you tell how miserable I am?' But I sit there and answer the questions. I share. I participate. Firstly, because we are still in therapy, and I have a promise to uphold. Secondly, because I walked in here with a perfect stranger, and Andie simply thought we had a terrible relationship.

But her advice has been good. I feel more attuned with everyone now. Even at work a few weeks ago, I had a moment with a team member where instead of brushing off the feeling she was having a bad day, I asked about it, and I found out that she'd lost her dog recently. I couldn't fix it, but her cubicle neighbor said the consolation flowers from the company had really touched her. I'm also feeling closer to Avery. I'm even planning on reaching out to my parents. Their absence is painful, but I don't know if they realize it.

And then, after what simultaneously seems like an eternity and the blink of an eye, therapy is almost over, and Andie leans back in her chair, looking at the two of us.

"I am so happy for you two," she says, her voice soft and genuine. "I don't know I've ever seen two people more committed than you two are. You have it in you to make it as a couple, as long as you keep on working at it.

"Now, even though we're not going to see each other again, I do have one more question for the two of you: Where do you see this relationship going? Long term. You don't have to answer me, but I want you to think it over and discuss it soon. I know from earlier sessions marriage is important to the two of you, at least individually. Where and when that happens, and if it happens to be to each other, what hurdles would need to be overcome? What questions do you two still have that need to be answered before you take that next step?"

Summer and I sit there in silence. I can't quite look over at her. Marriage to Summer. In the split second I allow myself to imagine that possibility, I know it couldn't be an immediate thing, but in the future? I see the flash of a beautiful woman dressed in white in front of me. She has Summer's smile, and Summer's red-brown hair.

And then I cut the dream off. Because that's all it is—a dream. I can't torture myself with something I could never have.

Though I would throw myself at that possibility if I had the slightest confirmation Summer cared the same way about me.

Just say something, and I'd do it. I would be yours forever, I promise her, as I look at her sitting next to me. *Just say something.*

"I know it's a lot to think about," Andie says with a smile. "But you two are becoming great communicators. Even if you're not ready or are scared to talk about it right now, I hope in time you will be. Benjamin Mee once said, 'Sometimes all you need is twenty seconds of insane courage. Just literally twenty seconds of just embarrassing bravery. And I promise you, something great will come of it.'"

Andie looks at the two of us. "I am so, so proud of you. This concludes your sessions. Good luck out there."

SUMMER

It's clouded over by the time we step out of the door to the office, hand in hand. It seems natural now to be holding his hand, to be close to him.

But it's over.

We did it.

We fooled the therapist.

And I feel terrible.

I've been trying to put on a brave face. To focus on the positive—finishing therapy, the situation with Louis getting sorted out, and simply being able to be here with Chase. But it feels like the ability to be happy is slipping further and further away.

I know this is goodbye.

He hasn't said he doesn't want to see me again, but I know if I can't be with him, have Chase hugs and Chase kisses, any sort of proximity would be pure torture. It would turn a beautiful friendship into a painful nightmare, and as much as I don't want to say goodbye, I can't do that to myself.

But I'm ... I'm scared. I'm scared I got caught up in the moment. In his touch and his kiss, and in the therapy, and the focus on building something based solely on a lie. And Chase ... he's so perfect. He's warm and loving, but I know that's just how he is. As much as he's been willing to teach me how to be a good partner, to teach me how to be loving, I'm not convinced it's been his love for me. Or at least, for more than just therapy.

We walk across the parking lot slowly. The wind is starting to blow, and dark blue clouds are approaching across the valley. Old dead leaves, the last offerings of the trees, a last-ditch sacrifice to appease the winter, skate across the ground as we finally reach my old Crown Victoria.

He stands close, blocking the wind, the collar of his black wool coat flipping up. He reaches out and takes my hands in his, warming my fingers.

"I don't know ..." he trails off and looks down at my hands. "It's probably not a good idea to meet up after this, huh? With the breakup and all."

The break up. Right. Tears prickle at the back of my eyes, and I clear my throat. I will not cry in front of him. I can't. Suddenly, his touch is too much, too painful. It's tearing my heart out, and if I don't break contact, there's no way I can walk away.

"Yeah," I say, dropping my hand from his. I try to smile, but I know it probably seems half-hearted. Chase's face falls.

Pull it together, Summer, I scold myself. *You're not angry at him. You're just going to miss him. So, so much.*

"It'd be a little difficult to explain." It sounds hollow in my ears. "Long term. To everyone."

Chase nods. "Agreed."

I want him to protest. To say he doesn't want to break up at all. That he wants to love me and cherish me until the day I die.

Joanie's voice floods through my brain. *Sometimes that's not enough, Summer. He has to want to be with you, too. Otherwise, it's not fair.*

He doesn't speak.

I want to tell him something, anything. Anything to keep him here longer, before we go our separate ways. "I know you said no at the beginning," I say, trying to keep my voice from breaking. "But if you want, I can pay you for all of this. You've done so much, and put in so much effort—"

"No," he says. It's a gentle exhale, but when I look up into his eyes, they're intense. "No, Summer. The therapy ... it's been so much more than I could have hoped for. If nothing else, I'm indebted to you."

My heart sinks. Indebted. It sounds so formal. So, this is where we're going. Back to business. Back to the way it was before. I don't want it to be. I don't want to leave Chase behind. But I can't force him into something he doesn't want. I love him too much for that. And as much as it hurts, I respect myself too much for that, too. So, I take a deep breath.

"We should make a clean break of it, then," I say, as much as declaration to myself as anything.

He nods, his expression serious. "It'd probably be for the best."

I press my lips into what could probably pass as an encouraging smile. "Yeah, it would."

He looks at me for a long moment, and for a second, I think he's going to say something.

But he never does.

Instead, he reaches for my car door handle. My heart breaks. Pulling it gently open, he looks down at me. His gaze is still tender, still kind, but there's something there I don't recognize, and I can't place what it is.

He looks down at his hand on the handle, and then back into my eyes. "I think this is where I leave you, then," he says. And he gives me a small smile. "I guess ... this is goodbye."

Chase gives me a small kiss on the cheek. And then he walks to his car, gets in, and drives away.

Chapter 23
The Problem Pt. 2

SUMMER

It shouldn't be sunny in April. When I think of April, I think of grey skies, and rainstorms, and late snowstorms and basically anything that will keep those ridiculous flowers in the ground. But no. It's the first week of April, and the sun is bright and shining. The birds are singing. The daffodils are blooming.

It's the worst.

I'm staring at the computer screen, trying to focus on the work in front of me. I should be working on my new project, which is due in the next week and a half. Instead, I'm barely getting by pretending I don't know the reason why I feel like I'm about to cry.

After all, everything is going fine now. Ana and I have kept in contact with HR, and with all of my evidence, and the fact that Louis tried to fight HR—by some accounts, literally—Louis got very, very fired.

It turns out he's not only done this to me, but the team lead Louis had replaced. She was also a young woman—who, admittedly, I didn't know very well—and she hadn't wanted to step forward.

At least, not until I did.

The sheer amount of justice that has rained down on Louis Granger has been cathartic.

Also, considering the sabotage he was involved in on my projects, there are even rumors the company might sue Louis. But those are only rumors. I told them I'd cooperate however I need to, but I'm not on a witch-hunt.

Mom and Dad took the news of me and Chase's breakup well. I'd told them a couple days after it had happened, when I went to family dinner alone. All I could manage was, 'It didn't work out." They didn't press for details.

Zen ... I'm not sure how she took it. At first, she looked shocked, and then there was this long moment of silence where she seemed to see into my soul. She had taken me into her arms and held me for a long time, and it was all I could do to not burst into tears.

It was then I had realized the reality of the situation: I'm depressed. And it doesn't take a genius to realize why.

I miss Chase. I miss his hugs, his reassurance, and, although I'm caught between blushing and crying every time I even think it, his kisses. I miss his company, his jokes, and I even miss his ridiculously gorgeous, dust-mopped house. I was worried I would regret becoming so close to him, but I don't. Instead, I think I made a mistake about not telling him how I feel.

But how could I? Even now, in the middle of my regret, I can see it wasn't the right thing at the time. But if not then, when should I have done it? The night on the mountain? The first time we kissed? Neither of those feel right either. But it doesn't feel right to be without Chase. Life just feels ... empty.

It's almost the end of the workday now. Forcing myself to

focus, I go through my teammates' work—which is, as always, almost-error-free. In fact, now that Louis isn't in there messing everything up, we've started a days-without-errors board. We've only gotten up to two days so far, because bugs and coding go hand in hand, but it's done marvelous things for focusing us as a team. It's one of the things I'm trying to focus on rather than Chase.

I have to drag my attention back from where it's been wandering several times before the day finally ends. Ana waves at me from her office as I walk past, and I wave halfheartedly in her direction.

She knows I broke up with Chase. She feels bad.

So do I.

I walk down the stairs and then out the door into the parking lot. I try not to sigh. It's even warm out here. Shucking off the coat I'd hoped I would need, I sigh and head to my car. I've just unlocked the door to the Crown Victoria, yanking the door open, when someone speaks behind me.

"Summer? Summer Weathers?"

The feminine voice startles me, and I turn toward the sound of the voice. There's a young woman standing by some sort of mid-sized vehicle. She's classically gorgeous, with perfectly straight long brown hair, and bold red lipstick. I can't see the color of her eyes, but her sunglasses, which look expensive, are practically opaque. I do know one thing, though—I don't know this woman.

I shift, still holding onto the door. "That's me," I say. "Can I help you?"

The young woman walks forward. Even though I can't see her eyes, she looks like she's early-to-mid-twenties. She's wearing four-inch black stilettos, and an asymmetrical black dress. The whole effect makes her look incredibly important, and I try not to fold my arms in discomfort.

"I was told you were dating Chase Merrill."

Suddenly, I know who this is. I stare at her for a full two seconds before, in a dizzying reversal, I find myself blisteringly angry instead of sad. Tossing my coat and bag across the front seat of my car, I slam Jennie's door shut.

"Well, Amanda," I say flatly, walking up to her, "whoever told you was wrong. We broke up. About two weeks ago."

The brunette doesn't seem perturbed I know her name, or my sudden shift in mood, but I'd dearly love to know the name of the person who told her about Chase and me.

She folds her arms. "I need you to give him a message from me."

I frown. "I'm not in contact with Chase anymore." It's a fact that stabs me every time I think about it, but it's true.

"I need you to get in contact with Chase." She says it like she hasn't heard me. I actually stop moving and stare at her, because I cannot believe what she just said to me. Not that I didn't think she had the audacity, but I didn't think she'd have the audacity to dictate to someone she'd never met before, let alone her ex's ex.

"No," I tell her.

"What?"

"No," I repeat myself. "I don't want to do that."

Amanda frowns at me. "You don't want to do that?" It's like she's repeating a sentence in a foreign language.

"No."

"He's not answering my messages," she whines. It probably is supposed to sound plaintive, but I've heard way too much about this woman's 'relationship' with Chase to believe it.

"What a pity," I say dryly. "What does that have to do with me?"

"I was told he'd answer if you texted him." Amanda flips her hair over her shoulder.

"I doubt it," I say, wishing it wasn't true. Actually, I don't know if it is, but the last person in the world I will try it out for is Amanda.

"I don't think so," Amanda said. "I have it on very good authority Chase would answer if it was you texting him."

I glare at her, the words digging in like knives. My sadness fuels my already simmering anger, which flashes. I take a deep breath to control myself. "Well, then. It's a very great pity you're not me, isn't it?"

She looks shocked for a moment. "I was told you—"

I'm done talking. All I want in my near future is a large bowl of ice cream and to watch my favorite TV show. Preferably, as soon as possible. "Amanda, I don't care what you were told." My voice is clear and cold, and she stops, those sunglasses staring back at me blankly. "Do you know what I was told about you?"

I shouldn't go there. It's Chase's insecurity, and the last thing I want to do is feed this madwoman. But a very clear boundary needs to be drawn here. If Chase were present, he would try to do it as diplomatically as possible, so he didn't hurt Amanda's feelings.

I'm not Chase.

"I heard," I say, "when you broke up—after cheating on him for several months—you told Chase he was old, boring, and toxic. That you were glad you broke up."

Amanda's mouth dropped open.

I tilt my head expectantly. "Am I wrong?"

I'm not, and she doesn't answer. Her jaw is still dangling, and it gives me strength. "I don't know what hold you think you have over him, but you don't. He's told me about what he went through with you, and how it affected him afterward, so we could avoid having a relationship like the one you gave him. And you know what? Turns out, he's not boring. Or toxic. And if you think thirty-five years old is old, I'm guessing you're a little too young to appreciate him."

Amanda takes a deep breath, full of bluster. She's probably going to deliver some sort of cutting remark. She doesn't know I've put up with coworker abuse for the last three months. She could literally call me anything under the sun, and it wouldn't faze me.

I put up a hand. "I don't care what you feel. I'm guessing either your new boyfriend cheated on you, or you're realizing what a good thing you had and lost. I honestly don't care. But leave Chase alone."

Amanda bristles. "You're not even dating him anymore! You said it yourself!"

I shrug. "You're right."

"If you hate him so much, why are you standing up for him?" She takes off her sunglasses, and frowns at me.

I take a deep breath. "Because I don't hate him. I've never hated him." I take a deep breath. "I love Chase Merrill more than I could ever love anyone else. And because of that, I will never help you."

"I wanted to say I'm sorry!" she exclaims, stamping her foot.

I turn and yank open Jennie's door. "Then find another way. You convinced the man I love he was broken, when the only thing wrong with that relationship was you. Do it yourself or leave him alone."

Then I climb in, slam the door shut, and drive away.

I don't go home. At first, I find myself driving towards Chase's house, but I immediately pull a U-turn and head in the opposite direction. I didn't realize my mom's house lies in the other direction until, without really thinking about it, I pull Jennie up in front of the brick-lined drive.

And everything caves in on me.

I didn't cry when Chase left. I'm not much of a crier anyway, but I didn't think I was supposed to. After all, he wasn't my real boyfriend, and I wasn't really supposed to have feelings for him. But sitting there in the Crown Victoria, looking at the ridiculous happy flowers in the ridiculous happy sunshine, it pounds down on my head like a waterfall.

It's true. All of it.

I love Chase Merrill more than I could ever love anyone else.

I miss Chase.

I miss him so much. So much I can barely breathe.

I don't want him to date Amanda. I don't want him to listen to Amanda. I want her to leave him alone.

I want him to date me.

I want him to love me.

Tears are streaming down my face, and I'm sobbing so hard my chest hurts. I'm grasping the steering wheel, holding myself forcibly upright, when the passenger side door opens.

It's Mom.

She seems to know. She's holding a box of tissues—the good kind, with lotion and aloe—and she offers it to me as she slides into the car. Her curls bounce a little as she tilts her head to the side, and she sighs.

"Oh, sweetie."

For once it's not cloyingly sweet. For once, it's not pity. There's understanding there, and compassion, and that ends every bit of control I've ever had. I reach out for her, and she holds me in her arms, rocking me from side to side as I sob into her shoulder. Holding me up. Being there for me.

It's something I've forgotten in all of this. The reason why she kept sending me those blind dates. Why she kept signing me up for subscription services. Why she and Zen sent me to therapy.

Because she loves me.

And no matter how crazy, no matter how overbearing, no matter how overstepping she is, I love her too.

And somehow, I think she understands. And that's why I tell her. Because I love her. Because I've never talked with her about this, and like Andie told me at the beginning of all of this, I think I need to give her something to work with.

"Mom," I whisper into her shoulder. "I miss Chase."

"Oh, sweetie," she says, rubbing her hand along my shoulder.

"I think I love him," I whisper. "But I've made a mistake. With him, but also with you."

Mom looks down at me. "What do you mean, sweetie?"

"I mean ... Mom, I never actually had a boyfriend. Ever."

Mom freezes. "Summer?"

I pull back. My nose is running, and Mom hands me a tissue. "Thank you."

"Of course," Mom replies.

I keep talking before she can question me. "I mean ... You know back when I turned thirty-two, and you started setting me up for blind dates and talking about dating apps?"

She looks unsure. "Yes, I do."

"Mom ... that was really hurtful."

Her expression flickers. I've started this now—if I don't finish, I'll have done more damage than good.

"I know you want me to be happy, and I'm so glad you're looking out for me. But ... Mom ..." I take a deep breath and pinch my eyes closed. "You always pushed me to get good grades when I was a kid. That was fine, and fun. I wanted to, and the things you were encouraging me to get into were great. But I also did it because I thought it made you proud. When I got older, and I graduated from school, it was like everything switched, and all you would talk about was me getting married. Like it had never occurred to me, or I never thought about it.

"It wasn't—and isn't—wrong for you to want and hope those things for me. But when that's all you talk about, it makes me feel like nothing else I've done matters to you. Like I'm playing a game, but you keep on changing the rules. I want to get married. I want to have children. But those things haven't happened for me yet. And the ways you were trying to help ... weren't helping."

Her face falls, and I reach out. "But I wasn't ... I wasn't helping either. I know I haven't talked to you about any of this. I guess I assumed you wouldn't care, or you already knew and already didn't care. I'm sorry for that."

"But what about Chase?" Her voice is small. It hurts.

I exhale. "You remember when you signed me up for all those apps?"

"Yes," she looks close to tears. I wrap my arm around her. It's time for both of us to be brave.

"I was so angry," I admitted. "And instead of telling you about it like I should have, I decided to make up a boyfriend. I felt like instead of constantly offering advice, you'd be happy for me, or at least be able to focus on the things that were actually happening to me, instead of focusing on what I didn't have. So, I lied." I take a deep breath. "I lied. And I made up a boyfriend. He didn't have a name, and I didn't try to make up anything about him. He was just there to exist. And I got carried away. It was easy to blame things on him or use him as an excuse to get out of things I didn't want to do. But also to get you to leave me alone about dating and being single."

Mom thinks about this. She looks undeniably sad, and it pulls at my heart, because I know she knows it worked. But I've hurt her, and it hurts more than angry me ever cared about. She was wrong, but I'm wrong, too, to have done this.

"How did Chase ... come into the picture?" Mom asks tentatively.

"I met Chase after you and Zen got me therapy."

Her mouth drops open. "That soon?"

"Yes. If it makes you feel any better, everything you know about Chase himself is true."

"He hasn't been terrible to you at all?"

The question hits like a shot to the heart. "No, Momma," I say, my eyes filling with tears. "Chase has never done anything to hurt me." Nothing except walk away, like we both agreed to do.

"And you love him."

My face crumples, and I can't stop the tears anymore.

"Yes."

"Oh, sweetie." She reached out for me, and despite the fact I'm much taller than her, she pulls me close and cradles my head as I sob.

I stay for dinner, and I end up telling Dad everything. He looks more relieved than angry, which I can't quite figure out, but I accept it all the same. After dinner, where Mom orders my favorite pizza, and Dad turns on an old TV show rerun, I curl up next to him like I used to do when I was a kid.

"Dad?"

"Yeah, Sunshine?"

"Are you mad at me?"

"No, I'm not."

"Why?"

At first, he doesn't answer, seemingly getting further and

further engrossed in the movie, until finally he answers. "Well, I guess it's because I love you."

"But I lied to you. I thought you'd be disappointed in me."

"And I am," he admitted. "But I'm more disappointed your mother and I made you feel like you couldn't tell us. We're your parents. We're supposed to be your first support in this world."

"I could have reached out more."

"And so could I, Sunshine," he says, and sighs. "I've known something isn't quite right for months. I wish I'd tried to talk to you about it."

We're silent for a moment, watching the TV screen, but not really watching the show.

"I'll try to do better, Dad," I promise.

"Me, too, Sunshine."

The next Sunday, Mom invites me over for dinner. It's not the regular monthly dinner, but I accept anyway. I figure if I have any hope of fixing the relationship with my mother, sister and aunt, I should put in the time first. Even if we never completely see eye-to-eye, I don't want it to be from lack of effort.

I'm not surprised when I see Joanie there. I've already called her and confessed. She took it better than I thought. She actually almost seemed relieved. Now, wordlessly, she opens her arms, and I step in.

"I'm sorry," I whisper in her ear.

Joanie holds me even tighter. "You're a punk, you know that?"

"Yeah," I say.

She presses her head into my shoulder. "I'm sorry, too."

"You don't need to be. You were watching out for me."

"But I'm sorry you felt like you couldn't confide in me. I'll try and do better. Will you let me?"

Joanie and I release each other. I've cried so much over the last week or so that it doesn't feel like I should have any more, but the familiar prickling behind my eyes says that I haven't cried myself dry yet.

"Only if you let me," I whisper. Joanie squeezes my arm and nods.

Zen walks in from the kitchen just about then. My sister squeezes my arm once more and walks into the kitchen. I think she knows I need to talk to Zen alone.

"Hi, darling," my aunt says, and pulls me into a close hug. I hug her back. I'd forgotten how good her hugs feel when I'm not busy resenting her.

"Hi, Zen," I whisper in her ear. "Do you have time to talk?"

"For you? Always."

I take Aunt Zen to the study and tell her everything. She looks a little nervous, but there isn't anything that I could do to prepare for her opening line.

"I have a confession," Zen says. "I knew you weren't dating anyone."

My mouth drops open. "But—Zen, you gifted me six therapy sessions?"

She presses her lips together and looks more than a little sheepish. "Yes. I ... well, in the spirit of full disclosure, I thought it would be a good way to call your bluff." I open my mouth and she puts up a hand. "I know it was wrong, Summer. I know that. But real boyfriend or not, we were worried. You were unhappy, and pretty much everyone could see it."

"I wasn't—" I start to protest, and then I close my mouth. I thought I'd only been angry because they were forcing a fake boyfriend on me. But I was unhappy, too. "I see. I'm sorry."

"I am, too."

We sit there for a long moment on the couch, not quite knowing what to say.

Or at least I don't. Zen looks over at me after a moment. "Why did you and Chase break up?"

I look over at her. My heart's taken a beating, but I can talk about it. "Well ... we were done with therapy. That's what we had agreed."

"But you didn't want to?" Zen asks.

I frown. "Not really."

"But he did?"

I stare at her. I opened my mouth to say, 'yes, he did.' But I find I can't say it honestly. I don't know. "I ... I didn't ask." Zen shifts in her seat, and I feel like I need to explain. "It's ... I wanted to be in a relationship with him. I didn't feel like I should ask. He's such a good man, Zen. He didn't go in expecting a long-term relationship, and I'm honestly worried if I did ask, he'd do it because he's nice. Besides," I say, and my voice breaks. "I don't think he saw me as more than a friend."

Zen mulls that over, pursing her lips. "But you don't know for sure? You never asked?"

I shake my head. "No."

"Hmmm." Then Zen speaks again, a little carefully. "You know ... maybe you should talk to him."

"I don't know if that's a good idea." I look down at the ground and bite my lip. "I don't want to make it harder than it already is. And I don't know if he wants to hear from me now that everything's over with."

Zen nods, like she understands. "I can see how that might be the case." Then she pats my shoulder and stands to go back into the kitchen. "But I still think you should talk to him."

I nod—in understanding, not agreement—and then I call to her as she starts to walk out of the room. "Hey, Zen?"

She turns back. "Yes, Summer?"

"I just ... thank you for therapy."

She turns around to look at me. "What?"

I stand and walk over to her. "Thank you. I know you meant it as a way to call my bluff, but I really did learn a lot about me. And I'm grateful."

Zen's expression softens. "I'm glad it did some good."

"It did," I say. "But it also helped me learn a couple of things about myself. About how I want to work out my relationships. And that's why ... Zen, I love you and Mom so much. Please don't set me up or sign me up for anything. Not until I tell you I'm ready for something like that, all right?" It will probably be never, but Zen seems to understand.

"I understand. And I'll talk to your mom, too."

"Thanks, Zen," I say, wrapping my arm around her.

She wraps her arm around my waist, and we walk into the living room together. "Of course, Summer."

A question pops into my mind. "Hey Zen, if you knew Chase and I weren't dating, did you, um ... tell Andie?"

Her eyebrows lift and she shakes her head. "No, no, no. That would have been a massive breach of ethics. No, she treated the two of you like you were the real deal."

I think about this as Zen shuffles forward to help Mom finish dinner.

It was real for me. The whole thing was real, honest-to-goodness love for me. I only wish I'd been brave enough to say something.

I walk over to the counter and start cutting vegetables to put in the salad, but the quote Andie gave us, the one Benjamin Mee had said, comes to my mind. *Sometimes all you need is twenty seconds of insane courage. Just literally twenty seconds of just embarrassing bravery. And I promise you, something great will come of it.*

Chapter 24
The Problem Pt. 3

CHASE

I used to be excited for spring. Now, three weeks into April, I'd give up almost anything to go back into the dead of winter.

At first, it's strange to me. Amanda's breakup had been so sudden and harsh, but I'd had little-to-no break in my regular routine. I'd been affected, but not lonely. Stressed by Amanda's words, but not by her absence.

I've always known I would break up with Summer. In January, it was a term of our agreement: we would go to therapy together, and then we would part ways.

I finally told Avery everything. It went about as well as I thought it would. She didn't speak to me for half a day while she processed and then called me and let me have it for fifteen minutes straight. And since then, she's been sending me a constant stream of funny memes and jokes—nothing relationship related—and lunch every day to try to keep my morale and energy up.

I don't know if it's working. It feels like a part of my heart walked away. I can't focus, at work or at home. The one time I tried going out on a date—if only to practice what I'd learned—I knew right away there was no spark. And not because my date wasn't interested, or desirable. It's because of me.

I'm missing something, and it's Summer.

I love her. I want to know how she's doing. I want to know the details about how it ended with Louis. I don't feel like I can ask Lacy, because it will undoubtedly get back to Summer, and I don't want to put that on her.

I want her to be happy. I know she did not take me on to be a real boyfriend to her. She wanted someone to go to therapy with, and although I think we became genuine friends, I'm not convinced she ever saw me as more than that. It's heart-rending and driving me absolutely crazy.

Which is probably the reason I've finally agreed to talk to Amanda. She wants to take me out to dinner to say sorry for everything. It's more personal than I want—hence the confusion about my sanity—but at least it's a neutral, public location. Not like when she broke up with me while we were on a date up the canyon, and we had to drive home together for thirty minutes afterward.

It's also on a Thursday evening, which means if nothing else, I can cry off early and blame it on an early morning meeting or something.

I pull up to the restaurant a couple minutes early. The sun is going down later and later, and there is enough light I can clearly see the young woman waiting for me as I drive up. And she looks young. Younger than when we broke up.

Why I thought it was a good idea to date a woman almost ten years younger than me, I will never know.

I'm glad she's already out of her car. I'm not angry at her, but the idea of opening the door to her car lends a larger degree of intimacy to the relationship than I'm comfortable with. Not that I'm willing to go so far as to not open her door on purpose, but ... well, I'm glad I don't have to make that choice.

I exit my car and walk up to the restaurant. It's a new Chinese place. Could it be, after never remembering once during our relationship, she remembers my favorite food now?

If that's the case, I'm a little worried about the ramifications.

"Chase!" Amanda says, bouncing up and down in little hops. "Oh, it's you!" She leans in and presses a kiss to my cheek before I can say anything. She probably would have gone for a hug as well, but after her lips make contact, I step back out of reach and straighten. She's not tall enough to reach me under normal circumstances.

Thank goodness.

"Hi, Amanda," I step up to the door and open it. "Shall we go in?"

Her expression freezes a bit, like she's trying to recalibrate. At one point in our relationship, I probably would have felt bad, but that was almost a year ago, and before Summer.

The pain hits as Amanda crosses the threshold of the restaurant, and I try not to let it show on my face. She might be insisting she's a changed woman, but I've never known a woman to smell blood in the water quicker than her. She was cutthroat, backstabbing, and never had a good word to say about anyone, and the way she wore me down for this meeting does nothing to dissuade me from feeling like she has changed.

I'm also starting to realize how anxious I am. Was I always like this with her?

We sit down to eat. Amanda wants to get dishes to share, but I ask the waiter gently to give me my own plates. Amanda looks up at me sharply. To cover for myself, I shrug. "I've been getting over a cold."

"Oh." Her hard look softens. And now I've lied to her so I don't offend her. Have I always done this?

My mind spins as we receive our dishes and begin to eat, trying to recall everything we'd gone through together. At the time I would never have called it bullying, but I realize quickly that she trained me so well—manipulated me so well—that I have been acting like this for years and never thought anything was wrong with it.

And now I'm getting a little angry.

Because all I can think about is how Summer didn't want even to have me put my arm around her because she was worried she was taking advantage of me. And now I have Amanda, who even after insulting me and lying to my face still assumes I want to share a dish with her.

Who does she think I am?

The Chase of eight months ago, my brain supplies. Pre-therapy Chase. The Chase before a winter of Summer.

"So, Chase," Amanda says, dragging a piece of sweet and sour pork across her plate, creating a trench through the sauce. "How have you been?"

I idly begin to wonder if I'm going to be footing the bill for this 'apology supper' and shrug. "Doing well."

"Oh?" Her eyes flick up to mine, and it's probably wishful thinking, but she looks a bit perturbed.

Good. I nod. "Yep. Work has been going well."

Amanda nods, still apparently taken a little aback by my sidestepping around the issue. She's a subtle sort of person. She won't bring up relationships unless I do, but I wonder what would happen if I avoid mentioning them at all.

"And ... how about outside of work?"

"Oh, you know," I say, looking around the restaurant. "Avery and I have been trying out a lot of different restaurants. Always looking for our new favorites."

Amanda pretends to brighten. "Oh, and how is Avery? I've missed her."

That's a lie. Throughout the whole time we were dating, Amanda tried to avoid Avery as much as possible—and tried to make me do the same. It gave rise to Avery-Tuesdays. It's also, I'm realizing now, a huge red flag.

At no point would I ever have considered getting back together with Amanda, but now I'm wondering at my decision to even meet with her for dinner today.

"She's doing well," I reply, a little late. It probably makes me look inattentive. I'm starting to be fine with that. "She's trying out for an official rugby league this summer."

Amanda looks like she couldn't care less. It's probably true, but now I'm looking for ways to get out. I don't get the chance.

"So, Chase ..." Amanda says, her voice carefully low and gentle. "I just wanted to tell you I'm sorry for the way all of this ended." She lowers her eyelids. "I know I might have made a mistake or two, and we weren't in a good place. But ... the longer I've stayed away, I've come to realize what I had all along. It was a mistake to let you go." She bats her big brown eyes and looks up at me through her eyelashes. "I think we should get back together."

"No." The word is out before I can even think, and I'm sure I look as stricken as she does in the next minute. It wasn't supposed to come out quite so harshly, but ... what?

"Well." Her voice drops into a huff. It's a tone so familiar I almost wince. "You might try to give it a little thought first."

"I don't need to." My voice is so quiet it's almost a whisper. "Amanda, you broke up with me."

"And now I'm trying to fix that." She says it slowly, like I'm the little know-nothing I used to be.

I stare at her. I am the CEO of a nationally recognized up-and-coming firm. I handle deals worth millions of dollars. I'm a university graduate, a couple of times over. I am a smart, capable human. How in the world did I get tangled up in ... this?

"There's nothing that needs to be fixed, Amanda." My voice is quiet, but it might be because I'm dissociating. "I don't know if you've noticed, but it didn't work because you didn't want to be in the relationship. And now that we're done, I don't want back in."

Amanda laughs in disbelief. "Excuse me? Aren't you Chase Merrill, king of second chances?"

And there it is. I fold my arms and lean back in the chair. "Your boyfriend dumped you, didn't he? He dumped you, and now you're alone, so you're coming crawling back to me? Do I look that desperate?"

Her face becomes a scowl so fast I nearly recoil. "I don't know what you're so gleeful about," she snaps. "You broke up with what's-her-name—Summer? You should feel sorry for me."

The bottom drops out of my stomach. I frown. "How do you know about Summer?"

"How could I miss her? It's the only thing Lacy wants to talk about. It's like she was rubbing it in. 'Chase and Summer get along perfectly' 'Chase and Summer look perfect together' 'Summer absolutely looooves Chase.' Kind of a jerk move, considering she was the one that introduced us."

It was a detail not many people knew—Lacy had introduced me to one of the undergrads she was mentoring at the time. That person was Amanda. Lacy had intended it as a summer internship, but I'd quickly gotten caught in Amanda's crosshairs.

But all of this had nothing to do with the really important part of that sentence. "Lacy said Summer loved me?" My voice is soft.

Amanda rolls her eyes. "Chase, everyone has told me Summer loves you. Even Summer herself said so when I dropped by—"

"Excuse me?" Disbelief drops through me, hot and cold at the same time. "When did you meet Summer?"

"About two weeks ago?" Amanda says, rolling her eyes. Apparently, I'm not following the script. I couldn't care less. "I found her as she was coming out of work. She was so rude."

My brain is spinning in circles. "She said she loved me?"

Amanda sighs and closes her eyes in feigned patience. "Yes. And then she told me to stay away from you. To be perfectly honest, it was kind of like a 'if I can't have him, no one can.' It felt really toxic." She gives me such a sanctimonious smile that even if she hadn't told me what she just told me, I'd leave immediately. As it is, I need to make a phone call.

"I need to go." I stand up before the words are finished coming out of my mouth.

Amanda shoots to her feet. "Chase!" I look over at her, and she looks at me. She seems to be floundering, like she's not in control of the situation, and doesn't know what to do about it. "What about us?"

I take a deep breath, and sigh. "Amanda, we're done. What we had wasn't good for either of us. You know that as well as I do."

Amanda's jaw clenches. She's about to say something. To try to make me stay. She still doesn't realize I made my mind up before I ever entered the building. I shake my head. "Goodbye, Amanda."

I turn away and walk toward the front of the restaurant. I pay the bill—for myself—and head out to the parking lot. If this is true, if Summer loved me all this time ... But what if Amanda was wrong? What if she's setting me up for something I can't see coming?

What if Summer didn't mean it? I knew she disliked Amanda. What if it was only a ploy to try to get Amanda to leave me alone? I could believe that of Summer—protecting me from Amanda without a second hesitation, regardless of whether she loved me or not.

But what if it isn't a ploy? What if Summer ... I pause on the sidewalk outside of the restaurant, battling with myself. I love Summer. And if she loves me, then this will be the beginning of something amazing. If she doesn't ... I don't know how I will ever recover.

But how can I stand still until I know? How can I call when I'm so afraid?

Suddenly, the quote Andie gave us the last day of therapy drops into my head. How did it go? All you need is twenty seconds of insane courage?

I've barely pulled my phone out of my pocket when it begins to ring.

I stare at it.

It couldn't possibly—

I answer it and put the phone up to my ear.

"Summer?"

Chapter 25
The Solution Pt. 2

SUMMER

I stand in the parking lot of the therapy building, bouncing on the balls of my feet as I wait for Chase to arrive.

It was simultaneously thrilling and terrifying to hear his voice after a month of utter silence. He'd answered on the first ring.

The first ring.

It was almost as though he'd been waiting for me to call. The conversation had been short and to the point. I'd told him I needed to talk to him. He'd asked when. I told him now. He asked where I was. There had been no hesitation in his voice. I'd told him where I was, and he told me to give him ten minutes.

That was ten minutes ago.

I think I might be hyperventilating, but I can't tell whether it's because of my nerves, or because I've paced back and forth across the parking lot so many times, I think there's a groove. I've been here since the end of work, trying to build up the courage to call.

I hadn't expected him to pick up. Or pick up so quickly. Could it be—

No. I cut myself off without mercy. I am here to let him know my feelings, not to assign feelings to him. I could very well be going home with my heart in tatters after this, but at least I'll know I've given everything I can to this relationship. I will not have regrets, and that will be enough. It might not be good, but it will be enough.

It's getting close to sundown. The sky is changing with the dying of the day, gold streaks running across the sky, cutting into the blue like a magnificent splash of color across an endless canvas.

I hear a car, and I turn toward the entrance to the parking lot. It's his. I can see him behind the wheel. He's wearing a white button down, with the sleeves rolled up to his elbows. He looks incredible. He must have come from work. I feel a little underdressed, in blue jeans and in a flowy green top. It's not what I usually wear, but I'd forgotten to do laundry again, and it's what was clean.

He's driving fast through the parking lot, turning into a parking spot only three spots away from Jennie. I'm along the back edge, almost by the therapy building itself. My heart is thundering in my ears, and I watch him step out of the car, looking around for me.

He hasn't seen me yet.

Part of me wants to run away. It tries to convince me loving him for as long as I did was gift enough. That I can enjoy the memory without ruining it when he says no.

But I don't move. I'm rooted to the spot, staring at the man I love as he finally finds me, and begins to move toward me, his brows set low, and his mouth set with unmistakable determination.

The terrified part of me screams at me that he's angry at me for interrupting his evening. That I've held on too much and presumed he wanted to keep in contact when he really didn't.

Maybe that's right, but I've got something to say first.

"Summer?" Just like on the phone, the sound of my name on his lips raises goosebumps on my arms. He stops about ten feet away, his hands hanging by his sides. His head tilts to the side. "Is everything okay?"

I'm staring at him, but I don't care. He's bathed in golden light, and it's easily the most glorious thing I've ever seen.

"I'm perfectly fine," I say quietly. I step down off the sidewalk and start walking toward him. I stop about five feet away and mirror his body language. Shoulders back, arms by my sides. He opens his mouth, but I know I need to speak first. Otherwise, it'll never happen. I can do this. I can be brave. Twenty seconds starts now.

"I have a confession to make," I say, closing my eyes. My mouth is dry. I swallow. When I open my eyes, Chase is standing there, lips parted like he was about to say something but has stopped himself.

"What is it?" His voice is calm. He wants to hear what I have to say.

"I've lied to you," I say, a small smile forcing its way onto my mouth.

He looks a little confused. "You have?"

"Yes." I'm breathless. "I have. Chase, I told you ... I told you at the beginning of therapy that we had to break up at the end. Through the whole thing I told you we were just friends and it wasn't real. And at the end, I told you the best thing would be to follow our plan and break up."

Chase doesn't say anything. He's studying my face, like he used to do, and part of me just wants him to read my mind. The other part of me begs him to stay quiet until I've said my piece.

"We did have the plan to break up. I want to believe we are

friends, and what we had ... we had a fake relationship. But Chase ... I lied." My voice chokes, and I have to pause to compose myself.

"How did you lie, Summer?" Chase takes a step forward, within reach now, his whisper patient and heartrendingly gentle.

"I didn't want to break up." It's barely a whisper, but I say it. I say it, and I know he hears it, because he goes still. His chest rises as if he's about to say something, and I interrupt him again. "I don't know when it happened, Chase, but it became real for me. Every bit of what I've said and done, I have meant wholeheartedly. It was why I felt like I was taking advantage of you—because I knew I loved you, and I didn't know whether you loved me back.

"And I don't know if you could ever love me back. I don't know if you feel anything but friendship for me. I don't want you to become my boyfriend just because you're nice and don't want to make me feel bad, but I love you more than I could ever say, and if there's any possible way you feel the same ..." I trail off and then take a breath. "I've never missed anyone the way I have you over the last month. If you could find it in your heart to love me, I beg you to forgive me."

Chase stares at me, his eyes shining. For a moment, he doesn't say anything, and then he moves. In a step, he's crossed the two feet between us, wrapping me in his arms and lifting me off the ground as he hugs me for dear life. I manage to exhale in relief, wrapping my arms around his neck, before he puts me down, and presses his lips to mine.

He tilts my head back, deepening the kiss, and I can't help the soft sigh that escapes my lips. There's no pretense now. No self-consciousness, and no apologies. His arms are tight, and I am safe here. I am whole here. I am loved here.

When he finally draws back, one arm wrapped around my back, and the other tangled in my hair, he smiles at me.

"I love you," I whisper.

"I love you more," he responds. His voice is low, almost a growl, and something flip-flops in my chest. "And for the record, if you made a mistake, I made the same one—times ten. And I'm sorry."

"I didn't realize this was a competition."

He smirks. "Only if you want it to be."

Then his lips are on mine. My eyes drift closed, and I'm lost to everything that isn't Chase. When we separate, I let one corner of my mouth curl into a cheeky smile.

"For therapy?" I ask.

He makes a noise in his throat that is definitely a growl. "Absolutely not."

And then he kisses me again.

Epilogue

SUMMER

December 21st

They say karma comes for us all. Today, I certainly hope so. Jennie has no concept of the idea that it's my birthday, and since returning home from work, has completely refused to start. Since Chase is finishing up stuff at his job and will head straight to my parents' house from there for my birthday dinner, I've called Mom. She's on her way.

There are benefits to having my dad cook my birthday dinner.

Knowing Mom's getting the house ready for a birthday party, though, I did try to get in touch with Lacy first, but she sounded harangued when she answered the phone. "Sorry, Summer, I'm in the throes of pre-Christmas prep at work," she'd said. "Maybe ask Rhett?"

My brother is also running late from picking up my other brother, Scottie, from the airport—they'd flown in for

Christmas on different days for reasons I had yet to understand —and they're expected to get there later than Chase.

I bounce a little on the sidewalk, looking for my mom's blue sedan as the enormous fluffy flakes fall from the sky. I'm most likely going to drive back to her house—she's not super comfortable driving in snow. Which, when I think of it, makes me feel kind of touched she'd even consider it. Then again, you can't celebrate a birthday without the birthday girl.

And I feel like thirty-four is going to be a pretty great year.

Mom pulls up in my parents' brand-new sedan, the tires crunching in the newly fallen snow. She opens the door and pops out.

"Happy birthday, sweetie! Now, get in, get in! I'm not driving this a moment longer than I have to!" She rounds the car to get in the passenger side. I grin, jog to the driver's side, and hop in. In a moment, we're on the road.

My mom's in a good mood. To be fair, she rarely isn't, but birthday dinner preparations and Christmas in a few days seem to have put her all in a flutter. As we drive to her house, she talks about how Dad is on hour eight of preparing the pork, and how she's picked up the most darling blankets for Rhett's new addition to his family, as well as finding something she's sure Joanie's oldest will finally wear. I smile as I listen to the love pouring out of my mother's mouth, as she talks about the tree and the Christmas Day plans. About my dad and the clock she's had custom made for him.

On a whim, I reach out and grab her hand.

She looked up at me, silencing herself mid-sentence, and then squeezes my hand back. "Oh, Summer. Everything okay? Am I talking too much?"

I shake my head, sending her a gentle smile. "I was just thinking how much I love you, Mom," I tell her. "Tell me more about Christmas."

And she does. I think I know what everyone is getting by the time we get back to the house—including, to my surprise, Chase.

"Really?"

"Of course, dear!" Mom says, almost sounding offended. "Just because he's not officially part of the family doesn't mean we can leave him out. You know how it is."

I'm not sure I do but considering I've bought five for him on my own, I don't really have much room to talk.

The last eight months have been an absolute dream. Things aren't perfect—we're both learning how to be in a relationship with each other—but even as we learn, it's been exciting and amazing to grow with him.

Chase and I both went back to therapy, but now it's on our own. Chase's relationship with Amanda, as well as with his parents, has taken a toll on him he said hadn't realized until that fateful dinner with Amanda. Every so often I'm invited to go with him, to discuss something he and his therapist want my viewpoint on. It's glorious to see such a loving man choose to remain kind, wonderful, and strong every day. I'm excited to see what kind of man he's going to become in the future.

I'm working on my relationship with my family. My relationships aren't perfect, but they are good, and better than they have ever been.

I pull into the driveway at Mom's house and under the canopy that doubles as their protected parking, noting the cars around the house. It looks like Joanie and Zen are already here. I also note there are a lot of cars around my neighbor's house. A new family moved in a few months ago. They must be having their own Christmas party, or something. Considering we usually sneak a few spots in front of their house, I hope we won't collide too much, but it looks like there's still a space for

Chase and Lacy. Rhett and Scottie will just have to get what they get.

Mom and I get out and walk to the kitchen door. It's locked, which is a little weird, but not unheard of. Sometimes, Mom locks it out of habit as she leaves. I spin the key ring to get the house key, like I've done more times than I can count, only to realize not only is this key ring as new as the car, but it is also empty.

"Um, Mom?" I say, swinging the car keys at her like a pendulum.

She looks confused for a moment, and then her eyes widen and she smacks a hand to her forehead. "Oh, good grief, sweetie. Cheese and crackers, I forgot I didn't have a house key on this keyring yet. We're going to have to use the front door. Come on."

Shaking my head at my mom, but in far too good a mood to be annoyed, I follow my mom around the side of the house, and up the main drive.

A Christmas tree stands in the huge window out front, exactly where Mom's put it every Christmas for the last forty years. The lights twinkle at me in the darkness as I approach, and I remember last year. I'd been angry then. Would I have been so angry then, if I knew how my life would change in only a year?

I smile and try to resist the uncharacteristic prickle behind my eyes. Stomping the snow off of my shoes as I walk up the steps, I grab the door handle and look back at my mom with a grin as I open the door.

"You'd better hope this door is open. Can you imagine trying to explain to Dad why both doors are lock—"

"SURPRISE! HAPPY BIRTHDAY!"

I nearly fall out of the door as the lights flash on, and my entire family, plus Chase, Lacy, and Avery jump at me. Mom's right behind me, and with strength belying her size, pushes me back into the house.

"Got you, sweetie!" she says cheerfully, like I didn't just nearly flatten her.

"Thanks, Mom," I say, looking around breathlessly. "Lacy, Chase—what're you—"

Lacy's grinning at me, and Avery is literally hopping in place. And Chase—Chase is—

He's on one knee.

Mom pushes me further into the house, and I stumble forward as she closes the door behind us.

Chase's hand is shaking. I'm shaking. I look at him, lips parted, but not daring to speak a word, as he holds out a red velvet ring box with a solitaire diamond ring inside.

"Summer?"

"Yes?" I breathe.

"Summer Sunshine Weathers?"

"That's me," I whisper.

It breaks the tension a little, and he huffs a laugh. "The last year has been the best of my life—except for a little stint from March to April."

It's my turn to breathe a laugh.

Chase continues. "In the spirit of always speaking our minds, I love you more than I can say and I never want to break up with you, ever. Will you marry me?"

I know the answer to the question, but for the life of me, I can't speak. My throat is closed, and I can't speak because of the tears suddenly trickling down my face.

So, I nod. And then sob. And then nod again. "Yes," I say, pressing my hand over my mouth as he slips the ring on my finger. "Yes."

He's standing in the next moment, gathering me into his arms, raining down kisses on me—my cheeks, my eyes, my lips.

I hold onto him for dear life, incandescently happy, and absolutely terrified I am dreaming. And then Chase kisses me and I realize no dream could ever be this perfect.

My tears subside as we part, and I have to laugh as I run my hand down his cheek. "You got me," I admit. "How long have you been planning this?"

"Since September, after we talked about marriage for the first time," he says, throwing me a not-so-guilty look. "I gotta say —I'm so glad I brought your mom and Zen in on this. They are masters. That thing with the front door? Seriously."

I snort and bury my face in his shoulder. "I knew it."

"Knew what?" he asks, dipping his head to look into my face.

I look up at him, and then I press a long kiss to his lips. "That I love you."

He smiles and pulls me into a tighter embrace. Burying his face into my neck, I hear his voice, deep, soft, and sincere. "I love you, too."

The End

Acknowledgments

Caylie—You are fantabulous. Thank you for immediately loving it, and forgiving me for not actually sending it to you as it was being written.

Nashelie—Thank you for loving Summer and Chase and for letting me send you the very rough first draft, haha. You're the best.

Brooke—thank you for loving this book, asking inconvenient questions, and being a WONDERFUL cover artist to work with. It's been great!!!

Janaya, Emily - Thank you for your eyes and encouragement!

MADELYN - MADE-EE-LEEN. YOU KHAVE BIN WERY KHELPFOOL. Seriously, you are a miracle worker. Thank you for helping all of my books SO much. You are a very big part of how it was finished.

Kayla, my faithful editor, thank you SO MUCH for fitting me into your very tight schedule, particularly this time!

Alexia - I got a 8/10 from you, when you were reading outside your regular genre. I will treasure this for the rest of my life.

Jesse—This is not your chosen genre. Thank you for working on it anyway, and encouraging me to do my best. 🩶

To my advance crew, ARC readers, and Street Team: Thank you for being willing to take a chance on me and loving my book!

And, to this meme, that started it all:

Anyone down to take couples
counseling and see at what point the
therapist realizes we don't even know
each other?

Content Guide

Please be aware that, while every effort has been made to include information about sensitive issues, not every eventuality or personal sensitivity can be accounted for. Thank you for your patience and understanding.

Content warning for The Heart of the Matter:

- Workplace Bullying
- Misogyny
- Themes and Discussion of Emotional Abuse (not between the main characters)
- Poor family relationships

About the Author

Rebekah Isert is a k-drama loving, romance reading, genre hopping menace. She's written a couple of Urban Fantasies, insists on publishing Science Fiction, and has now broken into Romance because it sounded like a blast. She hopes you enjoy her stories no matter what genre.

The Heart of the Matter is her seventh book.

Also by Rebekah Isert

Science Fiction

The Man From Delwaphria Series

Rescue

Recruit

Renegade

Rendezvous

Recoil

Urban Fantasy Standalones

Wednesday's Book

Oak and Ivy

Contemporary Romance

The Heart of the Matter